# PICKING UP THE PIECES

## BAYTOWN BOYS SERIES

### MARYANN JORDAN

Picking Up the Pieces (Baytown Boys) Copyright 2018 Maryann Jordan

Cover Design by: Graphics by Stacy
Cover and model photography: Eric McKinney
ISBN ebook: 978-1-947214-07-1
ISBN print: 978-1-947214-06-4

*My father-in-law served in the Navy during World War II.
He commanded a PT boat in the Pacific, alongside John F.
Kennedy, who would later become our president.
In Picking Up the Pieces, at one of the American Legion
meetings, an older veteran named Dennis talked about his
story. His words are the words from my father-in-law.
This book is dedicated to him, as well as all of the service men
and women who have served.*

## Author's Note

I have lived in numerous states as well as overseas, but for the last twenty years have called Virginia my home. All my stories take place in this wonderful commonwealth, but I choose to use fictional city names with some geographical accuracies.

These fictionally named cities allow me to use my creativity and not feel constricted by attempting to accurately portray the areas.

It is my hope that my readers will allow me this creative license and understand my fictional world.

I also do quite a bit of research on my books and try to write on subjects with accuracy. There will always be points where creative license will be used to create scenes or plots.

Four years ago, my husband and I discovered the Eastern Shore of Virginia and fell in love with the area. The mostly rural strip of land forming the peninsula originating from Maryland, has managed to stay non-commercialized. The quiet, private area full of quaint towns captured our hearts and we rushed to buy a little place there.

It has become our retreat when we need to leave the hustle and bustle of our lives. I gather ideas, create characters, and spend time writing when not walking on the beach collecting sea glass.

The moon hung over the Chesapeake Bay, off the Eastern Shore of Virginia, creating shimmers of diamond sparkles across the undulating water as it sent wave after wave upon the shore. The inky water caught the moon's reflection, but the night swallowed most of the illumination so even the ships anchored in the bay were only visible by the lights on their decks. The waterfowl were now silent, asleep on their perches, no longer searching for food. The waves cast seafoam, seaweed, and shells upon the shore as the tide rolled in.

And, the beach accepted the deposits of sea glass that the ocean deemed worthy to leave for whoever was lucky enough to discover the gifts.

Lance Greene might have appreciated the peaceful night, since sleep was elusive and his beachfront house had a perfect view of the bay. But, as usual on sleepless nights, he stayed inside in his spare room that he had turned into a studio.

The modest one-story home, nestled behind a large

dune, sat on a slight hill overlooking the bay. He had been immediately drawn to the house, the wide windows allowing light to chase out the dark corners during the daytime. The cedar frame had turned grey with age, but the previous owners had painted it with a clear, weather-resistant stain making sure it would last against the forces of nature.

The front of the house faced the road, a small porch framing the front door, almost as an afterthought. Lance knew the heart of the house would be facing the bay and the sunsets, so the foyer would only be usable as an entrance, not a place to gather. But that hadn't bothered him at the time...he had no one to welcome to his home anyway.

The realtor had wanted to show him other, more *exclusive* properties—code word for more expensive and larger—but Lance had walked away from the hawkish woman with his hand up, silencing her prattle. With a fierce glower sent her way, he noted she stayed outside while he had roamed inside by himself.

By himself—that was the way he liked most things. He found life was easier when he separated himself from others. Their needs, wants, desires no longer became his responsibility. Thoughts of his former self— before it all went to hell in Afghanistan—were pushed to the back of his mind.

Just as he suspected, the focus of the house was toward the back, facing the bay. And as he wandered through the empty rooms, he had no trouble visual- izing what his life could be, in this nowhere place on the shore. The former owners had taken the smaller rooms and opened them to create a large area, containing both the long living room and dining room, which flowed into the kitchen. A few upgrades in there were fine with him. He was not a foodie and had no intentions of becoming one. Off the living room was a screened porch, large and accommodating.

The lines of the space were pleasing with vaulted ceilings and large windows allowing the sunlight to spear inside. He had sucked in a deep breath, feeling as though he might have finally found a place where he could breathe.

The master bedroom was wide enough for his king-sized bed and the adjoining bathroom had been upgraded as well. Not a small man, he appreciated the oversized, glass-walled shower. Nodding to himself, he discovered the other two bedrooms. One faced the side of the house, positioned so it received both morning and afternoon sun. The lighted space beckoned to him and he recognized it for what it was. An out-of-the-way perfect place to land.

He had walked back outside, after glancing into the other bedroom, hall bathroom, and laundry room, and stalked toward the realtor, ignoring her eyes widening as he approached. "I'll take it."

Her gaze had jumped from him to the house behind and with a wide smile, she said, "Lovely! Let's go get the offer signed."

Her curious questions about his reasons for moving to the Eastern Shore went unanswered. She had given up her inquisition as his stoic persona left her with nothing to do but focus on filling out the paperwork, not gaining information on the newest resident-to-be.

Now, a year later, bending over the table, he sat on his stool, peering through his tabletop, lighted, magnifying glass, his hands holding the delicate wire and shards of sea glass that he used in his artwork. The work was meticulous, but he relished the creative process from idea to design to completion. An exquisite piece.

As he finished drilling the tiny hole in the glass, he wove the gold wire through and around, occasionally testing his work against the design drawing in the notebook next to him on the table. Once satisfied with what he had accomplished, he leaned back, stretching the kinks out of his spine and neck. He preferred working in the daylight, but sleepless nights were put to use as well.

Standing, he headed toward the door, stopping to look at his newest artistic endeavor. A mosaic created out of perfectly fitted pieces of sea glass lay on another table. The play of light off the multi-colors caught his eye and a slight smile escaped as he appreciated the work. With a final sigh, he flipped the light switch, plunging the room into darkness before he made his way through the house. He passed by the living room, now furnished with a long, comfortable sofa and several deep-cushioned chairs facing a flat screen TV on an antique wooden stand. Some of his artwork hung about the room, the only nod to living on the beach. He shunned decorating in commercial beach—wooden signs painted with sayings about how life is better with your toes in the sand or shells strung in a fishing net. Instead, he opted for comfortable. Masculine. Private. Uncluttered. The way he liked his life to be.

Opening the refrigerator door, he pulled out a bottle of water, draining the entire contents while standing in his kitchen, his throat working as he swallowed the cold liquid. Tossing the bottle into the recycle bin, he glanced at the clock on the stove. *2:17 a.m.* The time did not really matter to him as he had no place to be the next day. Or the day after that. Working from home afforded him the chance to create when the muse moved him and not worry about whether it was during the day or the middle of the night. Having no social calendar to contend with also made life simpler.

*Simpler. That's why I moved here. No expectations. No disappointments. No friends to lose in the middle of the desert. Removed from society, but with just a thread of connection.*

Pushing aside thoughts of his time in the Army, he was assaulted by the more recent naggings from his mother.

Walking into his bedroom, he sat on the edge of the bed, his head in his hands, willing his memories to fade into the background. He had been a fool, opening his email earlier and reading the note from his mother, once more berating him for disappointing his father. *"You know when your father is unhappy, he makes my life miserable. I would think you would care about me instead of being so selfish!"*

Forcing her out of his mind, he thought of the upcoming American Legion meeting. Two of the reasons he moved to Baytown were the newly charted AL and the desire to be in the company of good men and women who understood the military life. He hoped some of their spirit of camaraderie would rub off on him...eventually.

Laying on his back, staring at the slow-moving ceiling fan, he thought of Mitch Evans, the police chief of the small town on the bay that he now called home and the president of the American Legion. Mitch had been a chance meeting on the far side of the world several years ago. A tentative friendship that grew to offer him a lifeline. Baytown was Mitch's world, where he was raised and returned to take over when his father, the former chief, had to retire due to a heart attack.

Mitch had roots and, if Lance was honest with himself, he envied those roots. They grew deep into the land of the shore, connecting Mitch to his childhood friends who had also come back from military service. Connecting Mitch to the town that revered him. To the job that always called to him. To his family, that gave him the support he needed. And, back to the woman he left behind.

Lance had learned the reason for the name Baytown Boys—the group of men who had been fortunate enough to be raised on the shore, childhood friendships turning into sports teams in their adolescent years, military brothers after high school, and now adults creating their future. Grant, another police officer; Aiden and Brogan, brothers who owned the pub; Zac, the fire chief; and Callan, still with the Coast Guard.

Their ranks had increased with new blood—former

military men and women needing a place to call home. True to his nature, Mitch had extended the hand of friendship to him, to include moving to Baytown to put down roots as well.

He had taken Mitch up on his offer, but knew that roots would not grow. It takes a healthy plant, with a good root system to begin with, and he surely lacked those qualifications. But he was here and had no desire to leave.

Rolling over in bed, he stretched out his long legs, grateful the room was large enough to easily accommodate his California king. There were few luxuries he desired, but his comfortable mattress was one of them. Anything he could do to tempt peaceful slumber.

Closing his eyes, willing sleep to finally come, he prayed the screams in the night would evade him for once.

2

The sun was just peaking over the dunes, streaking the dawn sky with flashes of pink and yellow against the many colors of blue as the night began to fade away. During the week, Jade Lyons rose early to get ready for her job. A former first-grade teacher, this year she had been assigned to teach second grade at Baytown Elementary. But, Saturdays gave her the opportunity to get out of bed at dawn for an entirely different reason.

Smiling, she knew most of her co-workers slept in on the weekends, but once her newfound friends in Baytown had shown her the beauties of walks on the beach before the crowds came, she was hooked.

With binoculars hanging about her neck, she looked out onto the bay at the variety of ships anchored. There were large cargo ships waiting for their time to enter the Norfolk port or to travel north toward Baltimore, some laden with massive containers stacked on the decks. Others empty, waiting to dock and be filled for their trips around the world. Standing on the shore, she wondered where they sailed from and where they were bound. It was hard to imagine the lives of the men and women whose careers were spent on those large ships, traveling from port to port.

Fishing boats from the area grabbed her attention as they moved out of the harbor, heading into the bay toward the ocean, providing the restaurants and stores with their fresh-caught bounty. Other charter boats were taking individuals or groups out for a chance to bring in bass, trout, red drum, or flounder. Pulling out her camera, she snapped pictures, zooming in to capture as much detail as possible.

Lifting the binoculars to her face, she stared out at the multitude of sea craft, beginning to recognize many of the local fishing vessels. Carson & Sons had two boats that went out every morning, the Taylors did blue crab fishing in the bay, and George Caday handled his own boat with the help of a few deckhands, having no family to assist. She remembered one of her student's father and grandfather were the Carsons who owned that fishing business and he often spoke of wanting to become a fisherman as well. Fishing boats had sailed out of the Baytown Harbor for a century and Jade loved teaching her students about the history.

She had been thrilled to discover she could meet the local boats as they came in, buying fresh fish before their catch was sold to one of the restaurants.

Her gaze moved to the large merchant ships. Pulling out a pad of paper from her small backpack, she scribbled down the names and numbers she could identify on their sides. Later, she would Google the ships and where they were from, using the information with her class. The children loved to sit in their circle, surrounding the globe in her lab as she pointed out where the ships originated from or where they were bound. They may only be second graders but most had grown up on the bay, with many whose parents were farmers or fishermen. She knew some would never leave the shore, so expanding their world in any way she could was important.

Shoving her camera and paper back into her backpack, she carried her small sand bucket as she walked along, looking down, scouring the beach for sea glass. Since arriving in Baytown, she had been befriended by a group of women her age, all from the shore, and they had introduced her to collecting sea glass.

Tori owned the Sea Glass Inn, given to her by her grandmother. She smiled as she thought of the news that Tori and her police chief husband, Mitch, had announced at the last gathering. They were expecting a baby and she had been truly pleased. From the hoots and hollers from the others in their group, everyone else had shared their joy as well.

She had met Tori when she first moved to town, staying at the Inn for a few weeks until finding an apartment. That was where she also met Jillian and Katelyn, childhood friends of Tori's, both born and raised in Baytown. Jillian owned the town's coffee shop and Katelyn was part owner of the town's pub, providing both women with the opportunity to know all the shore's gossip. Jillian's fiancé was another police officer in town while Katelyn and her fiancé ran a private investigation business. Belle, a nurses' aide at the local nursing home, rounded out the group. These Baytown women had welcomed her into their circle and many sea glass-hunting trips turned into sharing and laughing. Helping to start the American Legion Auxiliary had been a thrill for her as well, now feeling like a Baytown woman herself.

Looking over the bay again, her heart was light, realizing how much she loved her life right now. Smiling, she bent over, snatching one of the colored pieces of glass deposited on the shore before the surf reclaimed it once again. With a whoop, she dropped it into her bucket, allowing it to join the others she had gathered.

Looking out toward the ships, she shouted, "Thanks!" before dropping her head to continue her search as she walked. She had learned that sea glass came from the glass bottles the sailors tossed overboard. The glass breaks and is ground by the sand and the surf so that by the time the small pieces wash upon the shore, their edges are rounded and smooth.

She had an ever-growing collection of jars filled with sea glass in her apartment, but always took some to her students to talk to them about the treasures the bay offers. Remembering their excitement when she first showed it to them, she was surprised to learn that many of the children had not ever searched for sea glass...

*"Where do you go on the weekends?" she asked.*

*One small boy replied, "I gotta help Daddy pick tomatoes on the weekend."*

*His answer stunned her, not realizing that for some of the children, they worked on their parents' farms even at such a young age.*

*"I go out on Gramps' boat to work with my older brother and dad," said another boy.*

*"Mama works at the grocery store on the weekends, so I gotta stay home," one girl spoke up. Smiling proudly, she added, "My older sister watches me and our little sister, and I help clean the house."*

Sucking in a deep breath through her nose to clear her mind, she faced the realization that the lives of many of her students did not include leisurely walks on the beach. *I'm in the right place, doing the right job. Even if my parents never agree.*

Baytown, part of North Heron County, on the Eastern Shore, was one of the poorest counties in Virginia, if not the poorest. It was the reason she had discovered it. The opportunity to work in a school that was desperate for educators who loved teaching and children, regardless of the pay, brought her to the shore. She loved her job and the children she taught, but knew the state was eyeballing their school, monitoring the progress.

Sighing, she continued her musing as she walked. It was so hard to deviate from teaching what you love to teach to the state tests, so she relished any opportunity she had to enrich her students' lives.

Lost in thought, she bent over continuously, picking up more and more sea glass as she walked southward on the beach. The sun rose slightly higher in the sky making the glint off the shiny glass easier to see. The gulls called out to each other, swooping down into the surf, ascending with a fish in their beaks. A Blue Heron stood like a sentinel, its long legs in the water as it eyed it, waiting for the instant it could plunge underneath and return with a crab.

She dropped another fragment into the bucket when she spied a large green piece at the edge of the water and scrambled forward to snag it quickly. Closing her fingers around the glass, she felt elated as it plunked loudly into the pink plastic container. Hopping in a silly dance of joy, she continued her walk southward, head down.

Eyes focused on the sand below, she startled when a large pair of flip-flop covered feet moved directly into her path and her body collided with another's.

A yelp left her lips as she lifted her head, stumbling backward, dropping her bucket. In front of her stood a man—tall, muscular, his legs planted widely and his hands on his cargo-shorts clad hips. A loose, wrinkled t-shirt blew in the breeze, allowing the material to plaster against his wide chest. Dark hair, dark bearded scruff, and square jaw. Sunglasses covered his eyes until he lifted one hand and raised them to the top of his head. Now that she could see his hazel eyes, she realized they were boring straight through her and she felt the heat of their pissed off sparks.

"Oh," she stammered. "I...I'm so sorry. I didn't see you."

He said nothing.

"Uh...I wasn't looking where I was going...really, I'm so very sorry."

Silence met her again.

Blushing, she sucked in her lips, dropping her gaze away from his intense stare. Seeing her bucket on the sand, she bent to pick it up, jerking when he spoke, his deep voice clipping each word.

"You're trespassing."

Eyes wide, she opened her mouth before snapping it shut. Her brows lowered as she looked around at the empty beach. Lifting her eyes back to his, she felt the anger radiating from his body. "I...uh...trespassing?"

"Yes."

Her head turned from side to side, searching for an indication of privacy. "There...there isn't a sign...or uh...anything—"

"You're on private property."

Licking her lips, wishing she had her sunglasses on to feel less exposed in front of him, her eyes darted behind him where she spied the roof of a long, low house just beyond the dunes.

"Oh...I'm sorry." The man's gaze dropped to the bucket in her hand and she could have sworn his anger ratcheted up another notch. Self-consciously she moved the bucket slightly behind her as she stepped backward. "Well, I'm sorry. I...uh...I'll just..." Walking backward a few steps, she hoped he would say something to lessen the embarrassment, but he just continued to glare.

"And that includes anything you find on this private property," he announced.

"Huh?"

He nodded toward the bucket in her hand.

Her mouth dropped open as frustration speared through her. "I picked this sea glass up as I walked...not here." Seeing his unyielding stance, she added, "Well, except for the last piece I picked up." She reached into the bucket and pulled out the large green piece, holding it out for him to take.

He kept his hands on his hips and she stood, feeling awkward as he stared. She pressed her lips together, not knowing what to say. He slid his sunglasses back down on his face and she slowly lowered her hand, dropping the glass back into the bucket.

His silence was deafening and the heat she felt on her face was not from the sun, as embarrassment flooded her. Uncertain what he wanted her to do or say, she decided the best option was to flee. Turning quickly, she hurried down the beach in the direction of town, no longer looking for sea glass, the enjoyment of the morning now ruined.

## 3

An hour later, walking into Jillian's coffee shop, a head jerk from the barista indicated her friends were upstairs. The murmur of voices blended together with the hissing of the espresso machine. The old, brick building had been bought by Jillian's parents, who turned it into a coffee shop. They kept the solid wood paneling, carved wooden support poles, and the glass display cases on the sides of the long room downstairs.

Antique tables and amber sconces on the walls, to soften the sunlight that came from the front, gave the quaint shop its ambiance. The unused upstairs had become Jillian's joy as she restored the second floor to the same glory as the coffee shop downstairs and showcased local artists' paintings on the dark paneled walls. Patrons could take their food upstairs and sit at the tables surrounding the area to enjoy the arts while relishing the treats, but usually she and her friends commandeered the upstairs when they needed a place to sit and talk.

The scent of the roasting coffee beans followed her as she ascended. Rounding the corner at the top, she observed Jillian, Katelyn, Tori, and Belle already sitting at a table next to a tall window overlooking Main Street. Tori's reddish hair glowed in the sunlight streaming through the glass. Jillian, with her blonde, girl-next-door looks and Katelyn, with her Irish blue eyes and dark hair always made Jade think what an interesting trio the original Baytown Girls made. Add in Belle's sweet face, and the kind hearts they all exuded, and she loved spending time with her friends. But now, approaching the gathering, she tried to meet their friendly smiles with one of her own, but failed.

Belle, more sensitive than most, immediately jumped up, her hands extended as Jade walked closer. "Oh, sweetie, what's wrong?"

Having gained the rapt attention of the others, whose faces now mirrored Belle's concern, she shrugged. "Just had an embarrassing encounter this morning, that's all," she replied, accepting Belle's hug.

"What happened?" asked Tori, patting the seat next to her.

She gratefully slid into the delicate chair, twisting her head toward the barista who had followed her upstairs with another coffee. Taking a sip of the sweet, steaming brew, she sighed as she leaned back. "I was out on the beach, checking out the ships and looking for sea glass. I had no idea that part of the beach was private."

Katelyn frowned, her head giving a slight jerk. "The Baytown beach isn't private. What on earth made you think that?"

"No, no, not the town beach. But south of town. Beyond the Dunes Golf Course." Seeing the now shared frowns of the others, she continued her explanation. "I sometimes go way past the golf course and walk along the beach. There's almost no one out in the early morning and the beach is so peaceful."

"And?" Katelyn prompted.

"Well, I didn't know that the beach was part of someone's private property."

"It's not," Katelyn and Jillian exclaimed in unison.

"Oh, but it is," Jade contended. "I met the owner."

Jillian shook her head, her blonde braid swinging back and forth. "Jade, I'm telling you the beach is not private. People can own to the dunes, but the actual beach is not private."

Her brow furrowed as she sucked in her lips, now more confused than ever.

"Tell us what happened—" Tori began before her attention jumped to the stairs, "oh, babe, hi!"

The others looked over, seeing Mitch Evans round the top of the stairs, his smile aimed at his wife. "Sorry to interrupt, ladies," he said, as he made his way to Tori's side. Leaning over, he placed a sweet kiss on her lips as his hand slid gently to her still-flat tummy.

The women smiled amongst themselves at the loving gesture.

Standing, Mitch said, "I hated I didn't get a chance to greet you this morning, with the call I got."

"Was everything okay?" Tori asked. She turned to the others and said, "There was a car accident past the diner on the way out of town."

Nodding, Mitch replied, "Yeah, it was. No one was hurt, but Zac checked them out anyway. Jason got an early morning call and towed both cars into his shop."

Jade knew Jason was another new transplant to town, like her. He came at the invitation of Zac, both having served in the Navy together. As the town's only mechanic, he snagged all the towing business as well. Zac was the fire chief and EMT.

Mitch was turning to leave when Tori halted him with her hand on his arm. "Sweetie, Jade was just telling us that someone told her the beaches south of town were private."

Blushing again, she quickly offered, "Oh, no, it's no big deal. I don't need Mitch to hear about my embarrassing morning."

Mitch turned his full attention toward her, his brow creasing. "What happened? Were you harassed?"

"No, not at all. I just wandered onto someone's private beach and had no idea I was trespassing. The owner made sure to let me know I was on his land." Offering a slight shrug, she added, "I was just embarrassed, that's all."

"He? Who told you this?"

"I...uh...I don't know. I was south of the golf course and, after I was stopped, I did see a low house over the dunes."

Mitch's hands landed on his hips, his brows still drawn down. "Can you describe him?"

"Uh...well, he was tall. Dark hair. Slightly scruffy beard...more like he just hadn't shaved yet. He was in good shape."

"And what did he tell you?"

She replied, "Well, that I was trespassing. I told him I was sorry but that I hadn't seen any signs. He stayed pretty mad at me so, after I apologized again, I started to leave. Oh, yeah, he also seemed really irritated that I had been picking up sea glass."

At that, a collective gasp went up as Tori, Katelyn, and Jillian all exclaimed, "Lance!"

Mitch dropped his chin, his head shaking, whether in irritation or mirth, she did not know.

Katelyn, blue eyes snapping, spouted, "I can't believe he told you that."

"That makes me furious," Jillian added.

"Girls," Tori's voice cut through, her eyes on her husband's face. Gaining their attention, she said, "Let Mitch deal with it."

He lifted his head, a slight smile playing about his lips. She watched as he squeezed his wife's shoulder and felt their powerful love expressed in a glance and a touch.

Mitch turned to her, saying, "I'll talk to him, Jade. The beach is not his, but…well, Lance likes his privacy." With one last kiss for Tori, he nodded to the others and headed back down the stairs, leaving her mouth hanging open.

"I…how…oh, my God!" she fumed. "How dare he! That man stood there, fire pouring from his eyes and dared to berate me for trespassing on *his* beach? *His* beach? What a jerk!"

Katelyn's temper flared as well, shaking her head in derision. "I've only been around him a few times, 'cause ever since he's been in town, he lives like a recluse—"

Belle, ever the peacemaker, her hands fluttering about, quickly said, "Maybe he was confused...or maybe he just didn't know...or maybe—"

"Nope, no excuse for assholery," Jade quipped, slapping her hand down on the table. The quartet was quiet for a second before laughter burst forth. She looked over in surprise, her frown still in place.

"Assholery?" Jillian giggled.

Rolling her eyes, she fought her own grin. "Well, that's my word for when someone has been an asshole."

"I like it," Katelyn declared, her eyes dancing.

"I hate to say this," Tori said, hesitating as she held Jade's eyes, "and I have no excuse for his behavior this morning, but I've gotten to know Lance...just a little... since he and Mitch became friends when they met in the Army."

Jade respected Tori's opinion so she sucked in a deep breath and said, "So, what was this morning about?"

Tori shrugged before replying, "Well, I know he is intensely private. I know he gives virtually no information out about himself, but he's made a few friends with the guys through the American Legion."

"I never see him around town," Belle commented, her voice heavy. "That's kind of sad, isn't it?"

"Well, he still didn't have to be so mean to Jade," Katelyn defended.

Beginning to rethink her anger, she sighed heavily. "Now, I don't know what to think." She noticed Jillian had grown quiet and, turning toward her, she cocked her head.

Jillian bit her lip as her fingers twisted the napkin on the table in front of her. "I just thought of something," she said, looking at her. "I know he searches for sea glass too—"

"Well, big deal," she huffed, trying to hang on to her irritation, curiosity getting the better of her. "Sorry, Jillian. What does the sea glass have to do with him berating me?"

Jillian stood and walked over to one of the pieces of local art she displayed in her galleria, an exquisite mobile created from sea glass. "This..." Jillian said, touching the piece reverently, "is Lance's work. He creates these."

She eyed the breathtaking artwork, her heart beating erratically in her chest. "Oh," she whispered, feeling foolish that she had never learned the identity of the creator of the beautiful sea glass works of art. "Well, damn, now I feel bad."

"Don't," Katelyn declared. "Honey, first of all, he was lying through his teeth when he told you that he owned the beach. And to do it in a way that embarrassed you and made you feel bad...well, that's just downright mean."

Suddenly Belle jumped up and threw her arms around her, saying, "Oh! I have to get to the nursing home, but sweetie, don't let him upset you. You should walk wherever you want!"

She returned Belle's hug and, standing, smiled down at the others. "You guys are the best. I'm exhausted and since it's Saturday, I'm heading home to spend the day relaxing."

Tori hustled over and placed her hands on her shoulders, peering into her eyes. "Are you okay? I promise Mitch'll talk to him."

"Oh, he shouldn't bother," she replied. "I'm a big girl and can take care of myself. And honestly, now that I think about all y'all have told me, there's no battle to fight. He was wrong to lie to me, but I'll just avoid that part of the beach in the future."

After hugs all around, she headed out to her car, sliding her sunglasses down as she turned her face toward the sun, allowing the rays to warm her heart. Realizing what good friends she had made actually had her feeling sorry for Lance. The sea glass artwork stayed in her mind as she tried to reconcile the creative talent with the grumpy man she met this morning. *He must be awfully lonely to be such an irritable man.*

## 4

The sun was already beaming into the studio windows when Lance heard a vehicle pull into his drive, the tires crunching over the crushed oyster shells and sand. Pinching his lips together at the intrusion, he stood, walking to the window, surprised to see Mitch climbing out of the Baytown Police SUV.

Leaving his studio, he walked toward the kitchen, knowing Mitch would eschew using the front door and come around to the back. Pouring another cup of coffee, he yelled that the door was unlocked and looked up as Mitch walked in.

Mitch slid his sunglasses off as he entered, his smile landing on him, or rather on the cup of coffee he was holding out toward him.

"Thanks man. My first cup of the day has already worn off."

"Long night?"

"Accident on the road leaving town early this morning. No one hurt. Old Man Copper pulled his tractor into the lane and a vacationer wasn't expecting farm equipment on the road. Slammed right into him. Zac was on call as the EMT and Jason got the car towed."

Nodding, he walked with his cup to the screened porch, knowing Mitch would follow. The two men settled into the worn, comfortable chairs facing the bay. Quiet for several minutes, they allowed the peace of the view to sink in. Gulls, dipping as they flew, called back and forth to each other. A flock of three black Pelicans glided over the surf. The tide had rolled in, chasing the crabs into their holes.

He remembered the first time he met Mitch, both serving in Afghanistan in the military police. Different localities, but their paths crossed when he was investigating military thefts of weapons that were being sold on the black market. The two men hit it off immediately. He had also decided to join the Army after high school, and served with the Criminal Investigation Command.

When Mitch left the military, he joined the FBI as an investigator after college. But it was not until Lance was discharged, then working with the Richland Police, that Mitch reached out and encouraged him to move to Baytown.

*"You'll love it here...quiet, not expensive, good people. Honest, hardworking people that would give you the shirt off their backs."*

Mitch was persuasive, or perhaps it was just the call of the bay. One visit was all it took and he packed up and moved. Now, a year later, he still enjoyed the peace, making a few acquaintances at the American Legion. Not friends…just good acquaintances.

"Awful quiet out here," Mitch said, appreciating the view.

"Yep," he responded.

"Don't get many visitors this way."

"Nope."

"Guess that suits you, doesn't it?"

"Yep."

Mitch chuckled at the short answers he was receiving, causing Lance to look over at him. Sighing, he said, "You got something you want to say? Or did you just come out here to watch the gulls and drink my coffee? Which, considering your cousin, Jillian, owns a coffee shop, I'm sure you didn't need to come all this way for."

Shaking his head, Mitch turned to him and said, "You always were a straight shooter." Sucking in a deep breath and letting it out slowly, he added, "So, why the hell did you tell Jade that you own the beach and she was trespassing?"

He jerked his head to the side, staring at his friend. "Are you shitting me? She went to the police? I can't believe—"

"Whoa, chill," Mitch interrupted, his gaze now hardened. "First of all, you're not the injured party here, and second of all, no, she didn't come to the police."

Dropping his chin, he grimaced, knowing he had been a jerk to the woman on the beach. Still, he hated having to explain himself.

Mitch explained, "She was talking to the girls this morning…she's friends with Tori and the others."

27

Lance knew exactly who Mitch was referring to—the Baytown Women. Tori, Jillian, and Katelyn. So, if one of them knew, they all knew about the incident.

"I just happened to stop by the coffee shop to check on Tori—"

Jerking his head around, he asked, "Is she okay?"

Smiling, Mitch nodded. "Yeah, she's good. I just had to leave this morning with the call-out and didn't get to kiss her good morning."

Rolling his eyes, he snorted.

"Hey, don't knock it until you've tried it," Mitch laughed. "Anyway, Jade was there and really upset. She was embarrassed that she didn't know this was private property. As you can imagine the others immediately told her that it wasn't."

"Great. Katelyn and Jillian are probably already planning my execution."

Throwing his head back, Mitch laughed. "Well, those two take their friendship duties very seriously."

"Jesus…" he sighed, now wishing he had left the beauty on the beach alone.

"Why the hell did you have to scare her?"

"Scare her? I just told her she was trespassing," he defended, but knew his words sounded peevish.

"Jade's a nice girl. Only been in town for a year…'bout like you. She teaches at the elementary school."

*Great…Now I'm the big, bad wolf to some little Snow White…or was that Red Riding Hood? Fuck, what's the matter with me?* Irritated, he growled, "Didn't stop to ask her about her life story…just wanted her to leave."

Mitch was quiet, sipping his coffee as his gaze stayed on the ever-changing surf.

Lance rolled his neck, wincing at the sore muscles from sitting at his design table for so long. He hated defending his actions, even when they did not make sense. Letting out a long breath, he said, "I just like my privacy, that's all. And she was picking up sea glass. Hell, had a bunch in a bucket."

"Yeah, I figure Jillian showed her your work since the girls were in the galleria." Finishing his cup, Mitch stood. "I love this view," he said. "I like the view from my grandfather's little cabin, but this is a really nice place you've got here." Looking over at him he added, "Too bad you're out here all by yourself. When I invited you to come here to live in Baytown I thought you'd enjoy the town a little more."

"Don't gotta surround myself with a bunch of people all the time to enjoy it," he countered, then hung his head. "Jesus, sorry Mitch. I know I'm an asshole...but I'm an asshole who prefers my own company."

"Nothing wrong with that. But I'd like to think that Baytown has something to offer you besides just the chance to hide."

"People know where I am, I'd hardly call that hiding."

"There's all kinds of hiding...I think you're mostly hiding from yourself. But then, I figure you got your reasons."

No response was needed so he clamped his lips together, his chest tight.

"Don't forget about the American Legion meeting

tomorrow night," Mitch said as he stepped through the door, letting it clang shut behind him, and began walking down the path. "Oh," he called over his shoulder, "and stop harassing the pretty teachers you come across. After all, she was gathering the sea glass for the kids in her class."

He watched Mitch round the corner, heading to his vehicle parked out front. Dropping his head back, he sighed, the face of the teacher—Jade—coming to mind.

Dark hair blowing from a ball cap perched on her head. A pink tank top and white shorts that revealed more of her figure than he wanted to notice. He had stood on the beach, feet apart with his hands on his hips in a threatening stance hoping she would see him and turn around. But she never looked up. She just kept her head down as she searched the beach. He watched as she rushed to the edge of the water, coming up with a large piece of sea glass before she looked out at the ships and yelled a thank you, dancing around in the surf at the same time.

Shaking his head at the memory, he had thought she was a young teen until she came closer, her head still down as she searched. Then, it was easy to see she was a woman, and a beautiful woman at that. And she never looked up.

*Not until she ran right into me.*

A slight grin twitched at the corners of his mouth as he remembered her huge eyes as they widened, taking all of him in. An embarrassed blush painted her cheeks as she dropped her bucket.

*That damned, pink, child's sand bucket.*

Taking the now empty cups back to the kitchen sink, he rinsed them before setting them on the drying rack. He knew Mitch was right—he shouldn't have scared her. Or lied to her. Or made her embarrassed. That was an asshole move. *But damnit, I like my privacy.*

He remembered a time in his past, though now it seemed like centuries ago. Friends. Fun. Drinks with co-workers. Dating. That confident young man was gone. Dead and buried in the hills of Afghanistan.

Walking back into his studio, he tried to focus on the new design he was creating, but as his gaze landed on the clear, plastic containers dividing and holding the different colors of sea glass, he found himself staring at the green ones. Walking over, he reached down, running his fingers through the green, smooth fragments. The various hues glistened in the sunlight. As he continued to stare at the pieces so resembling jade, they began to taunt him.

Jade. Fuck, her name is Jade. He remembered those green eyes staring up at him. The color of her name.

## 5

---

Saturday night, alone in her attic apartment. Baytown did not exactly offer a downtown nightlife, although drinks with friends at Finn's Pub was always a good choice. Jade loved Finn's, owned by the three MacFarlane siblings. Katelyn, who only worked part-time, alongside her two brothers, Aiden and Brogan.

But, tonight, the idea of being alone held appeal. Her day, starting with the run-in with the glowering hulk and meeting with the girls, had been busy with grocery shopping, errands, cleaning her quaint apartment, and preparing new lesson plans.

Standing at her kitchen counter, she poured a glass of wine before moving through the living room. She loved her home, small as it was, and felt lucky to have snagged it, knowing it would not have stayed on the market very long.

Tori once said it reminded her of the attic room she had at her grandmother's Inn, before she moved in with Mitch.

The elderly owners of the house wanted to rent the attic apartment to a female teacher and she had just stumbled across the ad in the newspaper the day they had it listed. One phone call and one visit later, she was in love and, gratefully, they thought she was a perfect tennant as well.

The large attic had been divided into a living area separated from the small kitchen by a counter. She easily fit a grey sofa with burgundy throw pillows, a comfy chair, and TV stand with her newly purchased flat screened TV. Scoring a small coffee table and matching end table off Craig's List rounded out the room. The hardwood floors were the room's glory and she only covered a small portion of the wooden planks with a deep burgundy rug.

The single bedroom was through a door off the living room and her well-appointed bathroom, with its gleaming white tile, included a white, claw-footed tub. She had carried the burgundy theme into her bedroom with a Walmart comforter in multi-tones of burgundy, grey, and white. Craig's List provided her bed frame and matching dresser. There was a window in her bedroom that overlooked the back of the property, including the owner's flower gardens. With her own private entrance from a staircase that rose from the back of the house, she felt completely free.

But it was the deck, off the living room through sliding glass doors, that sold her on the place. The small, but sturdy, deck was large enough for two chairs and a little table, and overlooked the bay. The sunsets filled her apartment each evening, casting the room in a golden glow.

Now, taking her glass of wine there, she sat, leaning her head back as she closed her eyes and let the breeze off the bay flow over her. The distant sounds of people leaving the beach met her ears, as well as the sounds from the restaurants on Main Street, and the muted conversations from a few people walking on the sidewalks. She loved being above it all—three floors high gave her the perfect view of the bay, while still making her feel connected to the town.

Connected. *Exactly what Lance Greene is trying not to be.* She could not stop her thoughts from wandering down that path once more. Truthfully, he had been on her mind all day, alternating between anger and sympathy. Anger that he had lied and intimidated to get her to go away. Sympathy that he felt the need to be so disconnected to others that he did not even want them near his house, which was out of the way to begin with.

She had toyed with the thought of going back the next day to give him a piece of her mind, and had not quite dismissed the idea. *Maybe he wants to be left alone, but he went about it all wrong! And he certainly doesn't have the rights to all the sea glass on the beach!*

Tired of thinking of the enigmatic Lance, she downed the rest of her wine in one gulp and re-entered her apartment. Sighing, she rinsed the glass out before making sure her door was locked and then headed into her bedroom. A long, hot bath while finishing the book she had started was the perfect ending to a day that had not started out perfectly.

Sunday morning dawned just as beautifully as the previous day, and as she finished her bowl of cereal she determined Lance Greene was not going to intimidate her into staying off the southern beach. It had the best view of some of the ships anchored in the bay and she was not going to change her weekend plans for him.

Grabbing her binoculars, shoving the pad of paper and her sunglasses into her little backpack, she settled a ball cap over her head, pulling her ponytail through the hole in the back. With her hand on the doorknob, she spied the pink, plastic bucket with yesterday's bounty of sea glass still inside. Hesitating, she grimaced as she grabbed it on her way out.

Thirty minutes later, she wandered down the beach, keeping a sharp eye out for where she was in relation to Lance's property, making sure to not get close. Stopping, she took note of the ships in the bay, jotting down their names and identifications as well as snapping more pictures. She loved the little camera zoom lens she had bought for her phone, surprised at how much more detail she was able to capture in her photographs.

Finished, she stared down at the sea glass she had added to yesterday's collection. The glistening shards caught the morning light, glowing and twinkling. Almost taunting. Sighing, she lifted her gaze in the direction of Lance's house, even though she was far enough away she could not see it. Her mind wandered to the beautiful artwork he created.

With a determined air, she turned and headed up the dunes toward the road.

———

Having stayed up late again last night, Lance slept in on Sunday morning, a rarity for him. He had spent part of the night working on his latest design, but needed a large piece of sea glass to create the perfect balance.

Rising from bed, he padded into his kitchen, scrubbing the sleep from his eyes as he searched for the coffee. Out. *Damn.* Realizing he had forgotten to pick it up at the grocery, he stood for a moment in indecision, hating the idea of a grocery run. But, the need for caffeine called, so he headed back into his bedroom. A quick shower later, he grabbed his keys on his way out the front door.

As he pulled the wooden door behind him, his foot tapped an object in his way. Looking down, he viewed a pink, plastic, child's sand bucket sitting on his doorstep. Incredulous, he stared for a moment, as though the item was an apparition and would disappear. Leaning over, he spied the sea glass in the bottom, more than yesterday's haul. Sucking in a quick breath, he jerked his head up, scanning the area. No one could be seen. *What the hell is her game?* The idea that someone had come to his doorstep while he was sleeping unnerved him.

Bending, he snapped up the pail, exposing a folded piece of paper underneath. Taking it, he unfolded the missive.

***Mr. Greene, I'm sorry I bothered you yesterday even***

*though I now know the beach is not privately owned by you. Nonetheless, I also know that you use the sea glass to create art and as I have plenty to share with my students, I will gladly return what I gathered yesterday.*

*Jade Lyons*

What should have made him happy, simply infuriated him. How dare she patronize him. *I sure as hell don't want her sympathy!* Angry, he left the bucket on the steps and stomped to his SUV. Driving away, he tried to focus on the coffee and whatever else he might need. But the green-eyed Jade continued to invade his thoughts.

---

Jade pulled into the parking lot at the Baytown Harbor, near where the fishing boats were docked. Discovering the local fishermen who would sell some of their fresh catches to individuals who came before the restaurant trucks was a bonus for living in a little bayside town.

Waving toward the Carson boat, she stopped just at the edge of the pier where they were moored.

"Hi!" she called out, seeing both Richard and his son, Rick, unloading crates of fish.

"Hey, yourself!" Rick shouted. "You in the mood for some striped bass or trout?"

"Ooh, yeah," she enthused, her smile aimed at the young fisherman.

Rick nodded and turned to his father, pulling one of each species of fish out of their tank. Rick walked over the gangway to the pier, moving with her to the table with scales. As he weighed the catch, he asked, "How's Ricky?"

Shaking her head, she laughed, "You know your father will have to rename his business to the Carson and Sons and Grandson."

Chuckling, Rick nodded. "I reckon my boy's got fishin' in his blood."

"Well, he's doing great in my class, so you've got no worries there. He's a smart little boy."

Rick's smile was joined by his father's as he came down the gangway, grinning toward her.

"My grandson behaving himself?" Richard asked.

"I was just telling Rick that Ricky is a smart boy, and I might add, a real pleasure to have in class. And, as you know, he loves talking about going out fishing with you."

Paying for her purchases, she waved goodbye, smiling as she passed the Taylors' crab boat. She loved crab, but never bought it fresh, the idea of boiling them making her feel ill. Continuing on, she walked several piers over to George Caday's boat. Greeting him, she checked to see what catch he had brought in.

"Hey, darlin'," George called out. "I got some flounder today. Not the greatest catch, but it's good enough to filet."

"I'll take one," she agreed, wrinkling her nose at the smell. His boat was older than the Carson's boat and the smell occasionally caused her to take a step back as he weighed her fish. Pulling out his long, sharp filet knife, he deftly slit the fish along the spine, easily separating the flesh from the bone.

"Ugh," she murmured, staring as he pulled the head and spine from the body. With a toss, he got rid of the insides, leaving the white flesh perfect for serving.

He handed her the wrapped, fileted flounder and she smiled her appreciation. "Oh, thank you, Mr. Caday. I'm terrible at getting all the bones out of the fish."

"Been doin' it for so many years, I can filet all kinds of fish with my eyes closed," he laughed, the lines emanating from his eyes deepening. Pushing his old cap back, he asked, "What'd you get from Richard?"

"I got a bass and trout from them," she replied. "With your flounder, I'm set for the week."

He placed his hands on his hips and sighed as he looked over at the Carson's new boat. "Sure is purdy," he stated. "My old boat needs replacing, but then Richard's got family to keep his legacy going. 'Fraid it's just me."

Seeing the sadness cross George's face, she was uncertain what to say.

George did not seem to notice her hesitation, as he continued, "My wife passed on about ten years ago. She got cancer and it took her fast, God bless her soul. We only had one son and he ended up all messed up on drugs. He's been in prison for the past few years and who knows when he might get out."

Stunned at the personal information he was sharing, she simply nodded in sympathy.

"My wife was like you...she'd get up early and come down here when I got in to see what I caught." Chuckling, he added, "She wouldn't wait till I got home. She'd go looking for sea glass and then head over here."

"Yes, me too," she enthused. "I love looking for sea glass. I like to go to the beaches south of town. They are empty and I have all the sea glass I can find."

Before they could continue their conversation, the harbormaster, Skip Morton walked over, clapping George on the shoulder in greeting.

"Is George telling you tales of the biggest fish he caught?" Skip asked after turning his bright blue eyes toward Jade.

George playfully pushed against Skip's shoulder. Just when it appeared he was going to say more, a truck rumbled up, interrupting them. She turned around and watched as the owner of the Sunset View Restaurant climbed down from his vehicle.

Thomas Fedor walked over, greeting George and Skip before seeing her holding a few packages of wrapped fish in her hands.

"You gonna be my competition?" he joked.

"Hardly," she grinned. "But I like to meet the boats once a week and see what I can find."

Nodding, he replied, "You can't do any better than fresh fish. I get my local catches from our harbor's fishermen."

Knowing he had business to conduct, she bid them goodbye and headed back to her car. As she drove away, she observed Thomas standing on George's boat, peering down into his tank of fish as Richard stood watching them from his boat.

Later in the afternoon, Lance tried to work in his studio, but his eyes continually drifted to the pink bucket taunting him as it sat on the corner of his table. Now, trying to remember why he brought it in, the large green piece inside called to him. He knew it would be perfect for his current creation, but the thought that Ms. Lyons' pity had left it on his doorstep made him want to refuse the offer.

A knock on the front door startled him and he tossed his magnifying headgear down as he stalked toward the door. He could not remember the last time someone came to the front door and now, today, he had two visitors so far.

"What?" he all but shouted, throwing open the door. Seeing Ginny Spencer, Baytown's only female police officer, standing on his front stoop had him glowering even more. "What? She's now got you after me? Mitch wasn't enough? I promise I won't scare the little bunny anymore," he grumbled.

Ginny, her hair neatly pulled back into her regulation bun, slid her sunglasses up to rest on her head as her eyes peered up at him. Placing her hands on her hips, she said, "What the hell are you talking about, Lance? What bunny?"

Realizing he was making a fool of himself, he clamped his mouth shut, his lips tightly pressed together.

"You going to ask me in or are we just going to stand here staring at each other, talking about small woodland creatures?" she quipped.

Dropping his head, he let out a deep sigh. "Sorry," he

mumbled, stepping back to allow her entrance. He led the way to the kitchen where he offered her a bottle of water before making his way to the screened porch.

Settling into the chairs, he could not help but think of he and Mitch just yesterday occupying the same ones. He glanced to the side at Ginny, one of the few women in Baytown he had taken the opportunity to get to know. Their shared past of being in the Army's military police gave them a silent camaraderie. Both being members of the American Legion also gave him the chance to observe her. Quiet, introspective, shunned crowds…in many ways, he understood her, probably better than most.

She had recently gotten together with Brogan MacFarlane, a stoic former Marine, and while he did not spend time thinking of matches, he had to admit the two were made for each other. Finally, his curiosity got the better of him, considering she had never visited before. "So, is this a social call or did you just want some water?"

She shifted her gaze from the bay to him, her lips twitching at the corners. "You bust Mitch's balls when he comes to visit?"

"Humph…sometimes." Sighing, he shook his head. "Sorry, Ginny. I'm not fit company for man nor beast," he admitted.

She nodded and he was glad she did not expect, or probably even want, an explanation.

"I've thought about something for a while now, but wasn't at liberty to talk about it. I'm still jumping the gun, but now I know it'll soon be public knowledge, so I wanted to bring it up to you. I kind of figure you might need some time to think about it, in case Mitch talks to you officially."

His interest captured, he turned to look at her more directly.

"The city's budget has allowed the police department to hire another receptionist dispatcher. You might have seen that Mildred's sister, Mable, has joined us."

Lance grinned, remembering the two older women, so alike in looks, one with grey hair tinged with purple and the other's tinged with blue. Nodding, he stayed silent, waiting for her to continue.

"What most people don't know is that Sam has been talking about retiring soon."

Sam Stubbis, the oldest member of the Baytown Police force, had a long, successful career, but lately, health problems had plagued the older man and he had hinted at the last American Legion meeting that his wife wanted him to retire. Looking up sharply at Ginny, he asked, "What's this got to do with me?"

Ginny turned her gaze full force toward him and said nothing, but her stare said it all.

Shaking his head, he responded to her unasked question, "Not interested, Ginny. Mitch has hinted for a year about a job here with the police force...wasn't interested then and not interested now."

She settled back, her eyes now facing the bay again, slowly nodding. After another few minutes, she said, "You got a nice view here. Brogan and I are on the north side of town with a similar view. Sometimes I find myself just looking out for a solid hour, letting the waves wipe away all other thoughts."

He nodded silently, agreeing with her assessment of beach living.

"You know I had no family support when I left the military…haven't heard from them in a long time. Sometimes, even as much as the town and the good friends I have here have adopted me, I still feel strangely alone at times. Lonely in a crowd…crazy, isn't it?"

Once more, completely agreeing with her, he turned his head to the side, staring at her profile.

"I still have nightmares, occasionally. Hell, so does Brogan. Thankfully, we haven't had them at the same time," she said, offering a rueful chuckle. "I got a feeling you have them too."

Seeing his pinched lips, she hastened to add, "Not asking you to share, Lance." She pulled out a card from her pocket, the information from the Eastern Shore Mental Health Group printed clearly on one side. Laying it down on the arm of his chair, she said, "A helluva lot of us in the American Legion have sought their services. It helps…more than you would think."

Suddenly, as though she had accomplished all that she had come to do, she stood and walked toward the back door. With her hand raised, flattened on the wood frame, she looked over her shoulder and said, "Respect your desire to be alone. Respect your desire for privacy. Respect the artwork you create. I think it's good for you…but is it enough? The town could use your investigative skills, Lance. The assistance you offered in the last big case we had was invaluable." Shrugging slightly, she said, "Think about it. That's all I ask."

With that, she walked out, leaving him still sitting in his chair, the business card on the arm, the damn pink bucket still on his table, and his mind racing instead of calm. Watching the surf roll in and out, he shook his head. *So much for a peaceful weekend.*

6

*Fuck it.*

Tired of staring at the large piece of green sea glass that would perfectly finish his work, Lance pulled it out of the pink bucket and walked over to the sink he had installed. Rising it off, his irritation at Jade for finding it, and then giving it to him, abated. He could not keep the smile from his face as he turned the fragment over in his hand, feeling its weight and edges. Perfection. Back at his table, he efficiently completed the mobile.

Holding the finished project up, he studied it for flaws, but the balance was perfect. The combinations of colors satisfied his discriminating eye. Smiling, he knew it was special and wondered if he should keep it or have Jillian display it in her galleria.

Walking into his living room, he took down the smaller mobile hanging from a hook in the corner and replaced it with the new one. The large, green glass twinkled at him as the sunlight came through the window. The memory of Jade's eyes, staring up at him wide with fright as pink stained her cheeks, hit him, but he pushed the thought away once more.

A flash of color by the side window caught his eye and as he hustled over, he stared toward the dune, watching the woman he had just been thinking about hurrying toward his front door, carrying something in her hand. Irritation returned, this time at his peace being interrupted yet again.

Grimacing, he stalked to the door and threw it open just as she was bending over to place the bag on his step.

"What the hell do you think you're doing?"

Jade stood quickly, her mouth open, but nothing came out other than a frightened yelp. She had been sure she would be able to sneak in again and leave the sea glass she had found. Blushing as embarrassment flooded her face, she took a step backward.

"You might not have been trespassing the other day, but you sure as hell are now," he stated firmly.

Swallowing deeply, she gathered her courage. "I just wanted to leave you some more glass...I thought you could use it—"

"I don't recall asking for anything from you...other than to be left alone."

Clamping her lips together, she sucked in a fortifying breath. Standing on the bottom step looking up, he appeared even larger than the other day. Dark hair, messy as though he just ran his hand through it, a day-old scruff on his jaw. His plain, dark grey t-shirt fit tight enough to showcase his muscles. Cargo shorts completed his outfit but, somehow, she doubted he considered his clothes to fall into the category of an *outfit*. More like whatever he grabbed when getting dressed. His hazel eyes bore into hers and she wished she had thought her plan of attempting to be nice and helping him through a little more.

Finally, gathering her wits, she rushed, "You can fuss and fume all you want, but the truth of the matter is, I like looking for sea glass, but other than giving some to my students for art projects I don't need what I find."

"Then why take it? What fascination could you possibly have with sea glass?" he bit back.

Her chest quivering, she stood her ground, staring at the infuriating—and furious—man. Dropping her eyes to the bag of colorful fragments, she wondered how to put into words what was in her heart without him trampling on her feelings. Slowly, she confessed, "Everyone looks at the ocean, but waves come and go. It's as though nothing changes, if the only thing we do is just stare out at the water. But the beach does change… it's full of what the ocean decides to leave for us to discover. Like little gifts. Sea glass is…" swallowing, she lifted her gaze back to him, "it's proof that things can change…for the better. Life can break us into pieces, but we can change, become more beautiful than we were before."

Lance sucked in a quick breath through his nose, her words striking a chord deep within. Letting his breath out slowly, he wondered how she managed to so eloquently state exactly what he had always thought… both about the waves and the sea glass.

Knowing her words sounded ridiculous, Jade

shrugged, adding, "I know you make beautiful things with your glass. I've seen them at Jillian's galleria. I've admired them for a while but never knew who made them."

Feeling foolish in the face of her poetic words about the very thing he cared about, Lance just nodded. "Yeah...okay...thanks. But...uh...you don't have to get any more sea glass for me. I'm good. I find what I need."

He watched her face fall and hated that it was his fault the shine had left her green eyes. She looked down, the bill of her ball cap now hiding her face. He noticed the long ponytail pulled through the back of the cap, the silky, dark tresses flowing down her back. Her make-up free face gave her an innocent appearance—*too innocent for me.* Shoving that thought back from wherever the hell it came from, he sucked in another deep, cleansing breath. "Look, I—"

Her head shot back up, her lips in a tight line. "No, it's all good. I shouldn't have come. I'm sorry, really...I'll leave you alone now."

Before he had a chance to refute what she was saying, she turned and ran back down the drive. Standing in his doorframe, he cursed, "Goddamnit!"

He watched her run from him, darting near the end of the lane to hustle back over the dune. He knew if he walked through the house, he would be able to see her still running down the beach. Away from him.

*Can I blame her? God, I'm such an asshole.*

For a moment, anger at her intrusion filled him, thinking that if she had not invaded his privacy, he would not have bitten her head off. But he knew that was only an excuse. Somewhere inside of him had been a decent person at one time. He knew when he lost that person...he just had no idea how to find him again.

Dropping his head, he stared at his shoes...and the bag of sea glass left next to his feet.

---

"Ms. Lyons, Ms. Lyons!"

Jade turned toward the excited voice and watched as the two little girls twirled the globe. "Did you find where the ships were from?"

"You said one was from Canada and I found it," one of the girls claimed, her small finger pointing to the correct country on the globe.

"I found the one from It-ly," said another child.

"Italy," she corrected, with a gentle smile.

Smiling, she gathered the children around in a semi-circle and together they found the latest countries that she had identified.

"Here are some of the pictures I took the other day when I was on the beach." She began to pass around the photographs she printed of the different ships in the bay. "Using the marine website, I have found the countries that the ships came from and which port they are traveling to."

"How come this one has funny writing?"

"That's Russian. Their language is different from ours and they have a different way to write their alphabet. So the letters on their ship spell the name, but in Russian and not English."

The children, all excited, passed the pictures around, each guessing what they thought they carried.

"I bet this one has cars on it," one little boy claimed, smiling a snaggle-toothed grin. "Daddy says all them *for-yun* cars come on ships from other countries."

"Oh, I'll bet this one has toys on it," another child exclaimed, their eyes wistful at the thought of an entire ship filled with toys.

She laughed, "Well, I haven't started looking to see if I can figure out what they carry, but I am finding more and more that are traveling to the ports in Norfolk and Baltimore—"

"I been there!" another child said, bouncing up and down. "I went to the aquarium in Baltimore."

That started another round of excited voices, all clamoring over where they had been. Bringing the lesson back to the ships, she took the pictures of the ships that had circulated and stuck them on the large map on the wall with push-pins.

The bell rang for the children to head to lunch and as the aide lined them up and walked them toward the cafeteria, she hurried to the teachers' lounge. Twenty-five minutes was not long for lunch, but she was grateful for the chance to have a quiet, although simple, meal with adults.

Just as she arrived, one of the fifth-grade teachers opened the door for her. Bill was a new teacher, his handsome face smiling with a surfer-boy grin as he walked in with her. As she sat and pulled out her sandwich, she watched as he talked to everyone, his flirtatious nature keeping the other teachers entertained. Finishing her sandwich and chips, she stood, glancing at the clock to make sure she had enough time to hustle to the ladies' room before having to pick up her class.

Bill winked at her as she passed by and she offered a small smile in return. Walking back down the hall, she thought of how, at one time, the idea of dating Bill might have held appeal. But for the past week, the dark, brooding Lance had filled her mind, almost against her will. Shaking her head at the irritating thought, she slammed the bathroom door open.

*Well, Lance made it clear...no more sea glass hunting for him...or near him!*

Pulling into the harbor parking lot, Jade observed with a smile that she was not the only one out buying fresh fish. Before she could step from the car, her phone vibrated with an incoming call. Looking at it, she sighed, but answered, knowing that to put off the conversation would only make it worse later.

"Hi, mom," she said, attempting to adopt a carefree tone.

"Jade," her mother began. "I'm calling to see if you were planning on coming home for Thanksgiving."

"I...well, I might...uh..."

"Your father and I are planning a cruise, but I told him I would attempt to see if you wanted to join us. His business partner's family will be going and we thought it would be a nice gesture if you at least made a showing of being with family."

"Mom—"

"No, Jade. There's no excuse for this self-imposed exile of yours. And your father has arranged for the son of another business associate to travel with us. He's most acceptable as an escort for you."

Sighing, Jade dropped her head, staring unseeing toward the ground. "Mom, I don't want to take a cruise and certainly not set up with a blind date."

Silence met her ears and she slowed her steps, knowing what was coming.

"I don't know how long your father will continue to make these offers, Jade, if you continue to live the way you do—"

"Mom, I'm a teacher, not a prostitute—"

"Don't be vulgar," she snapped. "I've got to go, but at least think about it. If not for your sake, think of your father."

Hearing her mother disconnect without saying goodbye, Jade tossed her phone back into her purse. Taking a deep breath, she tried to clear her mind. Continuing toward the docks, she waved at Tori, Jillian, and Katelyn. "Hey, ladies!"

They turned, each waving their greeting. Walking over, she saw Thomas Fedor already on George's boat so she moved to the Carson's, stopping at the gangway. Looking at the other women, she asked, "What are y'all getting today?"

"Mom is making her fish pie for Pops tonight and asked me to get some striper for her," Katelyn grinned.

"Ohhh, fish pie sounds amazing," Jillian groaned. "Maybe I'll get some too."

Tori held her nose as she looked toward George's boat. "Sorry girls, but I think I'm going to have to pass on the fish today."

The others looked on in concern, but Tori waved off their fears. "Just morning sickness that lasts all day long," she bemoaned. "And George's boat is too much for me to stomach. I'll go talk to Skip for a few minutes." Giving out quick hugs, she hurried back to the harbor master's building.

"Mr. Fedor doesn't seem to mind the smell," Jade said, "but I suppose if you run a seafood restaurant, you get used to all the odors."

"The Carsons' boat is so much newer," Katelyn commented, "I guess it hasn't had time to get all stinky."

"Has Mr. Fedor already bought from the Carsons?" Jade asked, wondering if they would have anything left for her.

Jillian nodded. "Yeah, he was here before meeting with George's boat, but don't worry...he held some back for us."

As Rick came down the gangway with the fish for the women, Jade waved at Richard, still on deck. He grinned before turning back to his tanks. She could not help but smile at the thought of Ricky joining his dad and granddad in the family business one day. *There's plenty of work to be done and fishing to be had,* she thought as she admired the Carsons' new boat.

The women walked to the Taylor's crab boat and Jade watched as Katelyn and Jillian bought crabs.

Standing to the side, she observed Harold Taylor tossed the crabs into a large pot of boiling water on the dock. Squeezing her eyes closed, she willed the scene from her memory.

"How can you eat crab in a restaurant and not get it fresh?" Harold asked, his smile firmly in place.

Opening her eyes, she wrinkled her nose and replied, "Well, do you think of a slaughterhouse when you order a hamburger?"

"Ugh," Katelyn blurted, narrowing her eyes at Jade. "Now I'll have that thought in my mind when I serve lunch today at the pub!"

"How about I occasionally cook and pull out some fresh crab meat for you and then you can just get it here and not have to worry about the prep?" Harold asked.

Eyes wide, she grinned. "Oh, my goodness, yes!"

Walking toward her car, she stopped to talk to Skip, still standing with Tori. "Hey, I was just thinking that a field trip to the harbor would be good for my class. We could do it the same day we go to tour the Coast Guard," she said, pointing to the CG's small base, just on the other side of the harbor.

"I'd be pleased to have the kids come," Skip said, his wide smile bright against his tanned face. Weather-worn lines, from sun and sea, creased his face as he pushed his ball cap higher on his forehead. "I love to show off what we have here."

Making the arrangements to call him as soon as she talked to her principal, Jade walked Tori to her car where the two friends stood for a moment.

"You are such a good teacher," Tori said, smiling at Jade.

"I just feel like so many of my students don't get to see some of the wonderful things that go on right here in their hometown. Afterall, that's one of the reasons I came to this area to teach."

"And I, for one, am glad you did," Tori said, with a hug.

As she watched her friend drive away, she smiled. *So am I!*

---

Lance stood as Mitch, commander of the local chapter of the American Legion, rapped the gavel on the podium, calling the American Legion meeting to order. He had arrived early to help set the chairs in the meeting room, an act which had not gone unnoticed by Ginny, who usually worked by herself or with Grant, another police officer and Jillian's fiancé.

She had lifted her eyebrow at him, but he had just shrugged and begun to open the folding chairs, setting them in rows. He could not even explain it to himself, but staying in his house began to feel restricted, so he figured helping was as good as anything to pass the time until the meeting started.

Mitch called out, "The Color Bearer will advance the Colors."

Brogan, the Sergeant-at-Arms, closed the doors of the meeting room of their new space. Jason, standing in the back with Brogan, marched forward, the American flagpole in his hands, and set it in the floor stand as all eyes focused on the flag.

"The Chaplain will offer prayer." This month, the Presbyterian minister stood and prayed as the group bowed their heads in unison.

Next was the part of the meeting's agenda that he hated. The POW/MIA Empty Chair Ceremony. A chair was designated as a symbol of the thousands of American POW/MIAs still unaccounted for from all wars and conflicts involving the United States of America. The POW/MIA flag was placed on the Empty Chair.

He knew every eye was facing the chair, but it felt as though they were watching him as he stared at the chair. That goddamn chair. He knew more than one good soldier that did not come back, but it was the one that haunted his nightmares that had his heart pounding and his palms sweating. A gentle touch on his arm brought him back to the here and now, his eyes jumping to Ginny as she turned her concerned face up toward his.

The meeting continued, Aiden reading the past minutes and Zac reading the treasurer's report, but he tuned them out as he worked to quiet his thoughts. Before he realized it, Brogan was assisting one of the oldest members to the front, wheeling him in his wheelchair, as Mitch handed the microphone to him. One of the agenda items Mitch had adopted was encouraging AL members to share a story from their time in the service, especially difficult ones. He imagined how hard it was to face the group and share, but appreciated the gesture from the others.

The veteran's hand, as well as his voice, shook as he held the microphone. "Name's Dennis. I'm ninety-seven years old. I was a young Lieutenant...Navy...fought in the Pacific...World War II." He rested a moment, but no one in the room was in a hurry.

Glancing sideways, Lance recognized the same expression on everyone else's face that was on his own as they listened to him—one of rapt attention.

"Commanded a PT boat...served along with my buddy Jack...you know him as former President John Kennedy."

At that proclamation, Lance leaned forward, his heart in his throat as he listened.

"We were young...innocent...didn't know nothin', although we thought we did. It was easy sometimes... firing them guns off our boats. Watching the Jap's sink..." Dennis' wrinkles settled deeper into his face. "That's what we called 'em. Japs....and a lot of other names. Most weren't very nice. I 'spect some o' you had names for who you were fightin' also."

A few small grins appeared around the room as well as some shifting in seats.

Sighing, he added, "It makes it easier, I suppose, to not think of the enemy as real humans...with families back home wondering about 'em. If we just gave them a nasty nickname, it made it easier to do what we were told to do."

Understanding nods now replaced the smiles, as the members' faces registered the truth in the older vet's words.

Dennis sat for a moment, his hand holding the

microphone resting in his lap. Aiden, closest to him, scooted his chair forward, taking the microphone from his shaking hand and holding it for him, gaining a nod of appreciation.

"Thank you, son. Don't got the strength I had when I was younger." His voice now stronger, without having to deal with the microphone, he continued, "Things got rough...sure, we had some pictures taken of us on islands, fishing, hanging together. We got tanned and felt invincible." Shaking his head, he said, "Young bucks, all of us. Thinking that shooting down other boats was the greatest thing ever."

After another pause, he said, "But when things get desperate, men do desperate things."

Lance's heart was thundering in his ears and he was sure the others could hear it pound. He watched as the memories moved over Dennis, recognizing that despair.

"We'd taken prisoners and transported them to some of the island camps, but," he shook his head, "we had too many. The last thing our superiors wanted, was live Japanese. Didn't want anyone to come back and take up arms against us again. So, we were given orders." He lifted his rheumy eyes toward the gathering of the former military from many different wars and said, "And we followed them orders. Didn't know anything else to do. Were told to put them in the water and run 'em down with our boats. If there were Japanese sailors in the water, we ran 'em down." Shaking his head, he said, "I can still see it...sixty years later. Bodies...pieces of bodies. A PT boat ain't that big. So, when we did what we were told...we knew it.

Felt it. Saw it. That kind of horror…can steal your soul."

Sucking in a breath, he added, "No different than a lotta you had to face. We all did what we were told. Saw things no man should ever see. Did things no man should ever do. I've lived with it for a long time. Never told my wife. Never told anyone until tonight. But, I spent years making peace with God, so I could live with myself. No one ever told us these things when we joined the service."

Aiden continued to hold the microphone and, with his other hand, held the old man's hand as well. Lance knew Aiden as the happy-go-lucky MacFarlane, but at that moment, he could see he was connecting with Dennis, as all of them were.

Finally, Dennis nodded slightly, and said, "That's all any of us can do with the orders we followed. Make peace with God. And make peace with ourselves."

As Aiden pushed Dennis back to his place, the crowded room was silent, other than the sound of a few sniffles as people wiped their eyes. Lance felt something on his cheek and lifted his hand, feeling the moisture. Blinking rapidly, he realized it was a tear trailing down his face. With a quick wipe, he leaned back heavily, glancing to the side, thankful Ginny's gaze was still on the front of the room.

Sliding his hand into his pocket, he felt the card she had given him earlier. The idea of talking to someone about what he experienced scared him more than his nightmares. But then green-eyed Jade came to mind and the hurt expression on her face when he rebuffed her simple offer of sea glass sliced through him. Gripping the card tightly, he knew he would never have a chance to be whole again without help. The chance to have friends. The chance to care. With that thought swirling in his mind, the idea of being around the pretty teacher did not scare him shitless.

## 7

"Lance? Hell, man, this is an honor," Aiden declared as many of the American Legionnaires walked to Finn's Pub after the meeting.

Brogan cuffed Aiden on the back of the head, "Shut up, bro." Looking over at him, he just gave an approving chin lift.

He nodded in return, appreciating Brogan's stoic demeanor, not making a big deal about it. He had never gone to an after-meeting, preferring to avoid public gatherings.

Aiden, never losing his grin, opened the door as they arrived and the whole group poured through the door. Heart pounding, Lance stopped just inside, taking in the crowded space. He had never hated crowds earlier in his life—it seemed to develop about the same time the nightmares began. *One more thing to talk to someone about when I finally make that appointment.* Shaking his head slightly, he walked toward the back where it appeared the group was gathering. Katelyn brought pitchers of beer over and other servers arrived with platters of wings.

It did not take long to see many of his friends pairing off in their natural couples. Gareth tucked Katelyn underneath his arm as Mitch slid in next to Tori, his hand immediately going to her stomach. Grant's lips were already on Jillian, and Ginny had found Brogan's lap.

The others quickly settled all around. Callan and some of his Coast Guard buddies made their way to the dart board, a rousing game ensuing. Aiden checked with the bartenders to make sure everything was in order and then made his way to a table nearby with Jason and Zac, who waved him over, pointing to an empty chair.

Taking it, he nodded at the server who poured him a beer and drank quietly, listening to the multitude of conversations flowing all around as music played in the background. Slowly the nerves decreased as he found that the situation was not as awkward as he always assumed it would be.

Jillian, leaning her head around Grant, asked Lance about some of his artwork she was displaying, Mitch was organizing another beach cookout for everyone, and most of the others were in quiet conversations and checking their phone calendars for Mitch and Tori's party.

Tori touched his arm and said, "Lance, I hope you'll come."

With a short smile, he nodded, "I'll try."

He noticed the looks shared amongst the group, intuitively knowing they were stunned at his attempts to be sociable. He heard a roar of cheering from the front and looked up toward the dart game, observing a few women standing nearby, clapping for the winners.

"Belle! Jade!" he heard Callan call out. His gaze shot to the front door, seeing the two women walking in, both wearing huge smiles. Belle was pretty, but it was the dark-haired, green-eyed beauty that snagged, and held, his attention.

Tonight, she was wearing make-up—not heavy, but just enough to illuminate her eyes and giving her cheeks and lips a bright color. And was standing right in the middle of a bunch of single guys. He wanted to look away. Tell himself it did not matter. But he could not— on either account. He continued to stare, uncertain if he wanted her to look over at him and possibly frown when she saw him, or keep her eyes on the dart game where the smile was sure to remain on her face.

He did not have to wait long for, in a moment, she turned and shifted her perusal over to the back of the bar where most of her friends were. He felt the instant her eyes met his…the widening of surprise followed by an immediate blush as she ducked her head. Turning away in haste, she leaned over and whispered some-thing to Belle, whose face immediately fell before she nodded and gave her a hug.

Without a look back, she moved toward the door and walked out into the night. Belle, her name called by one of the other women, smiled her shy greeting as she approached. Even from way in the back, focused as he was, he could hear their conversation.

"Where's Jade?" Jillian asked, looking toward the front.

"Oh, she said she had a headache and decided she needed to get home so she could take something for it," Belle explained, as she slid into a seat next to Katelyn.

*She left because of me*, he thought, remorse filling him. Having had enough socialization for one night, plus the overwhelming desire to check on Jade, he stood, excusing himself. Slipping out the door, he looked up and down the street, dark except for the lights above casting faint illumination down on the sidewalk. No Jade. Hearing a car engine start, he looked over, watching as she drove by. He stood, staring, until her taillights were no longer in view.

Walking back to his vehicle, he climbed in but instead of putting the key into the ignition, he sat for a few minutes, his decisions now coming to haunt him. *I came to Baytown to start over...but have I really? Or am I still stuck in the same shitty place I was when I got out of the Army?*

Later that night, lying on his back watching the ceiling fan slowly turn as he did every night, he made two decisions. Call the Eastern Shore Mental Health Center for an appointment, and next, see if he could repair whatever he fucked up with the beautiful teacher who just wanted to share her sea glass.

He remembered her words as he drifted to sleep... *Sea glass is proof that things can change...for the better. Life can break us into pieces, but we can change, become more beautiful than we were before.*

Feeling foolish for having left the pub early, Jade walked into her apartment, kicking her shoes off at the door and tossing her bag onto the kitchen counter.

"I didn't even stay long enough to get a beer," she grumbled to herself. Grabbing one from the refrigerator, she moved over to plop onto her sofa and downed half the bottle at one time.

Sighing heavily, she started to turn on the TV but soon recognized there was nothing interesting on. *Plus, I've got morning bus duty*, she remembered, accepting that she did not need to spend half the night channel surfing to try to drown out the memory of seeing Lance sitting with their friends.

He had never been there before, at least not that she had seen. She had heard his name mentioned occasionally, but since he did not frequent their gatherings, nor hung out at the pub or other town establishments, she had never seen him until their run-in on the beach.

*Why does he have to be so gorgeous? It would be so much easier to push him out of my mind if his looks didn't draw me in.* The first time she met him he wore sunglasses and, when he took them off, the anger on his face kept her from focusing on his unusual eye color. On their second fateful meeting, he stood in the shadows of his doorframe and it was difficult to discern much about his eyes. But tonight, even across the bar, she had been able to see his hazel eyes piercing hers. As usual, no smile, but just a stare that scorched right through her.

"Ugh," she proclaimed out loud, as she stood and

poured the rest of her beer down the drain. Moving into her bedroom, she grabbed her pajamas and headed into the shower, hoping the warm water would wash away the thoughts of him. Later, lying in bed, she had to admit, the shower was cleansing, but no such luck forgetting Lance Greene.

---

Another email. That makes one a week for the past three weeks.

Lance stared at the electronic missive, wondering what his mother's motive was, other than ruining his morning. Always the same. He was selfish, he needed to stop running away and help his father run their business, he needed to see to his trust, take accountability for becoming a soldier, policeman, and then an artist, and recognize how each had only alienated his father more.

His finger hesitated over the reply button before moving to delete. His thoughts slid back to the the American Legion meeting, seeing some of the families represented. Three generations of MacFarlanes, from Finn, the grandfather, to Eric, his son and father to Aiden and Brogan. Mitch and his father, Ed, as well as Ed's brother, and Jillian's dad, Steve. Families that shared...cared. A foreign concept to Lance, but one he would have liked to experience.

He knew Ginny was estranged from her family after she left the military, but with Brogan and now the whole MacFarlane clan in her corner, as well as the police department and the American Legion and Legion Auxiliary, she was well connected.

Rubbing his hand over his face, he shoved thoughts of his family from his mind. Looking at the early morning dawn painting the sky, he suddenly moved into action. Pouring a cup of coffee into a travel mug, he hesitated for a moment, then poured a second travel mug full of the steaming brew. Uncertainty crept in, but before he gave into the indecision, he added sugar and cream into one of the mugs. Screwing the lids on tightly, he headed out the back door, hoping his hunch would pay out.

He had walked for almost a quarter of a mile toward the north, when he spotted someone coming south. Too far away to clearly discern who the early morning walker was, he stopped and, moving back slightly from the edge of the water, sat in the sand.

His eyes stayed on the person, satisfied as they neared that it was Jade. The early morning breeze had become chillier and today she wore a green t-shirt with tight, black pants with the legs rolled up her shins. Her head was down as she walked along, occasionally stopping to pick up what must have been sea glass. As she came closer, she still had not noticed him. Pausing to lift her binoculars to her face, she peered out toward the bay. Pulling something from her backpack, he watched as she alternated between looking through the binoculars, looking on her cell phone, and writing on a small pad. After a moment, she put the paper away and picked up her small bag containing her collection of sea glass.

She drew nearer, but still had not noticed anyone

else on the beach. He grew concerned, realizing how vulnerable she was, out here alone and, seemingly so unaware of her surroundings, focusing only on the ships or the shore.

Not knowing what to say, he cleared his throat loudly.

Squealing in fright, she jumped back, eyes wide, as she jerked her head around to see him now standing about ten feet away. Immediately her gaze moved from his face to over his shoulder, and she blurted, "I'm not near your property. I keep track of where I should stop. And I—"

Hating that he put such restrictions in her mind, he raised his hands up in supplication. "No, no. It's okay. It's no problem for you to…uh…be here."

Jade sucked her lips in, staring at Lance, wondering what he was going to berate her about today. He slid his sunglasses up on his head, exposing his hazel eyes for her perusal, noting the golden flecks, causing her breath to catch in her throat. Hating that he had a mesmerizing effect on her, she dropped her gaze to his still raised hands, both carrying travel mugs. Before she had a chance to ponder that curious fact, he spoke again, once more drawing her attention back to his eyes.

"I…thought you might want…uh…coffee?" he stuttered, holding a mug out toward her.

Not moving, other than her nose scrunching in confusion, she stared dumbly, first at the proffered drink and then up to his face again.

"I didn't know if you might be thirsty…you know… uh…from your walk." His gut tight, Lance realized how rusty his social skills were, cringing at the sound of his own voice.

Staring at him, she tried to ascertain some hidden meaning in his words.

He observed her hesitation, as well as the doubt in her eyes, and rushed to say, "Honest...I just wanted to offer you some coffee."

"Why?"

Her hand wrapped around her middle, an unconscious act of protection that did not go unnoticed by him. Heaving a sigh, his shoulders slumped at what he knew would be her blatant rejection. "No reason...other than to just apologize."

At that, Jade visibly started, blinking several times, trying to figure him out. The idea of shutting him down —hard—was tempting, but she knew it was not in her nature to treat him the way he had treated her. "Apologize?"

"We've only met twice and both times, I was a complete ass—"

"Agreed," she quickly interrupted.

"I know I don't deserve it, but I'd truly like to apologize and hope you will accept it." Lance watched as she stared at him for a moment and felt as though she was inspecting him as much as the ships out in the bay she was so fascinated with.

"I'm Lance. Lance Greene," he continued, fear of her rejection creeping along his spine.

Jade carefully observed the man in front of her. Seeing him standing there, so large but so cautious, the coffee still held out in offering, her lips began to twitch

71

into a smile. Nodding slowly, she realized how difficult this exchange must be for him and her heart softened.

"My name is Jade. Jade Lyons. And I accept your apology," she said, her smile now fully in place. "I'd also love some coffee."

Reaching out her hand, she took the mug from him, her fingers gliding along his hand. The warmth she felt had nothing to do with the temperature of the mug, but everything to do with the man in front of her. Eyes wide at the tingling exchange, she watched as he snatched his hand back, obviously feeling the same effect.

## 8

---

Taking a sip, Jade was pleasantly surprised at the flavor, having expected a man like Lance to drink his coffee black. Smiling up at him, she approved, "Wow, this is good."

Letting out a breath he had not realized he had been holding, Lance offered a slight smile in return. "I wasn't sure how you took it, so I...uh...just guessed you might like cream and sugar."

Him taking the time to think about what she might like, caused Jade even more confusion, wondering what he was thinking. Nodding, she took another sip, not having any idea how to respond to the sudden and complete change in his demeanor.

"Would you like to walk...or sit...whatever?" he asked, hesitation lacing his words.

"We can walk some more. I'm parked fairly close today, so..." her voice trailed off as she watched him turn toward the south, as though he no longer minded her walking closer to his house. Deciding to not fight what was going on, she moved along with him, noting he shortened his stride to make it easier for her to keep up.

They walked in silence for several minutes, sipping their coffee as the sun rose high enough to paint the pink dawn a brilliant blue.

"I noticed your binoculars," he began, glancing down at her. "What do you look at? I thought maybe the birds around."

Smiling, she replied, "I do love the birds, but I was looking at ships."

Lifting an eyebrow, he repeated, "Ships?"

Laughing, she explained, "I like to identify the ones anchored in the bay. I write down their information, if I can see it, and take pictures. Then I use an app on my phone or, when I get home, my computer to determine which ships are out there. From that, I can see where they came from and where they are going."

Lance stayed silent for a moment, trying to figure out why she would care about the ships, but hated to ask. Looking toward the dunes, he could tell that they were only a few minutes from his house and wondered how she would react, considering how much of an ass he had been the two previous times she was near. His thoughts were interrupted when she stopped suddenly, shoving her coffee at him. Taking it, he followed her line of vision out to the bay, noting the cargo ship anchored closest to them. It had floated so that the side was clearly visible.

She positioned the binoculars over her eyes, her lips turned up into a smile. Dropping them, she shifted her backpack so that she could pull out her pad of paper and a pen. She jotted down the name and numbers from the side of the ship.

Looking up at his curious expression, she smiled as she reached for her coffee again. "I'm sure you must think me odd," she began, "but I've been trying to get a picture of that ship all morning, but was never able to see it clearly."

"Okay," he mumbled, his brows drawn down.

"You've gotta be wondering why," she teased, still grinning as she turned her face up to his.

At that moment, with her beaming face shining toward his, he did not care what her reason was for watching boats—he just wanted her to keep smiling. Seeing her look at him expectantly, he grinned in return, the smile feeling odd on his lips. "Yeah, I'm curious." As her eyes drifted behind him, he looked over his shoulder and realized they were in front of his house. Jerking his head around quickly, he asked, "Would you like to sit for a bit? I've got some chairs at the top of the dune."

Biting her lip, she hesitated before replying, "That's okay...um...I'd better be going—"

"I'd really like for you to stay," he hurried. "I'd like to hear more about the ships..." His voice trailed off as he realized how desperate he sounded. Waiting for her refusal, his heart skipped a beat as her smile returned.

"Okay," she agreed, then laughed as she added, "If

you don't mind being bored, I'll fill you in on my ship spotting!"

Walking up the dune, he reached out and grasped her elbow to offer steadiness in the shifting sand. Wondering what had come over him, he almost laughed at the long-forgotten social niceties, glad they had not left him entirely.

Arriving at the top, Jade had the opportunity to see the back of his house, noting the large screened porch on the side that led to a plank deck containing a few wooden rocking chairs. The back of his house was mostly windows, through which she could make out living room furniture. She followed him to the deck and settled in one of the chairs, smiling as she immediately began to rock back and forth. "Oh, I love rocking chairs," she exclaimed. "They remind me of my grand-mother's front porch."

It was the first personal tidbit she had shared and Lance considered inquiring about her family, but caught himself. *Asking her opens the door to her asking me about mine...and I have no desire to go down that road.* Settling into the chair next to hers, he moved the conversation back to her beach activities. "So, why do you try to identify the ships in the bay?"

"It's for my kids. I taught first grade last year, but have moved up to second this year and I love it. It's amazing the change in just that one year of age. In first grade, so much of our time is spent teaching reading, but in second grade, I can be more creative with other subjects, like science and geography."

She held his attention and he welcomed her enthusiasm, noting that the more she talked, the faster she rocked. Nodding, he encouraged her to continue.

"I check the ships anchored in the bay and see if I can find out where they've come from. We have a large map, as well as a globe, and we pin pictures of the ships onto the map. It helps the kids to learn about the oceans and basic continents. Obviously, at this age, we don't get into memorizing the countries, but it helps to expand their minds while realizing that the world comes to the bay right next to their town."

Her hands had fluttered about as she talked and now settled onto the arms of her seat as she continued to rock, her smile firmly in place.

"That's really interesting," he said, his eyes never leaving hers.

Blushing, she ducked her head. "I guess it sounds pretty lame to some people, but," she looked back up, "I really love teaching."

Desiring to ask her more, he hesitated again, not wanting the conversation to turn toward him, so he just nodded instead.

"Also, I've gotten to know some of the local commercial fishermen and can watch them go out into the bay as well. George Caday, the Carsons, and the Taylor family fishermen."

"I've met George and the oldest Carson at the American Legion. Can't say I know them, but I recognize their names."

Grinning, she added, "Sometimes, I meet the ships when they come back into the Baytown Harbor and will buy some fresh fish before their catch heads to the restaurants. George Caday is a sweet man who doesn't mind filleting the fish for me, because I am terrified of fish bones. Oh, but talk about terrifying—I can only chat with the Taylors because they go crab fishing and I hate the squiggly crab claws. The Carsons are a family run business and I have the littlest one in my class." Laughing, she said, "They are Richard, his son Rick, and the next generation is Ricky."

Realizing he had lived in Baytown for over a year and had not discovered buying fresh fish from the local fishermen, he watched her obvious enjoyment as he pursed his lips.

Easing into silence, Jade looked at the bay. Confused by his change in demeanor toward her, she wondered if she were overstaying her welcome. Slowing her motion, she pushed up on the arms of the rocker, standing. "Thanks for the coffee, Lance. It was a surprise…uh…a nice surprise."

He stood quickly, taking the empty mug from her hands, replying, "I really am sorry…I'm out of practice being…well, I'm sorry for the way I acted."

She turned her face up toward his, her attention held in place for a moment by the look in his eyes, knowing she could so easily stare into their depths for a long time. Reaching out, she placed her hand on his arm, offering a little squeeze, loving the feel of his warm skin underneath her fingertips. "See you later," she said, just before turning and walking back down the dune to the beach.

Wanting to look over her shoulder to see if he was watching, she finally gave in and sent a quick glance back. He was standing on his deck, his hands on his hips, his eyes on her, and to her disbelieving eyes, he threw his hand up in a small wave. Smiling, she waved back before breaking into a jog as she continued up the beach toward her car.

When she was finally out of sight, Lance faced the bay, seeing the ships on the water in an entirely different light. Shaking his head, he turned and walked inside, still feeling the touch of her hand on his arm and the way her sparkling eyes lit her face.

---

Jade laughed along with the others as Callan, Zac, Jason, and Aiden battled in beach volleyball, goofing off as much as slam-dunking the ball over the net. Mitch and Grant manned the grill as Brogan carried out a large ice chest filled with beer and water bottles. Tori placed covered dishes out on the picnic table on the deck, Jillian and Katelyn assisting. The sound of gentle waves washing upon the shore mixed with their laughter and music from the deck.

Tonight, they gathered at Mitch's bayside cabin that once belonged to his grandfather, who used it as a fishing cabin many years ago. It was stark compared to the nice rental cabins, being furnished simply, but the family had enjoyed many meals on the wooden deck and sing-a-longs around the fire pit. Now, it belonged to Mitch and Tori and they used it to host parties and cookouts with friends.

Mitch and the rest of the Baytown Boys had hauled

large logs from a neighbor's farm and cut them to place in a circle around the fire pit. The area was big enough to hold most of their group, with a few others in beach chairs to the side. The configuration allowed visitors to either sit on the logs or recline in the sand and have something to lean back against, which is what she was doing now.

"Hey," a soft voice greeted and as she looked up, she saw Belle sitting on the log next to her.

Smiling at her friend, she glanced at her clothes, surprised to see her still in her nursing scrubs since she usually showed in her cute sundresses.

"I know, I feel stupid," Belle admitted, blushing, as she nervously tucked a long strand of hair behind her ear. "I totally forgot about the cookout and then Tori called just as I was leaving work to ask if I could pick up some more potato salad at the grocery. I didn't want to make everyone late, so I hurried over, still in my uniform."

"Sweetie," she rushed to assure, "you look beautiful."

Blushing more, Belle smiled in return. "By the way, have you been able to avoid Lance since your run-in with him?"

She had not told her friends about leaving sea glass on his stoop, or getting caught when doing it a second time, or about the apology, served with coffee, the other day. "Well, I've seen him and we just talked...a little bit."

Belle's wide eyes and dropped jaw showed her surprise. "Really...you talked to him?"

Snorting, she said, "Yeah, he apologized and we

chatted a few minutes. Nothing major, but I thought it was nice for him to make an effort."

"Wow...other than the American Legion and a few of the guy-only cookouts, I didn't know he made an effort to get to know anyone at all."

Ginny plopped down on her other side and said, "Sorry, I was eavesdropping. Lance actually helped Brogan a few months ago when I got shot. I was kind of surprised, but he's really a good person. He's just private."

Nodding, she agreed, but kept her opinions to herself, afraid her true interest in the iconic man might show. Watching Ginny hop up as Brogan came over, she heard Belle say under her breath, "I hope there's someone out there for me someday." Before she could assure her, Belle stood and moved over to the tables.

Leaning her head back she closed her eyes, enjoying the breeze coming off the bay, the scent of sizzling meat, and the sound of her friends' laughter. For the millionth time, she thanked God she had landed on Tori's doorstep when she first came to town and that the close community of friends easily added her to their tight group.

A body plopped down next to her, bumping into her side, and her eyes jerked open. "Callan, what on Earth?" she laughed. "Can't you find another seat that doesn't include landing on me?"

"Just thought you looked lonely, sitting here by yourself," he joked, shoulder bumping her.

Sitting up quickly, she turned toward him and said, "Oh, but you are just the person I wanted to talk to."

Winking, he said, "See, I knew I had a purpose for coming over here."

Playfully pushing against his leg, she said, "No, seriously."

"Okay, Jade. Shoot."

"I really would like to bring my second-grade class to tour the Coast Guard facility here. I am working with Skip as well. Do you think that would be possible and, if so, who do I need to talk to?"

"I don't see why you couldn't. You want me to get the commander in touch with you?"

"Yes, please. The kids would love it since we study the ships coming into the bay."

Eyebrows raised, he listened with interest as she described her process of identifying the ships, looking up their origins, and then having the children find them on the maps. By the time she finished, she looked around and saw that she had the attention of several of his fellow Coast Guard buddies as well.

*What more could a girl ask for*, she thought. Surrounded by handsome, single men...but not the one she dreamed of. Sighing, she smiled as Callan winked at her just as someone called out, "Lance! Good to see you!"

Her head instantly whipped around, eyes landing on the man filling her mind. He was standing on the deck near the grill, his eyes boring straight into hers. Blushing, she wondered how long he had been there and if he had seen how close Callan had been sitting.

*It shouldn't matter*, she chastised herself. *Other than*

*coffee, he's never attempted to stake any claim, so he has no interest.*

And yet, as she tried to convince herself he had just been trying to make amends the other day, she wished it had been more.

# 9

Lance had stood outside the front of Mitch's cabin, the sound of laughter and the scent of the grilled meat from the back greeting him. Hesitating, he wondered for an instant what persuaded him to come but, truthfully, he knew the answer. When he ran into Mitch and Tori at the grocery store earlier that day, they reminded him of the cookout. Tori rattled off the names of their usual friend group who would attend, and even though he knew them all, he decided it was not his scene. Until she mentioned *her*. Jade. Once that name crossed Tori's lips, he knew he would give in to the urge to see her again.

Now, he was here, on the deck, and a quick glance revealed she did not lack for male company. It did not matter that the men had all moved on to grab food or go back to their game, just seeing her surrounded had shot a bolt of jealousy though him—an emotion he was totally unfamiliar with. The desire to flee ran through his mind, but then he looked at her—really looked at her.

Her gaze was on him. Her smile was directed his way. Her body leaned forward slightly, and as he continued to stare, she stood up, dusted the sand from her hands, and walked toward him, moving with a natural grace. Now the desire to flee was replaced with the desire to stay, if only to be in her presence a little longer.

Her jeans fit her hips and thighs perfectly and the green t-shirt under her navy sweater made her eyes appear larger and brighter. With no ball cap on, her long, dark hair flowed over her shoulders, the tresses lifting slightly in the bay breeze.

He continued to hold her gaze as she stepped up onto the deck, making her way over, but he noticed that, as she slowly neared, her smile tightened. Recognizing her nervousness, he cursed himself, knowing she was still gun-shy. Determined to erase that look on her face, he turned his body and directed his attention toward her, his lips curving in a slight smile. The relief in her eyes was amazing to watch, the dark green lightening as her smile relaxed.

"Hey," she said, so close now she had to lean her head back to hold his gaze. "I'm surprised to see you here... pleasantly surprised, I should add."

"Thanks," he replied, his eyes leaving hers only to shift around the gathering before landing back on her face. "I don't usually...well, I guess you know I don't tend to socialize much."

She placed her hand on his arm and leaned in. "It's okay, you know. Not everyone has to be Mr. Sociable, like them," she said, jerking her head toward the beach where the volleyball game had resumed its rowdiness.

"I noticed you captured their attention," he said, then immediately wished he had kept his mouth shut instead of letting his jealous insecurities show.

Grinning, she replied, "Come on. Come sit with me. I assure you, there's plenty of room and no one else I'd rather talk to."

At that proclamation, he breathed easier, nodding at the others as he followed her to the fire pit, trying to ignore their surprised expressions. Walking behind her, his gaze inevitably dropped to her ass, perfectly silhouetted in her jeans with her long legs tapering to her bare feet with pink-painted toenails. Sucking in a quick breath, he felt the pang of jealousy again, knowing he was not the only man there who was interested.

She bent over, grabbing the towel she had been sitting on and gave it a shake, knocking the sand off. Laying it back down, she spread it out wider before sitting down, her back against the massive log. Patting the other side of the towel, she looked up at him expectantly.

Settling his large frame next to her petite one, he was conscious of the space—or lack thereof—between them. Sliding his leg over to give her more room, she shook her head slightly.

"Don't worry, you're not crowding me."

Following her lead, he leaned back, finally relaxing, as others settled around the fire pit as well. His trepidation about being in a group of people lessened as he watched the camaraderie amongst the friends, old and new. The men he knew from the American Legion. The police officers he knew from assisting with one of their cases a few months earlier. And most of the women he knew from their men. Watching the couples interact, he rubbed his chest absentmindedly, the idea of a relationship seeming foreign and yet, now, with Jade sitting so near, he could almost imagine his arm around her possessively.

An elbow punch from the side jolted him and he dropped his gaze to her.

Grinning, she said, "You're staring so intently at everyone, I thought maybe you forgot I was here."

Heat flooding his face, he shook his head. "I can guarantee that would never happen."

"Do you like to people watch?"

"Not usually, but with this group, it's nice to see the way everyone interacts."

Her face brightened, as she nodded. "I know exactly what you mean! When I first decided to teach here, I didn't know anyone. I ended up staying a few weeks at the Sea Glass Inn, where I met Tori. She immediately befriended me and began including me in her gatherings. That's how I came to know Jillian, Katelyn, and Belle. They all went to school together here and, since they have known each other for years, I felt honored to be included. Recently, Ginny's joined our crazy group as well."

"They're the lucky ones to have you be their friend, if you ask me," he commented, his eyes still roaming her face.

Before Jade had a chance to respond, Mitch called

out that the food was ready. Lance jumped up, holding his hand out to her. Smiling, she placed her smaller hand in his much larger one, feeling the power in his grip as he assisted her to stand. Turning toward the deck, she observed the other women all staring at her, huge smiles on their faces. Blushing, she walked next to him as they got in line.

Soon, they were all gathered around the fire pit or in chairs around the edges, plates balanced on their laps, beers and sodas nestled in the sand to keep them from tipping over.

"Hey, Jade," Callan called out. "Just got a text back from the commander. He said a field trip would be fine. You just need to figure out a day and time that'll work and coordinate it with him."

Grinning widely, she nodded in appreciation. "Thanks! That was quick. I want to combine it with the trip to the harbor to visit Skip. I think he'll be easy with the dates, so I'll work with your commander first. I'll have to do the paperwork with my principal and then I'll get in touch with him. The kids will be thrilled."

"How you handle twenty-five little ones every day is amazing to me," Katelyn said. "I'd lose my mind. It's hard enough for me to handle my brothers."

Everyone laughed as Aiden and Brogan both threw their wadded paper napkins at her, easily deflected by Gareth.

Shrugging, she replied, "I love it. Second grade is wonderful...they're young enough to still be interested in learning and yet old enough to have some responsibility."

Listening to the conversations, Lance realized he was discovering more about Jade than he had on his own. His desire to keep the topics from being too personal had also kept him in the dark about her life.

Peeking through her lashes toward him, Jade noticed his quiet introspection and had the feeling there was very little going on around them that escaped his attention. Curious as to why he normally eschewed social gatherings, she wanted to know more about him without making him feel self-conscious. Not sure how to do that, she determined to watch and listen, seeing what she could pick up on.

"Lance, I've sold a few more of your sea glass mobiles. When do you think you'll have more for me?"

"I've got some ready. I can bring them by this week, if you'd like."

"Oh, that'd be great," Jillian enthused. "There are two wedding parties in town next weekend and the guests always end up in the galleria looking for unusual gifts."

"I wondered what was going on," Tori added. "My inn is fully booked."

"One of the waitresses at the Sunset View Restaurant came into the pub and was talking about the increased wedding business they were getting," Katelyn remarked.

"I love what the new owner of the Sunset is doing," Tori said. "I know a lot of townspeople were concerned when somebody from New York came down and bought it, but he's turned what was a nice, but slowly dying, restaurant into a real destination place."

Katelyn nodded, "I was very skeptical when he

bought it at the auction, but the marina is gorgeous and they are going to start a simple breakfast during the summer out near the water."

"The empty building next to the restaurant is now a nice reception area," Belle said. "One of our part-time nursing assistants was going to get a seasonal job there."

"Who's the new owner?" Jason asked.

"Thomas Fedor," Tori replied. "He was great to work with when I was planning our wedding reception."

"Well, your wedding there was gorgeous," Jillian said, smiling as Tori grinned at Mitch, receiving a wink in response.

"And we're next," Grant stated, throwing his arm around Jillian's shoulders.

"It's only a month away and the ceremony will be on the pier, but the reception will be at the Sunset," Jillian said. "We've been working with Thomas' wedding planner and the Sunset reception area will be perfect."

Ginny leaned into Brogan, saying, "Glad we're doing a little ceremony at our house on the beach," and received a gratified nod from him.

Katelyn, sitting on the sand, looked up at Gareth, and said, "Yeah, between Jillian and Grant and then our wedding, the town'll have a couple of big celebrations."

"Then send me all the sea glass artwork you can, Lance," Jillian called out. "Looks like we'll have lots of shoppers in town!"

As everyone continued to eat, Jade looked over, her voice low, saying, "I don't know if you ever show anyone your art as you're working on it...and if not, that's fine," she rushed, "but if so, I'd love to see it sometime."

Warmth infused deep inside as he met her eyes. Nodding slowly, he said, "I normally don't let anyone into my studio...but for you, I'd gladly make an exception. Maybe...later today?"

Grinning broadly, she leaned back, finishing her hamburger, now excited for what was coming after the cookout.

Tori had gone into the house to get the dessert when she suddenly appeared at the door, her face pale and her hand clutching her stomach. "Mitch!" she cried before doubling over in pain.

Paper plates full of food were tossed into the sand as everyone jumped up at once. Mitch, by her side in an instant, grabbed her, pulling her into his arms. "Babe, what is it?"

"Cramps," she gasped.

The crowd parted for Zac as he rushed to her other side. Looking at Mitch, he said, "Let's get her to the hospital."

Mitch stood, gathering Tori in his arms, as Zac ran to get his SUV. Grant and Jillian rushed forward.

"I'll drive," Grant said, as he and Jillian hustled after Mitch, "so Zac can be in the back seat with Tori."

Katelyn and Gareth headed out as well. "We'll take our car so Grant and Jillian will have a way back."

Mitch called over his shoulder, "Someone call my parents!"

"On it!" shouted Katelyn, digging her cell phone from her purse.

A moment later, they were all gone, leaving a somber group standing behind, feeling helpless.

"Shit," Jade breathed, her voice trembling. Lance immediately circled his arm around her shoulders, pulling her in, willing his strength to carry over to her.

She liked the warmth of his arms around her, the steady beat of his heart next to her cheek. Reluctantly she pulled back, sliding her arms from around his waist. She, Belle, and Ginny moved to the deck to pack the food as the men gathered the trash and policed the ground. The hush over the crowd was tangible, each feeling the fear for their friends. Lance brought a garbage bag from the fire pit area, filled with refuse.

"You can put it in the can over there," she said, pointing to the garbage can at the back of the cabin.

"I'll take it to the dump so Mitch won't have to worry about it later," he replied, walking toward his SUV.

She watched him move away, her heart pounding as she viewed his quiet, take charge manner, doing what needed to be accomplished.

"A natural leader, isn't he?" Ginny said, coming up behind her, startling her.

Whipping her head around, she nodded as she saw Ginny's warm gaze on her.

"Never really knew much about him until he helped out with a case. Still don't know much about him, but I respect the fact that he likes his privacy."

Not knowing what to say, she just nodded again.

"But, I'll be honest, Jade," Ginny continued. "I think he's got demons like the rest of us...think he soothes them with his art. I figure that's as good a way to work on them as any other...hell, it's a lot healthier than many ways of dealing." She turned, looked her in the eyes and added, "I'd love to see him find someone he can trust. Someone he can have fun with. Maybe even someone he can protect."

With that, she walked away, leaving Jade both agreeing and confused. *Love, trust...yes. But protect?*

---

After the group left Mitch's cabin, they migrated to Finn's where the pall remained over the gathering. To her surprise and happiness, Lance came to the pub as well, rarely leaving her side. Comforting or staking a claim she did not know and, honestly, at that moment, did not care.

Finally, Katelyn and Gareth came in, reporting that the hospital had admitted Tori overnight for observation, but the good news was that she and the baby appeared fine. With hugs and handshakes all around, the friends called out their goodbyes as they headed for home.

Lance walked Jade outside to her car. Standing under the street light, he saw the remnants of worry in her eyes. Wanting to offer comfort, he knew platitudes were empty. Lifting his arms to her shoulders, he felt her shift, moving into his embrace, her face planting against his chest as her arms encircled his waist.

They stood, silent as the night, offering wordless warmth. After a moment, she slid her hands down, stepping back slightly, looking up. A little smile curved her lips, as she said, "Thanks, Lance. For everything. For just making me feel better."

It had been a long time since he had offered comfort to anyone, but it felt good. Tucking a strand of her hair behind her ear, he nodded. "Are you going to be safe getting home?"

"Yeah. I just live a few blocks over."

Hating to leave her presence, he knew she needed to get to bed. "All right. I'll…uh…see you…sometime?"

"I hope so," she chuckled. "You still owe me a tour of your studio."

"Absolutely," he agreed, opening her door and watching her slide into the driver's seat. Closing the door, he tapped on the window. After she rolled it down, he asked, "Hey, would you mind letting me know if you hear anything about Tori?"

"Sure, but I'll need your number."

Taking out his phone, he entered the digits as she rattled them off and then called her to get his number into her phone. Watching as she drove away, he turned toward his SUV, smiling, his heart lighter than it had been in years.

## 1 0

The moon hid behind the clouds, casting shadows over the bay. Inky water slapped against the side of the boat, muffling the sounds of the argument taking place on the deck. The craft floated dangerously close to the large ship anchored in the bay, but none of the occupants seemed to heed the danger, as their voices raised.

"I'm not doing it. I told you, I want out."

"You can't get out…not now. Soon, but not now."

"This wasn't what I signed up for. The money, yeah…that I needed. But this? Hell, no. You changed the deal on me and I never agreed to nothin' like this!"

"How sanctimonious can you be? Fuck, man, you didn't have any moral objection to what we've been doing. You can't quit now. We gotta go through with this. Don't you get it?"

Another voice joined the fray, this one deep and sure. "Enough. What did you do with it?"

Silence was the only answer.

"Come on, tell 'em. Tell me. For fuck's sake, don't do this," came his friend's plea.

The deep voice of the man in charge turned to the men with him, ordering, "Do it."

The sounds of a scuffle along with pleas for mercy cried out.

The deep voice intoned, "This is what happens when we don't get what we pay for." The sound of a gunshot echoed across the water, followed by a loud thud. Turning back to the man, left shaking as he watched his former friend lie still on the deck with blood pouring from his head, the leader demanded, "Get me what he took. I want it back or you will find yourself in a similar situation."

"I...I can make this right," he panted, his Adam's apple bobbing in his throat. "I'll deal from now on...by myself...I can make this right."

The man in charge stepped closer, looking into eyes now full of fright. "I want what is due to me. Get it." With a glance downward, he added, "And get rid of that." With the threat lingering in the air, he and his cronies moved back to their craft, leaving the lone man to decide how to get rid of the body and what to do with the boat that now had a deck slick with blood.

Placing a shaky hand over his mouth, he choked back the fear, trying to decide what to do next. *So close... so close to all that money and now this...fuck.* Pushing all thoughts from his mind, he got to work knowing the dawn would come soon.

With her phone tucked into her backpack, Jade began her walk down the beach the next morning. She hoped Jillian would text soon with an update on Tori but found that sitting at home only increased her anxiety, so she decided to head to Lance's place by way of a beach walk. Head down, her gaze scanning the surf, she picked up sea glass as it caught her eye. She had left her apartment without a bag and, since Lance still had her pail, she simply dropped the fragments into her pocket. A piece of plastic churning around in the surf snagged her attention and she grabbed it, assuming it was trash and could be disposed of later. As she looked at the Ziplock baggie, she realized it had pieces of sea glass in it.

Eyes wide in surprise, she looked up and down the beach but did not see anyone else. Grinning to herself, she was pleased with her find and emptied her pocket's treasures into the baggie. *Someone's loss is my gain!* Giving it a jiggle, she loved the way the colors—blue, green, amber, and purple—combined with the clear pieces.

Just then, a figure coming from the dune ahead came into view. *Lance.* With something in both hands, assuming it was coffee mugs again, she wondered if he had been watching for her. Breaking into a jog, she ran straight to him. He stood, his smile sliding slowly over his handsome face. Sunglasses perched on top of his dark hair. A day-old scruff on his jaw. Cargo shorts again, paired with a black t-shirt. Stopping a few feet away, she beamed up at him.

They stood for a moment, neither speaking, both

drinking the other in. She dropped her eyes to the travel mug and said, "Is that for me?"

At his nod, she reached out, taking the proffered drink and they fell into step heading toward his house.

"I was hoping you'd come today," Lance said. He noted she sported a pink ball cap with her long ponytail pulled through, pink capris paired with a long sleeved, navy t-shirt, and pink tennis shoes on her feet. Unable to keep the grin from his lips, he shifted his gaze back to his house behind the dune.

Smiling, she replied, "And I was hoping to see your studio."

"Absolutely," he grinned in return, taking her elbow to assist her up the shifting sand of the dune. As he opened the porch door he found his palms were sweating and realized that, other than Mitch and Ginny, he had had no other visitors. Self-conscious, he wondered what she would think about his home.

"Oh, Lance, this is really nice," she enthused, looking around as they entered the house from the porch. The room contained a long, comfortable sofa and several deep-cushioned chairs facing a flat screen TV on an antique wooden stand. Looking up, she spied some of his artwork hanging near the windows.

Pleased she appeared to like his house, he said, "Come on back. I use a spare bedroom as a studio."

Jade tried not to be nosy, but it was hard, now that she was inside his home. A quick glance exposed a neat kitchen and, as she moved down the hall, she peered into his bedroom, also decorated in clean, masculine lines. He turned to the room on the opposite side and she followed him in, her breath catching in her throat. A large window flooded the room with light. A long table sat against the wall, plastic containers holding sea glass divided by color and size. Near the window was a workstation, complete with drills, magnifying head-wear, lamps with magnifiers connected, glue guns, and a tall wooden stand with a hanger at the top, where he was able to create the mobile while keeping it balanced.

As she walked around, she asked questions, inter-ested in everything she saw. Lance was thrilled to talk about his art with someone who had a genuine desire to learn.

Jade stopped at one of the tables, a partially finished, large mosaic created from sea glass capturing her gaze, as well as stilling her heart. "Oh, Lance," she gasped, "this is magical."

Lance swelled with pride, releasing a held breath. "It's something new I've started. Creating something whole from the many pieces I find." He watched as she turned toward him, her eyes, now a light green, piercing him.

Taking in the beauty, Jade moved around the room, fascinated with his collection of sea glass. "Oh, guess what I found? Someone must have been collecting sea glass, put it in a plastic baggie, and then they lost it. I just tossed in the pieces I found today as well." Holding the bag up, eyes wide, she rushed, "I didn't think to ask if you were the one who lost it."

Grinning, he shook his head. "Not me. And no," he added quickly, "you keep it. I don't need it."

Shoving it back into her pocket, she glanced at the

side of the table. "Hmmm, nice pink bucket you've got there."

Chuckling, he said, "Yeah, funny thing...some girl left a bucket of sea glass for me. I never asked if she needed her bucket back."

"I'd say, if she gave it to you then it's a gift, so you have something really cool to collect your sea glass in from now on. Unless you think your masculinity will take a hit by carrying a pink, plastic, sand bucket."

"I think my masculinity is safe."

Standing in the light-flooded room, she cast her gaze over him, knowing there was no question about his masculinity. *Oh, yeah...it's safe.*

"Are you okay?" he asked.

Blinking, she quickly nodded. "Yes, yes. Sorry, I just...uh...was thinking of something." Attempting to hide her heated cheeks, she turned back to his table of sea glass. Her fingers sifted through the beautiful fragments and she looked up at him. "Can I ask you something? I mean, it's kind of personal, so if you don't want to answer, then you can just—"

A sliver of nerves slid through Lance but he choked them back. "Jade," he interrupted, his eyes holding hers. "It's okay. Just ask."

"I..." she fiddled with some glass, her head down, "know you used to be a police officer...in the Army... and you don't have to tell me anything about your former life...but I just wondered how you became a... uh, you know...do all this beautiful work?"

Familiar anxiety rushed over him—the churning in

his stomach as his chest tightened. Swallowing several times, he opened his mouth but nothing came out.

Her eyes darted to his face and she hurried to say, "It's okay, it's okay. I was just being nosy, it's not my business…"

Jade turned to leave, realizing the demons Ginny eluded to were real and staring her in the face. Hating that she ruined the moment, she headed toward the door.

"No…" a whispered voice stopped her.

Turning, her heart melted at the man standing in front of her. He portrayed a combination of stoicism and nervousness. Placing her hands on his arms, she gave a little squeeze, forcing her lips to curve slightly.

"Don't leave," he begged, his eyes searching hers. "Please."

"I'll stay," she promised. "But you don't have to say a word—"

"I never saw sea glass until I came here."

She gripped his arms tighter at his words, then lessened her hold as she continued to stare into his face, knowing there was so much to his story and wondering if he ever talked to anyone.

"When I left the Army, I got a job in Richland, worked Vice with the police department there. Things weren't really working out. It was all a bit…too much. Mitch was already in Baytown and contacted me, invited me to come. I took one look at the bay the first morning I was here and decided to stay." Looking down at the table next to them, small plastic containers filled with organized sea glass, he said, "I started seeing this on the beach, and couldn't believe my eyes. Little pieces of broken glass bottles...blue, green, amber, clear...they should be shit...you know... broken bottles? But, instead, they're like jewels."

Honored he was confiding in her, her breath caught in her throat as she stared at this strong man, both wondering what had happened to him and utterly fascinated by his unique personality. Afraid to speak and break the spell, she prayed he felt her strength through her touch.

Swallowing audibly again, he shook his head slightly before adding, "I don't know, really, what made me want to do anything with them. I started collecting... then organizing..." With a rueful snort, he added, "I'm a natural organizer, I guess. I like things to fit neatly into categories. Anyway, I saw a magazine article talking about pictures that people made with sea glass. I'm not a trained artist. I'm just a man who wanted to make something whole out of all the broken pieces. But as I worked with it, combining them, using glue and wire to create groupings, I first thought of a mobile...searching for balance. And then the idea of putting them together for a mosaic came to me."

Lance's gaze moved slowly from the glass on the table to Jade's face, fear etched in the lines around his mouth, but the light in her eyes eased his concern. Her smile wrapped around his heart, warming the chilled corners.

Her hand on his arm slid down until she was clasping his fingers, a gentle squeeze relaxing his fist, allowing her fingers to link with his. "Thank you for sharing that with me," she whispered, stepping closer.

He slid his free hand around her back, hesitant until she moved forward, placing her cheek on his chest. They stood silent, barely breathing, barely touching. He rested his chin on the top of her head, the fresh scent of her shampoo wafting through the air, and he felt his body relax.

He had shared a tiny piece of his life and she had taken it, held it, and thanked him, turning the first of his pain into something beautiful.

## 11

"Thank God she's okay," Ginny greeted Mitch as the Baytown Police Department meeting began.

He grinned, his smile showing his relief. "Yeah, Tori's fine. Doc said it was probably something she ate, but the baby's all snuggled in safe and sound. So, while it was a scare and I've got her at home for a few days, she's fine."

Grant, Burt, and Sam sat at the table with Ginny and Mitch, rounding out the BPD. Burt was a young officer, married with two children. Sam, the oldest member of the department, had served when Mitch's grandfather was Police Chief and when Mitch's father was as well. Mildred, their purple grey-haired, steadfast police transcriber and reporter, as well as her sister, Mable, their blue grey-haired, receptionist, flitted in and out, checking on Mitch as well as bringing in snacks for the officers.

Mitch, getting down to business, began the meeting, assigning duties and reviewing open cases. Thankfully, most of the cases were minor. A bucket of pecans had been stolen from someone's carport. The town manager was upset because people were parking backward on Main Street. The owner of the town's trailer park wanted police drive-bys at random times, fearing there might be drug sales taking place.

As the meeting came to a close, Sam, rubbing his chin, said, "Mitch, before we break, I need to talk to you all about something."

The officers shared looks, each figuring they knew what he was going to say.

"I know this won't come as a surprise, but I'm ready to retire. Wife's been on me about my health for the last couple of years." He sighed heavily, adding, "Don't know how I'll take to retirement, but she's got trips planned and, well," he smiled, "I'd like to see my grandkids more."

Mitch nodded, saying, "I knew this day was coming Sam, but I hate like hell to lose you. You served with my granddad and dad, and made my transition to this office so much easier."

"What timeframe are you looking at?" Burt asked.

Rubbing his chin some more, he said, "Well, I can be flexible. I was on the state retirement system website and checked my employment dates and what my income would be, and I can leave at any time. I'd like to stay at least another month to give you a chance to find someone."

"I appreciate that, Sam. You'll have to file the formal paperwork with Mildred before we can advertise, but," Mitch said, "as you may know, the town's budget has a part-time officer open. I wondered about the feasibility of this, but if we can find a full-time officer to fill your position, we would still have a part-time position to fill."

Ginny, her gaze on Mitch, asked, "You got anyone in mind you'd like to apply?"

Chuckling, he said, "Well, I think we'd all like to see Lance apply for either position. When I met him in the Army, he was a helluva criminal investigator. But...I have no idea if he would consider it."

"He helped us on that voyeur case a few months back," Grant remembered. "I know he prefers his privacy, but he had no problem coming to help when we needed him."

"There's a big difference between helping on a case and actually reporting in to work every day," Burt commented. "But, Mitch, you know him best...so we've got nothing to lose by asking him."

---

"Here is some more sea glass," Jade called out, wandering amongst the tables of children as they glued the pieces to the edges of picture frames. "Once you're finished, we'll set them on the bookshelves. Since your name is already on the back, yours will be ready for you when we get the photographs to insert."

Lance's mosaic had given her the idea to have the children glue pieces of sea glass to frames for holiday presents. The Thanksgiving holiday was coming soon and she knew their long winter break was just around the corner. The children loved the opportunity to decorate their own frame with the beautiful, multi-colored fragments of glass.

"What's your favorite color of sea glass, Miss Lyons?" Cindy asked.

"I love them all, but I have to admit that when I find a blue or deep green one, I feel like I've won a prize."

"I think they look like jewels," Ricky added, holding up a piece in his fingers, a wide smile on his face. "It's like giving our moms jewels for a present."

Remembering that Lance also compared the sea glass to jewels, she grinned as she agreed, "You are exactly right. And they will love them. In fact, I found some great sea glass the other day and meant to bring it in to show you, but I forgot."

"Did you leave it on the beach?" Caroline asked.

"No, I've got it in my house." Laughing, she added, "I've got lots of sea glass at my house. But, I've become friends with an artist who creates beautiful things out of sea glass, so maybe I'll give more to him."

"Can we see the stuff he makes?" Manuel asked, his eyes wide.

Biting her bottom lip, she wondered if Lance would agree to come visit her class and bring some of his work. "Well, I'm not sure, but it can't hurt to ask."

---

Lance led Mitch out to his porch, taking the same seats they had occupied the last time he visited. Only this time, he knew he was not here to berate him for being mean to Jade. Settling in the chairs, he looked over at his friend but stayed quiet. He knew Mitch would talk when he was ready.

After several minutes of enjoying the afternoon shade while staring out over the bay, Mitch caught him by surprise when he asked, "Tell me why you decided to be a cop?"

While in the Army, the two had shared meals, as well as worked on a few of the same cases, even though they were not assigned to the same platoon. They had clicked professionally and Mitch had been the only person he confided anything about his family to.

"You fishin' for something?"

Chuckling, he said, "I know Ginny mentioned Sam's imminent retirement to you. Just wanted to get a feel for you, that's all."

Leaning back, he nodded, appreciating Mitch's honesty. "Loved the idea of being a cop. Hell, growing up, my friends wanted to play video games where they could rob banks and shit. I only wanted to be the cop and catch them." Sighing, he continued, "I was fourteen years old when 9-11 happened. Sitting in a history class watching the Twin Towers fall. At that moment, like so many others, I saw the world change right before my eyes, and all I wanted to do was to join the military. I talked to the recruiter at school and discovered I could be a cop in the military. My old man hated any talk of me doing anything else but going to his Alma Mater and then joining the family business. You know he cut me off as soon as he found out I had signed up with the Army?" Shaking his head, he added, "He was determined to make me pay for what he considered to be a family betrayal. But my grandfather left me a trust in my own name, so I didn't need his money."

Nodding, Mitch took a long drink of the water he had handed to him. "I had law enforcement in my blood, as you well know. Only thing I ever thought about either, but then it was the only thing I was ever exposed to."

"Your dad's a good man and, I've got no doubt, your grandfather was just as good." He looked over at Mitch, before adding, "You had men in your life who taught you right from wrong, good from bad. The only lesson my old man wanted to impart was how to step on anyone and everyone to get ahead, make more money, and then rule his little kingdom."

"I joined out of high school and then did Military Police school. By the time I met you, you were a criminal investigator with CID. I tried to act all badass, but gotta tell you, Lance, I was in awe of your investigative skills."

Ruefully chuckling, he nodded, remembering a younger Mitch in the Army. "I was only a year older than you."

"I was always glad you answered that email I sent when I decided Baytown would be perfect for some of my old buddies."

"Yeah...I went to work in Richland right out of the Army, but it was too soon. I needed...a break."

"So, you still need a break? The art you create... damn good outlet and if it's your next vocation, hey, that's great. But, we could use someone of your caliber on our staff. And...what you don't know, besides Sam retiring, is that the city is going for a part-time officer as well. So...if you don't want full time..." He let the unspoken offer hang in the air as he kept his gaze on the bay.

Several minutes went by, neither man speaking, letting the whoosh of the gentle bay waves fill the void.

"I don't know, Mitch. Part of me thinks the timing isn't right. There's still shit in my mind...things I haven't dealt with. I will tell you that I made a call...hell, Ginny kept handing me the Mental Health Center cards, but I haven't gone yet. A police officer needs to be sharp...ready at a moment's notice."

"If you were an investigator...a detective...even only part-time, would you consider it?"

Shaking his head slightly, he wondered why he did not just tell Mitch 'no'. *I'm too fucked up to be any good to anyone.* But then, the pretty, green-eyed teacher came to mind. Jade. *If I don't get un-fucked...I've got no chance with her.* Rubbing his hand over his face, he turned to Mitch. "No promises, man. But, I'll think about it."

"That's all I can ask, Lance." Nodding, Mitch stood and shook his hand, before he headed back into town.

---

"I'm not sure I believe in this process."

Lance sat in the chair facing Charles, the counselor at the Eastern Shore Mental Health Group. Going on Brogan's recommendation, he chose this counselor, figuring if Brogan could get past whatever haunted him, then maybe there was a chance for him to get help also. Maybe.

"But something prompted you to call...to come in."

Sighing heavily, he nodded. "Feels like I'm at a crossroads."

"Tell me more about this."

"Is this how our sessions are going to go? You prod shit out of me that I bring up and then tell me how to deal with it?"

Chuckling, Charles shook his head. "As a counselor, my job is to listen to what you think your difficulties are, help you discover emotionally where you would like to be, and then assist you to get there. There's no judgment here. No preconceived ideas of what you should have done differently or should do in the future."

Shaking his head, Lance apologized, "Sorry. That was a jerk thing to say. I'm...not much for talking."

"And yet you're here."

Sucking in a deep breath before letting it out slowly, he said, "Yeah...here I am." Rubbing the back of his neck, he shifted his gaze around the room before settling back onto Charles. "I'd give anything to be able to sleep all night without waking up to nightmares. I'd love to have a conversation without feeling like I was going to choke on fear. I'd like to have a friend without being afraid..."

As his voice died off, Charles peered at him, but did not ask what he meant. After a moment of silence, he asked, "And the crossroads you mentioned?"

"My life was mine...my decisions...my career. First military police and investigator with Army CID. I actually thought about staying in the military...career military police. But...wartime...things happen. I got out...started working Vice in Richland...but the nightmares began." Drawing in a ragged breath, he continued, "I've got an opportunity for a future again in Baytown...but I'm scared shitless."

"Then let's talk about what happened."

He looked over at Charles' kind face and knew it was time. Time to unburden himself. Leaning back in his chair, he began to talk.

## 12

The sun hid behind clouds, but Jade barely noticed as she walked, head down, completely focused on the slivers of glass on the shore. The storm last night must have churned up the surf, because the sea glass pickings were plentiful. She even found a fragment of purple glass, the bottom curved as though it may have come from a cup. Excited, she slowed her pace to gather every piece she found.

Spying a large amber colored piece, she squatted in the sand to inspect it before placing it in her bag. She had decided to use an old, net laundry bag for gathering and carrying her new sea glass collection as she walked. The lightweight bag was easy to transport and the netted material allowed her to dip it in the water to wash off the glass all at one time.

Standing, she looked out at the ships with her binoculars and viewed several that were there the other day and some that were new. She recognized Carson & Sons' fishing boats and decided to check their catch out later in the harbor. She needed to talk to Skip about the class fieldtrip anyway. Shifting her bag to hang over her shoulder, she quickly jotted down the information she noted on the sides of the ships. As she slid her gaze over the horizon, she smiled at the fishing boats already coming back from their first hauls. A beautiful sailboat glided across the water, its white sails billowing in the morning breeze.

The sun peeked out from behind a cloud and she leaned her head back, face to the sky, allowing it to warm her skin before moving back into hiding. Sighing, she trudged on, torn between wanting to get to Lance's house and wanting to collect every piece of sea glass she could possibly spy.

A whiff of something unpleasant from the breeze brought her head back up quickly and she looked up and down the beach, wondering what the waves tossed up to the shore. Perhaps it was a dolphin, like last summer when a dolphin plague caused multiple carcasses to wash up on shore. Last winter, when she was walking with the girls, they came across a five-foot-long sea turtle carcass that had just landed on the beach.

Her eyes focused on a lump on the sand, right where the waves could still wash over it. White. Bloated.

*Eeww, I wonder if it's a shark.*

She covered her nose with her hand as the odor became more offensive. Walking away from the shore, she decided to give it a wide berth as she headed toward Lance's house.

At about twenty feet away from the washed-up animal, she turned her head to see if she could identify the species when her feet stumbled to a halt, her stomach dropping.

A body. A human body.

With a gurgling scream in the back of her throat, she raced toward the body, but as she neared, it was apparent...there was no chance of life...not with part of his face missing. Falling to the sand on her knees, her meager breakfast came back up.

---

Lance fixed two travel mugs of coffee, making sure to add extra cream and the sweetener he bought just for Jade. He grinned as he remembered the look on the cashier's face when he bought flavored creamer and sweetener. *Guess I've been a creature of habit, and I sure as shit don't seem like a flavored creamer sort of guy.*

Popping on the lids, he moved to the screened porch and then out onto his deck. The day was cloudy, but the breeze blowing off the bay was warm and he inhaled a breath of fresh, clean air. Letting it out slowly, he thought about everything that had roamed his mind last night. Talking with Charles had his thoughts churning as much as the surf. His parents, who would never be pleased with him. His skills as an investigator lying dormant in the face of a job offer. His artwork, which had helped him move through the wartime memories more than he realized. And Jade. *Jesus, no wonder I couldn't sleep.*

He looked to the side, seeing Jade jogging toward him. Smiling widely, he headed down the dune, figuring she must want her coffee—*or to see me*—hustling as she was. As she neared, he discerned she was not jogging, but running full force. Her mouth was open but any sound being emitted was carried away by the wind.

The hairs on the back of his neck stood up and if there was one thing he had learned in all his years in law enforcement—always listen to his gut feelings. Quickly setting the coffee mugs on the beach, he began running toward her, his heart pounding in fear, now close enough to see her pale, wide-eyed face. And to hear her screaming his name over and over.

As he reached her, she collapsed in his arms, her ragged breath tearing from her lungs. "Bo...bo...bo..."

He recognized hyperventilating and immediately swept her body into his as he lowered them both to the sand. Forcing her face to his, he tried to get her to slow her breathing, but to no avail. Shifting around, he placed his palm flat in the middle of her chest and pushed.

"Push against my hand. Breath out and push against my hand," he ordered. Getting in her face, he began slow inhalations and exhalations, saying, "Breathe with me. Breathe with me."

Her body shook as her breathing slowed enough she could create words and she croaked, "Bo...dy. Back... there. Bo...dy. Dead...bo...dy."

It took a few seconds for her chopped words to penetrate, but when they did his eyes widened in understanding. "There's a body? A human body?"

She nodded in jerks and he stood quickly, his eyes scanning the shoreline before he dropped his gaze back to hers. "Stay here. I'm going up the beach. I'll call it in once I see what's happening."

Her body in full-blown shakes, she just stared numbly at him.

He hated to leave her but knew he had to find out what she had seen. "Jade. Honey, do you understand? You stay here? I'll be back. Okay?"

Jade nodded, now feeling light-headed with oxygen finally getting into her lungs. She watched as he stood, shot her a concerned look, and took off running up the beach.

---

Approaching cautiously, making sure to not disturb the area, Lance viewed the body. Unable to stop the instinct to investigate, he began analyzing the scene. Pulling out his cell phone, he called Mitch.

"Hey, Lance—"

"This is official. Called you instead of 9-1-1 to keep down any unwanted listeners. There's a body washed up on the beach, just north of my place."

"Fuck!" Mitch cursed. "On my way. I'll call it in."

"I'm here. Gonna stay to make sure nothing happens. Come down Turner's Lane and park at the end of that road, closest to the beach. It's just inside the town line, so Colt may want in on this as well. Hell, probably the Coast Guard also."

"Got it. I'm calling it in. By the way, did you find it?"

Inhaling sharply, he replied, "No. Jade did."

"Shit," Mitch cursed again.

"She's a fuckin' mess. Got her up at my place. She ran to me, couldn't even breathe enough to tell me what happened."

"See you in less than ten minutes."

For the next eight minutes, he walked the scene, categorizing his observations so, by the time sirens sounded he had already begun the investigation. First on the scene were Mitch and Burt, both heading down the slight dune. Grant and Ginny followed right after them. He heard another siren and watched as Zac and another EMT came toward him, carrying a stretcher with an accompanying body bag. Before they reached him, he heard even more sirens before Colt Hudson and two deputies walked down the dune. Colt, the Sheriff of North Heron County, had also been an investigator in the Army, but they had never served together.

As the gathering of law enforcement and EMTs made their way toward him, he glanced to the side and saw Jade slowly making her way up the beach.

"Damnit," he cursed and Ginny hustled over.

"Mitch said Jade found the body?"

"Yeah, I told her to stay at my house," he said, concern etched on his face.

"I've got her. I need to interview her anyway, so I'll stop her from coming closer."

"No," he snapped, his voice sharper than he meant. Her face swung back his way, and he quickly added, "I want to be there when you talk to her. She's shaken."

Saying nothing, she stared at him a moment before giving a short nod and jogged toward Jade.

Blowing out a breath, he turned back to the scene,

stepping next to Grant and Mitch. Zac was in the sand, his phone out, calling the medical examiner.

Looking up, he said, "Dr. Warren says he'll come out now, but doubts he can tell anything from here. He's only about five minutes away. As soon as he takes a look, we'll transport the body back so he can do his examination."

Mitch nodded, standing with his hands on his hips, before moving toward the body. Lance followed suit, as did the other officers.

"Looks like some of the injuries we would see in the war when someone was shot at close range," Mitch began.

"Look at his wrists," Lance added. "They were bound at some point."

"So, we've got an execution on the shore...Jesus, that's fucked," Grant said, his frustration palpable. "The only concrete clue is the body itself. Who knows what else might have been washed away."

"It wasn't done here," Lance indicated. "The body's too bloated. It was done somewhere else then the body floated here. Probably been in the water a whole day, maybe more."

"Is Callan coming?" Burt asked, then turned as he heard noises from behind. "Never mind, there's my answer."

Callan and his superior officer made their way to the body as well. Shaking hands with Mitch and Colt, the officer said, "Anything for us?"

Mitch nodded and said, "From our first preliminary scan, he was killed somewhere and then possibly tossed from a ship or boat. Can your office help coordinate identifying any ships that might be missing someone?"

"Absolutely," Commander Tarson said, before turning to Callan. "Captain Ward, I'm giving this assignment to you. You'll report to Chief Evans as well as to me."

"Yes, sir," Callan agreed.

The gathering turned once more to greet the latest arrival. Dr. Warren, one of the town's physicians and medical examiner, came over the dune and down to the beach. Wearing his golf clothes, he frowned as he approached the group.

"Yes," he quipped, "I was on the golf course. But I should thank you. I just shanked the ball, so to be called away was fortuitous."

Kneeling over the body, he checked the temperature before examining the extremities. Nodding, he stood and said to Zac, "Load him up. I'll start work immediately." Turning toward Mitch, he asked, "Any particulars I should know?"

"Not a one," Mitch responded. "No identification on the body, so we're starting with a clean slate since we can't make a visual identification."

"I'll have a preliminary by tomorrow." With that, he followed the stretcher as Zac and his assistant moved toward the ambulance.

Lance looked up at Mitch, seeing his gaze focus over his shoulder. Turning to look down the beach, he viewed Ginny with her arm around Jade, and he wanted to be the one to offer comfort. "I want to be there when you interview Jade. Already told Ginny that."

Nodding, Mitch silently agreed. "Colt," he called out. "We're right on the county and town line here. Can my men search north toward town and your deputies take the south?"

"No problem," Colt acknowledged.

He directed two of his deputies to begin the search as Mitch ordered, "Burt. Grant. Comb the beach for at least half a mile toward the north."

Without wasting any more time, Lance began jogging toward Jade, his heart soaring when she looked up at him and broke away from Ginny, rushing toward him. Wrapping his arms around her still shaking body, he held her close. As much as he hated the reason why she sought his embrace, he closed his eyes in a silent prayer that she found shelter with him.

## 13

Lance sat on his sofa with Jade tucked close to him. His leg touched hers from hip to knee, his arm on the back of her cushion, barely managing to keep his hand from curving down to her shoulder.

Jade's hands shook as she took a sip of the water Lance had given her, before turning her gaze to Mitch and Ginny. Calmer, she still felt ill and, as the water passed her lips, she covered her mouth with her hand, holding back a gag. Blushing, she mumbled, "Sorry," before everyone rushed to tell her not to worry about it.

"It's the smell," she said. "I can still smell it even though there really isn't a way that could be possible."

"Your nerves are holding on to the scent," Ginny said, her face sympathetic. "I still remember my first time."

For a second, she was unsure what Ginny meant, and then it hit her. Ginny was referring to being around a corpse.

Swallowing audibly, she lowered her shaking hand. "I

don't know what I can tell you. I was just walking along. I was looking down for sea glass...I stopped to take note of the ships on the water. Um...that's something I do for my class' geography lesson. And then I had just started walking again when the smell...oh, God, the smell hit me. I've come across dead dolphins and even, a few months ago, a huge sea turtle that had washed up on the shore. Its smell was bad also, but this..." She gagged again, bending over, horrified she was going to throw up.

Lance immediately began to rub her back in gentle, circular motions while Ginny jumped up and headed into his kitchen. She grabbed an orange from a bowl on his counter and cut it into quarters.

Coming back to the living room, she bent in front of her and said, "Honey, take a whiff of this. Just breath it in."

She began to slowly deep breathe, the tangy scent of the orange filling her nostrils. Sitting up, she offered a slight smile toward Ginny, mouthing her thanks.

Mitch stood and said, "That's all we need, Jade." He cast a glance down and added, "Do you need a ride home...or back to your car—"

"I've got her," Lance interrupted.

Mitch eyed his friend, his lips twitching as he nodded. "Okay, Jade?"

She licked her dry lips as her gaze moved from Mitch to Lance, not wanting to impose. His face was hard, but his eyes implored hers, as though silently begging her to stay. "Yes...it's fine. Thank you."

Lance breathed easier as soon as she agreed and he

assisted her to her feet, where they walked Mitch and Ginny out to the deck. Watching for a moment while the officers moved back up the beach toward the crime scene, he pulled her in closer, his arm tucking her tightly to his side.

"You need to eat, Jade." Seeing her about to protest, he said, "Salad. I'll fix a fruit salad. That'll at least get some food in you but won't overload your stomach."

Nodding, she offered a weak smile as he guided her off the deck and back into the house.

---

The man's eyes darted around, thankful the house he was entering was at the end of a lonely strip of land with no neighbors around. His gaze took in the yard and he shook his head as he broke the poor excuse for a lock on the back door.

Once inside, he grimaced at the old house. Small. Messy. Shaking his head to rid those thoughts, he began to search methodically. When all the obvious hiding places turned up nothing, he felt a snake of panic unfurling in his stomach. Standing with his hands on his hips, he willed his mind to clear.

Looking at his watch, he worried about his vehicle parked outside, even though he had pulled around to the back. Unable to keep the fear of what would happen to him if he did not find what he was looking for at bay, he began to tear the small house apart. *It's not like he'll be coming back here anyway.* Ripping cushions and beddings, dumping the contents of drawers onto the floor, he searched everywhere.

Sweat poured off his face as he panted in fear. *I've searched the boat and now the house. Where the hell is it? Maybe he buried it. Maybe he sent it to someone. Hell, maybe he gave it to someone.*

Knowing time was of the essence, he pulled out his phone. At the answer, he said, "I've looked every-where...searched everywhere...it's not here."

He grimaced as the phone jiggled next to his ear when his hands shook.

"The bastard must have hidden it somewhere. Find it."

"I looked on the boat and in the house."

"That's your problem. I suggest you complete your task."

Just when he thought his contact was going to hang up, he heard, "You added weights to the body before tossing it into the bay, right?"

He gulped, the idea of telling his contact he had not even thought of doing that caused the pain in his gut to intensify. Sucking in a deep breath through his nose, before letting it out slowly, he replied, "Yeah, yeah. He won't be found."

---

Lance glanced over at Jade, sitting in the passenger seat, as he drove the mile back to her car. Pulling beside it, he put his SUV in park, but left it running.

Jade sat perfectly still, her hand not reaching for the

door handle. Steeling herself, she inhaled sharply. Forcing a smile on her lips, she said, "Thanks, Lance. For everything. I don't know what I would have done this morning if it weren't for you."

Lance's hands gripped the wheel as he tried to think of something to say, but the only words that came out were, "Don't leave."

"But I have to get home. I need to get home. I'm desperate for a shower." Her weak voice gave evidence to her nerves.

Refusing to think of the image of her in the shower, he explained, "No, I mean, let me take you home. I can get someone to come back and get your car later. But, I just don't think you should be alone right now."

Puffing out a breath that blew her bangs from her face, she nodded. "I know I should refuse your offer, but I'm not sure my legs would hold up pressing on the accelerator right now." She turned to him, her brows lowered in concern. "Do you think my car will be all right here?"

"It's fine for now, and I promise to get someone to bring it to you." After she rattled off her address, he put the vehicle in gear and headed into town.

Less than ten minutes later, he parked in front of a large house, his eyes widening at the size. Hearing a slight giggle, he looked over.

"I'm sorry," she said, "it's just that the look on your face was funny. And no, I don't own the whole house... or actually, any part of it. I lease the little attic apartment, but it's all I need for now and the owners are sweet. Plus, I have my own entrance. It's around the back."

She waited as he jumped from the SUV and stalked around to her side. Assisting her down, he kept his hand on her lower back as they made their way down the driveway to the back of the house.

Using her key, they entered the narrow stairwell that ascended to a small second-floor landing and then turned to ascend to the third floor.

"This house is over a hundred years old," she explained, "and the attic stairs were there for the servants. Mr. Poletta told me that according to what he can find from the history of the previous owners, they had two servants...a maid and a cook. They shared the attic room. The Polettas have lived here for over twenty years and they had the attic redone as an apartment that they could rent."

At the top of the stairs, she opened the door and he followed her into the kitchen. He was surprised at the amount of space she had. The kitchen was small but, for a single person or couple, it was enough. An eat-at counter divided the area leading to her living room.

Jade looked around, realizing it probably looked very girly to Lance, suddenly uncertain about having him in her apartment. Turning around, she looked up into his eyes and heaved a sigh. "Thank you, again...for everything."

He reached his hand out, tucking a strand of hair behind her ear. "You don't have to thank me for anything, Jade. It was my pleasure...no...it was my honor to be there for you."

She cocked her head to the side, his words confusing her, but a shy smile curving her lips none the less.

Giving a small shake of his head, he explained, "I… haven't felt very…uh…useful…for a long time. So, I kind of stepped back…from everyone." His large shoulders shrugged, "To be able to help you, was good for me as well." His face scrunched as he grimaced. "I feel like I'm fucking this up."

Taking a step closer, she placed her hand on his chest. "You're not messing anything up, Lance. Not at all."

"It's not just this…what happened today. It's been getting to know you that's made a big difference in my life. Today was just a chance I could give back to you. It felt good to have someone need me and me be able to help." Heaving a sigh, he reached up and clasped her hand on his chest. "I guess that sounds kind of…" his words drifted off, unable to think of what to say.

"I know what you're talking about. I feel that way a lot as a teacher. Like I've been given the opportunity to be at the right place at the right time for someone. And yes," she added, "you were exactly that for me." Cocking her head to the side, she asked, "Can I show you something?"

Curious, Lance nodded, his heart lighter. "Sure."

Jade continued to hold his hand tightly, leading him to the end of the living room. Pulling back the lace curtains and opening the sliding glass door, she stepped onto her deck.

The sun was high in the sky as white, fluffy clouds floated by. The sounds of families on the beach could be heard as they peered over the few rooftops between them and the bay, seeing the town beach.

Lance shifted his gaze from the beautiful scene to the woman standing beside him, her face turned up toward his.

"I know it's not much compared to the view of the bay that you have, but this is kind of my special place. I have my morning coffee or my afternoon tea or my evening glass of wine out here." A nervous giggle bubbled up from her and she shook her head. "I make it sound as though I can't be out here without drinking something."

"Nothing wrong with that," he said, loving the way the breeze blew her hair back from her face.

Sighing, she held his gaze, her words soft. "Thank you again...for everything, but mostly just for being here with me."

Unable to resist the desire, he leaned down, halting just a breath away from her lips, giving her a chance to tell him to stop.

Instead, she rose on her toes, circling her arms around his neck and whispered, "Yes."

With his heart pounding in his chest, he cupped his hands on her cheeks and angled his lips over hers. Pulling her closer, he reveled in all that she was. The taste of her combined with the flavors of the fruit she ate. The scent of her shampoo, the vanilla wafting in the breeze. The feel of her in his arms, her breasts pressed tightly against his chest. Closing his eyes, he willed his knees to hold him upright as her essence overwhelmed him.

Jade angled her head slightly, opening under Lance's gentle assault on her senses. His tongue slipped between her lips and the jolt sent shock waves to her core. Glad for the strength in his hold, she wondered if she even could stand on her own.

As they continued their slow kiss, exploring the first taste of togetherness, the breeze off the bay swept all other thoughts from their minds. Only two hearts syncing to beat as one.

14

_____

By the afternoon, Jade's cell phone had not stopped ringing. Jillian. Tori. Katelyn. Belle did not call because Jillian had called her, asking if she would pick up Jade so the girls could gather at Tori's house. Knowing they needed to see that she was all right and needing to have their morbid curiosity satisfied, she agreed to meet them.

Tori and Mitch lived in one of the older, brick houses in town, outside the main grid. A big yard with plenty of space for children to play encircled the stately home. She loved the wide front porch, with its porch swing and cool shade. As soon as she and Belle drove up, Jillian rushed down the steps and hugged her.

"I couldn't believe it when Grant called," she worried.

"I'm fine, I'm fine," she assured, as they walked up the front steps. After being enveloped in hugs from Katelyn and Tori, they settled quickly. She knew they wanted to hear about the body, but she wanted to make sure Tori was okay.

Rubbing her tummy, she said, "Honestly, it's embarrassing. I just had some cramps and, looking back, they probably weren't as bad as I thought at first. I'm not on bedrest or anything...just told to take it easy for a few days, but Mitch has practically bubble-wrapped me. I can't move without him fussing."

Sitting on the porch swing next to her, Jade patted her leg, saying, "I was scared for you, sweetie. We all were."

Smiling at the group, Tori acknowledged, "Thank you. That means a lot. But enough about me...what happened this morning."

Jillian, Katelyn, and Belle pulled up their chairs, ready to hang on her every word.

"Ladies, I don't really know what to tell you. I was walking on the beach, looking for sea glass—"

"Which beach?" Katelyn asked.

"South of town. I was heading toward Lance's—"

"Lance?" Jillian interrupted, her brows shooting toward her forehead. "Is there something going on? He's been coming out of his shell and I thought you two might be—"

"I feel sorry for him but I think he's a little scary sometimes," Belle added, her soft voice barely heard over the others.

Jade leaned toward Belle and said, "No, no, he's not scary at all—"

"It doesn't matter if he's scary, as long as he's good with her," Katelyn interjected.

"Stop it," Tori laughed, "I want to hear about this morning."

"Well?" Katelyn prodded, as though she had not halted the story's progress.

Sipping the lemonade provided, she continued, "I smelled something horrible and saw what I thought might be a dolphin in the surf at the edge of the beach."

"Oh, my God...I never thought about the smell," Jillian said, shaking her head.

For a second, Jade's stomach started to revolt, but she pushed the memory down. She held the tart lemonade glass under her nose, remembering how Ginny had used the citrusy orange scent to quell the nausea. Swallowing deeply, she continued, "Anyway, as soon as I saw it was a human body, I ran to get Lance."

"That's romantic," Belle said, immediately drawing wide-eyed, dropped-jaw attention from the others. Rushing to explain, she said, "I just mean that she had someone she trusted so completely that she would rush to them, knowing they would take care of it."

Jade smiled at Belle, thinking that she was right—it was nice to have Lance to run to, even in the worst situation.

Katelyn leaned back, her gaze speculative, "Back on track, ladies. So, who was it? Did they have any idea?"

Shrugging, she shook her head. "I don't know. It was a man, but I don't even know how they will find out who specifically. It was...uh...not pretty."

Tori held her hand over her mouth and said, "Ugh... just the thought is enough to make me gag. I don't know how you didn't throw up."

Scrunching her nose, she admitted, "I did. I threw up in the sand and then kept gagging as I was interviewed later at Lance's."

"He must have come from one of the big cargo ships on the bay," Jillian surmised. "No one in town has mentioned anyone missing, but he could be from anywhere on the bay's coast."

"Well, someone will report a missing person. You just can't fall off a boat without being missed," Tori declared.

---

"No one's reported anyone missing," Grant said, looking around the table at the other officers. Sam was present, but had gladly agreed to take the extra beach and town patrols while the others worked the murder case.

Scanning the group, Grant made eye contact with everyone, including Colt, Callan, and Lance. They all sat at a large table in the Baytown Police Department workroom.

Callan agreed, "Checked with the Harbor Masters in Baytown, Fort Story, and with Norfolk and Portsmouth, as well as any other Masters all the way to Baltimore."

Mitch looked at his watch and said, "I'm heading to the medical examiner's office for the preliminary report before the body's taken to the North Heron hospital for a more in-depth autopsy." His gaze shifted to Lance. "You in on this?"

Lance sat for a second, the war battling deep inside

ever since Jade had thrown herself into his arms. He knew she was in no danger, but just having her shaking body held by his sparked something, awakening a protective emotion he thought long dead.

Nodding slowly, he said, "Yeah...I want in."

The others nodded and grinned, clearly glad to have an experienced investigator on their team. Their smiles dropped off at the sound of raised voices from the station lobby.

"You cannot just barge in and expect to—"

"Ms. Score, you know, as Mayor, I can go where I want!"

Mitch sighed heavily, joined by the others, as Corwin Banks came barreling into the workroom. "Corwin," he greeted with little enthusiasm.

"I just heard that a dead body was found on the beach! Who the hell was it and why is there a dead body on the beach in Baytown?"

Lance watched the blustering mayor's jowls, reddened and jiggling, as he ranted. He had been around Corwin a couple of times since moving into town, but this was the first time he saw him in action with the police.

"Yes, there was a body found. No, we don't have an identification yet. Yes, we are actively pursuing identification and cause of death."

"Cause of death?" Corwin said, stepping back slightly. "Please, tell me he died of natural causes. Some guy just dropped dead of a heart attack or something."

"We don't know anything for certain at this time, but we're treating it as a suspicious death." Mitch replied.

Lance noted Mitch avoided mentioning the evidence of the victim's hands being restrained. *Probably the best thing to do considering the odd purple shade of the mayor's face.*

Corwin opened and closed his mouth several times, blustering, "Sus...sus...suspicious?"

Another commotion sounded outside the room. "Wait—"

"Get out of my way!"

The town manager, Silas Mills, strode in as well, his scrawny chest puffed out as his narrow-eyed gaze shot around the room. "I just heard. What the hell is going on? We've got the Fall Oyster Fest coming up and the last thing we need is bodies dropping from the sky—"

Slamming his hand down on the table, Mitch stood, his patience snapping. "Enough. We are investigating... we have no answers now...we will keep you informed. But until then, you two can do a lot by keeping your mouths shut until we know more."

Corwin nodded his head, his jowls shaking vigorously once again. Silas' eyes, already narrowed, became slits as his gaze landed on Lance. "What is *he* doing here? Why the hell do you have an *artist* sitting in the police station's workroom?"

"Because he's working with us on this investigation and because he found the body."

He was glad Mitch left out Jade's name, figuring Silas would find a reason to hound her.

Rearing back, Silas' sneer made his weasely face even more unattractive. "Him? Working on the case—"

"He's a former decorated Army criminal investigator

and worked Vice in Richland. So yeah, he's been taken on as a part-time investigator under my jurisdiction, which is allowed by the town's police code," Mitch declared in a voice not to be questioned.

Corwin's eyes lit with renewed interest as he stared at him. "Well, well, that's all right, isn't it? Yes, indeed, Mr. Greene, I had no idea. Good, good…this could be good for the town's reputation to have someone of your caliber—"

"Out, out, out!" came a call from Mildred as she shook her hand at the intruders. "You've taken up too much of their valuable time as it is!" She marched into the workroom and grabbed Corwin and Silas by the sleeves, dragging them out with her.

As Corwin hustled out, Silas jerked his arm from her and sneered as he left the room, casting a final threat over his shoulder.

"Well, if he's so good, then get this case solved before the Oyster Fest!"

The room sat in silence for a moment, before Lance turned to Mitch and asked, "When is the festival?"

"This weekend."

"Damn, he must watch too much cop TV if he thinks murders get solved that fast." He dropped his head for a moment before looking back up and saying, "I was going to ask if I can reconsider joining your department, but I think instead, I want to stay, just to shut those two fucks up."

Laughter from the group eased the tension as he and Mitch left, the medical examiner's office next on their agenda.

## 1 5

---

"He's been dead for at least twelve to fifteen hours, gauging from the time I first saw him on the beach."

Lance and Mitch both nodded as they stepped toward the body lying on the table.

"He was shot at close range. The bullet entered the forehead, obliterating that side of his head, then exited out that back. The angle indicates that the weapon was fired at a downward position. The bruising on the body suggests he took a beating before being shot. The bruising on his wrists and ankles suggest he was bound," Dr. Warren continued. "He was definitely dead before entering the water."

Looking at Lance, Mitch said, "We need Callan to give us his opinion on the coastal tides and directions to have an idea where he might have come from."

He nodded quietly, as he stepped closer to the table. The body was bloated, but part of the face was visible. Dark grey hair, trimmed short. Taking out his phone, he snapped pictures of the tattoos on the upper arms before moving down to the legs. Another tattoo was on his lower leg.

"They look like Navy tattoos," Mitch commented.

Nodding, he shifted his gaze from the corpse to Mitch. "I'd agree, but we should have Jason look at these photos. As a tattoo artist, who was also in the Navy, he's our best bet."

Thanking the doctor, he and Mitch walked outside. Turning to him, Mitch said, "Let me know what Jason says."

With that, Mitch headed to his BPD vehicle, leaving Lance standing on the sidewalk. Sliding on his sunglasses, he realized the job was now in full swing and he was officially investigating. The familiar feeling of following a trail, putting the pieces of evidence together, slid through him and he smiled.

Lance walked to the town's only garage, seeing the bay doors wide open and two vehicles being worked on. Calling out, he motioned to Jason as his head popped up from under the hood.

"Got a minute?"

Wiping his hands on an old rag, he came over, greeting him. "Sorry to keep you waiting, man. The noise sometimes keeps me from hearing who might be out here."

With the grease gone, Jason shook his hand and they moved into the garage's office.

"Got something for you to take a look at," he began,

then noticed Jason's gaze shift to outside. "No, no. It's not a car. It's a tattoo."

Jason had told them he learned the art of tattooing when he was a kid, but the Navy taught him the mechanical skills to work on engines. Loving both, he took over the closed garage when he came to town, but also bought the building next door to open a tattoo shop. With a full-time mechanic working with him in the garage, he was able to work part-time as an artist.

"Sure, whatcha need?"

Lance handed him a picture of a clearly dead man's shoulder. "Can you identify this for me?"

"Have you joined the force? Think that's great, Lance," he said, as he carefully perused the photograph.

"We thought perhaps the victim had been in the Navy—"

"Nah," he replied quickly. "If I had to give you my best opinion, I'd say he was in the Merchant Marines." Looking up, he said, "But around here? I'm afraid that includes most of the people out on those ships in the bay."

---

Back at the station, Callan listened as Lance and Mitch gave the doctor's early medical report. He looked at Lance, repeating, "Navy?"

"I thought so, but Jason says he thinks its Merchant Marines."

"Jesus, with the number of sailors on all the ships

around here, that might be harder to narrow down," Callan said, shaking his head.

"That's just what Jason said."

"The medical examiner is sending his fingerprints into the state," Mitch informed them.

"If he came in on one of the ships out in the bay, he wouldn't have to have any ID," Callan added. "But, then, he wouldn't be able to leave the ship, either. The crews are barred by post September eleventh federal restrictions that prevent foreign seafarers without U.S. visas from getting shore leave on American soil."

"So, they don't go ashore at all?" Ginny asked.

"Before nine-eleven, an entire crew often was given a 'crew visa,'" he explained, "but the concept of visas is that each individual is interviewed with a security check and, obviously, no one is doing that with a whole crew."

Grant leaned his tall body back in his chair, his eyes pinned on Callan. "Is this a new policy, since terrorist threats have heightened security across the country?"

Callan shook his head. "Actually, suspicion of merchant sailors from foreign-flagged vessels has been around for a long time. During the Cold War, crew members from Russia and Eastern Bloc countries had to leave their ships before the vessels could even enter the Norfolk port. With the largest U.S. naval base, security was always high."

"So, stuck on a ship, something happens and our victim is killed and ends up on our shore," he summarized, wishing it had been anyone else other than Jade who found the body.

Ginny speculated, "And none of the ships have reported someone missing. Even if a crew member had shot him, someone would have missed him and reported it."

"We need the full post-mortem to have any real evidence to go on," Lance said, "but until then, I'd say we need to get hold of the ship employee lists that have been in the harbor for the past few days." Standing, he nodded to the officers at the table. "Glad to be part of this, but right now, I'm heading over to check on Jade."

Walking out of the workroom, he missed the knowing smiles of the others.

---

Arriving at Jade's apartment, Lance realized he did not know how to get to her stairs without having her with him. Walking around to the back, he discovered an intercom buzzer pad. Pressing the button, he wiped his hand on his jeans, suddenly nervous, wondering how she would feel about him dropping by.

"Yes?"

"Uh, Jade? This is—"

"Lance? Oh, thank goodness! I was hoping you'd come by!"

Breathing a sigh of relief, he heard the outside door lock click and, with a turn of the knob, he was inside. Heading up the first set of stairs, he looked up as the rapid sound of soft footsteps came closer. Rounding the corner at the landing, Jade barely skidded to a stop before slamming into him.

His hands instinctively reached out, grabbing her upper arms. Steadying her, he searched her face, seeking the reason for her rush to meet him. "Are you okay? Is something wrong?"

Laughing, she shook her head. "No, no. I'm fine. Sorry, I just was really hoping I'd have a chance to see you again." As the blush stained her cheeks, she said, "Can you come up?"

"That's where I was heading until you came crashing down," he chuckled.

Her eyes twinkled and she turned and led him up the narrow staircase and into her apartment. Looking over her shoulder, she asked, "What can I get you to drink? I've got soda, water, tea, beer, wine—"

"Water's good," he replied, his eyes roaming over her face before shifting downward as she moved into the kitchen. A light blue tank top and jean capris replaced the outfit from this morning. He studied her face as she handed him the water. She was still pale, but other than the circles under her eyes, she appeared revived.

"Come on, let's sit outside," she said, leading him through the doors to the deck. Settling in, she took a sip of water. "I want to ask about today. What happened after you left me. I haven't heard anything, so I was concerned."

"I went back to the police station to meet with the team." Her hand on his arm halted his words and she looked deeply into his eyes, her face a mask of concern.

"Oh, Lance, are you sure you had to do that? I know being around everyone isn't something you really like."

Her touch, as well as her concern, reached deep

inside, warming the sliver of cold around his heart. Smiling as he covered her hand with his, he rubbed his thumb over her petal soft skin. "Yeah…it's fine. It's all good. I want to do this."

She smiled her encouragement, nodding slightly.

"Don't have much to tell you…uh…well, you'll hear this soon enough, but he was shot before he went into the water."

Jade's eyes bugged out and she gasped, "Sh…shot? Like killed? He didn't drown?" The idea that she had found a drowned body had been upsetting, especially since it looked like it took a beating on its way to the shore, but to think she had discovered someone who was murdered caused her breath to leave her lungs in a rush.

Grabbing her shoulders, Lance steadied her as he peered into her eyes. "You okay? I'm sorry. I know this is a shock."

Leaning her head on his chest, his steady heartbeat calmed her. "I can't believe it. It's so awful." Tilting her head back, she looked up. "Oh, Lance…just think how horrible it must have been if he knew it was going to happen."

Keeping to himself that the victim's hands had been tied, so he definitely knew what was going on, Lance pressed her head back against his chest. They stood, silent, for a few minutes, holding on to each other for strength.

"Are you going to keep up with the investigation?"

Her words, soft and gentle, moved through him. "Right now, I'm joining the Baytown Police Department on an advisory basis. Mitch and I talked about that as well. Then," he shrugged, "I can see. They'll have a position or part-time position for me...who knows."

"I think they'd be lucky to have you," she said, her eyes warm on him.

"Mitch has been a good friend. I was lost after the Army. Lost my direction. Lost my drive. Lost my will to give a fuck. But Baytown's been good to me. It's time I gave back."

The silence that followed was comfortable and he realized it was nice to have someone to talk to or just be with. He kept his hand on hers, loving the feel of her touch on his arm.

Jade smiled, deciding he had shared all he wanted for the moment, and announced, "I went to see the girls today. My phone was ringing like crazy and, since Mitch has Tori staying at home for a few days, we met at their house."

"News travels fast around here."

"It's both the curse and the blessing of a small town," she laughed. "Grant told Gareth, so he could do some searching, and Gareth told Katelyn. She called Jillian, who immediately called Grant to see what was happening. And then, just to round out the group, Jillian called Belle."

Shaking his head, Lance tried to remember what it was like to have a circle of supportive friends, then realized, if he were honest with himself, he had those friends in Baytown. Quiet for a moment, he allowed his mind to drift back to his military friends—

Shutting that thought down, he lifted his bottle of

water with a shaky hand, hoping she did not notice. Glancing over, her eyes were on him, a thoughtful expression on her face but, to his great relief, she did not ask him anything.

Jade knew he had just sent his thoughts down a road that he did not want to travel. Wisely, she said nothing, instead taking another sip before turning her attention back to the lowering sun over the bay. "It's always so pretty, isn't it? Whether sunny, cloudy, summer or winter...the sunset is always a special time. It reminds me of..." her voice trailed off.

"Reminds you of what?" he prodded.

Shrugging, she said, "It's silly, but it reminds me that every day will end. No matter how horrible the day might have been, when the sun paints the sky at the end of the day, I know there will be a tomorrow. A new day. A new chance to make changes. To make it a good day."

Her words washed over him and Lance closed his eyes for a moment, letting the evening sun warm his face. *A new chance to make changes.* Opening them, he met her smile and reached out, linking fingers with her as they watched the sun slide into the horizon.

---

A few days later, Jade noticed Lance hesitate slightly as they alighted from his vehicle and faced the large crowd at the open, grassy field near the Sunset View Restaurant, host of the town's Fall Oyster Fest. Sliding up to him, she wrapped her arm around his waist and said, "We don't have to go, you know."

Casting a smile down at her, he nodded. "I know we don't have to, but I want to. This is the first chance I have to actually step into a large group like this since I've been here. Mitch didn't want me to work tonight since I'm just part-time, so I can just try to take it in." Giving her waist a squeeze in return, he added, "And, this is my first public appearance to be seen with my beautiful date."

Laughing, she replied, "Oh, I like that reason."

Taking a deep breath, he moved them forward toward the gathering. A large tent had been erected on the grounds, filled with tables and chairs underneath. Smoke billowed from steaming pots frying oysters and fish, and barbeque smokers were filled with pork and chicken. Another table was laden with corn on the cob and big bowls of salad. Yet another table held cakes and pies, all donated by the local churches.

The huge crowd was milling about, plates in hand, as they moved between the different food stations. Lance watched the moving masses and shook his head. "How do you even know where to go in a madhouse like this?"

"Follow me," Jade encouraged. "I'm a pro at making my way through chaos. I work at an elementary school, remember?" Taking his hand, she led him to the nearest pile of heavy paper plates, snagging one for each of them. With her leading the way, they made it to the fish and oyster fry station, filling their plates with the seafood.

Admiring her ability to remain calm and focused in the middle of mayhem, he stayed close to her as they headed to the barbeque. Allowing his plate to continue to be piled upon, they darted to each station until no more food could be held.

Jade found seats with some of their friends and soon the two were settled, enjoying the food and camaraderie. She noticed the smiles the others sent her way and knew they were happy to see Lance out as well.

He glanced over, distracted by the melted butter dripping on her fingers from the corn. She popped them into her mouth, sucking the deliciousness and he shifted in his seat, mesmerized at the unwitting, sensual movement.

Appraising her plate, she realized her eyes were too big for her stomach. Leaning over, she whispered, "I'll never be able to eat all this."

"Is that why you already ate the piece of cherry pie?"

Elbowing him in the side, she said, "You're not supposed to notice things like that!"

Chuckling, he replied, "I'll remember that. But, seriously, what you don't eat, I will."

She soon moved her leftovers to his plate and watched in amazement as he dug in. As he finished, he leaned back, placing his arm on the back of her chair, his fingers gently rubbing her shoulder. She settled to the side, her body fitting neatly next to his.

"How are you doing?" Katelyn asked, sitting across from them, curled into Gareth's side.

"I'm fine," she replied. "I confess that I gave a small interview to a Baytown Gazette reporter this morning. I hated to do it, but she was rather insistent. God, I even let her take a picture, which I regret. But, I figure it's just a little town newspaper...no one will ever hear of it."

Music began at the other end of the tent and many of their friends moved to the dance floor. Just as she was about to suggest they leave, Lance asked, "Would you like to dance?"

Surprised, she nodded, a slow smile curving her lips. Standing, he led her to the grassy space just outside the tent, where the shadows mingled with the inside lights. Tucking her close, he held her tightly, her head nestled underneath his chin, and they swayed while the music swirled around them.

---

Stepping into her car after the school day, Jade's phone vibrated with an incoming call. She sighed, hating to hear what her mother had to say now.

"Hi, Mom," she greeted with little enthusiasm.

"Hi? That's it? Just hi?" her mother asked. "Your father almost had a stroke at the breakfast table this morning! Estelle had just served the coffee when guess who showed up on the morning news? Oh, yes, indeed. There's a picture of our daughter…a rather unflattering picture, I might add…on the news telling us you discovered a dead body on the beach!"

*How in the world did I end up on the news the day after I gave an interview? Or at all for that matter?*

"Mom—"

"No, Jade. There is no excuse for you not warning us about the possible bad press."

"Bad press? Mom, I didn't do anything wrong. I was just the one who discovered the unfortunate person—"

"You should have called and warned us. Your father

could have had someone keep your name out of the press. Now, we have done nothing all day but field calls from our friends wanting to know what is going on with our daughter."

Sighing, Jade lifted her eyes in silent prayer for her mother to end her tirade, but knew she would have to run out of steam before that happened.

"And furthermore, your father wants to know if you have finally come to your senses and decided to come back home. That lovely job at the private school you attended is still available."

"Mom, I have no intention of leaving, but even if I did, the school year has started—"

"That doesn't matter. With your father's pull, any new teacher they hired could be pulled out and they would let you in."

The idea that her parents would so callously have another teacher fired just so she could come back incensed her. "Mom...for the last time, that's not happening. Listen, I have to go. Tell Dad I'm fine and I'll talk to you soon."

Disconnecting before her mother had a chance to berate her more, she tossed her phone back into her purse.

---

"Did you see the news?"

Grimacing at the sound of the strident voice, the man looked around, making sure no one could hear his phone conversation. "Yes, yes I saw it."

"What are you going to do about it?"

"Me?" he bit out, failing to keep his frustration out of his voice.

"Your partner fucked over our arrangement and now you are left to clean things up. The chain continues, you know. You still haven't gotten what I'm owed and now I'm on the radar since I haven't been able to pay the next man up."

"I don't know what else to do," he said, fear curdling his stomach.

"I suggest you take care of the latest problem."

"But we don't know if it is a problem," he protested, bending over, fear now beginning to cripple him.

"It is a problem. It's your problem. And I'm no longer willing to let your fuck-up become mine. So, deal!"

With that, the phone connection went dead, but he continued to hold his phone to his ear as though some guidance would appear. Nothing happened...silence was all he heard.

---

"Ms. Lyons, my mommy saw your picture in the newspaper but told me she couldn't tell me why!" Chad announced.

"I know, I know!" Sandy cried. "I bet you're getting married."

Grimacing, Jade forced a smile on her face. "Uh, no, I'm not getting married. The newspaper just picks out people to do interviews, that's all."

She hated lying to the children, but in the past few days, her quiet life was turned upside down. News of the body on the beach had circulated the town and her part in the discovery became known. The small Baytown Gazette that interviewed her apparently released all the news as fast as possible, reaching beyond local posts and airwaves. She was not only mortified to see that they had her picture in the local paper, along with the interview, but also to hear that it had reached as far as her parents. She had little information to give people and certainly kept her comments to just the facts, but nonetheless, she found the small-town notoriety embarrassing.

"My mom said you were on the news this morning, too."

Eye wide, she said, "What? I don't think—"

A knock on the classroom door interrupted their discussion and she realized it was time for the students to go to lunch. Hurrying them out the door, she hastened to the teachers' lounge. As soon as she walked in, she was peppered with questions.

"Here's our celebrity," Bill quipped, a smile on his face as he patted the table next to him, offering her a space.

"What are you talking about? Did something else happen?" she asked one of the teachers who also mentioned seeing her on TV. Her nerves were rattled as it was, she wasn't sure how much more she could take. "I was only interviewed by the Baytown Gazette."

"The TV stations always pick up human interest

stories from local papers. It's making its way across the networks."

Rolling her eyes, she gave the other teachers her abbreviated version, not wanting to discuss the details of her find, especially at the lunch meal.

Bill fiddled with his phone for a few minutes finally declaring, "Here it is. It's only about thirty seconds of fame, but nonetheless, it's all about you."

As he turned his phone around for all to see, she was assaulted with the photograph of her, taken by the Gazette, as it flashed across the screen behind the perky broadcaster from the Virginia Beach station, saying, *"Last Sunday, a Baytown Elementary School teacher received an unexpected surprise when she was on the beach searching for sea glass. Jade Lyons, a second-grade teacher, was alone on the beach, picking up sea glass, when she stumbled upon a human body washed up on the shore. The local police are still investigating the death and we will bring you the updates as they are reported. According to the Baytown Gazette, who interviewed Ms. Lyons, she often searches for sea glass and finds all sorts of interesting things on the shore. She uses the sea glass for art projects with her students, but admits the find the other day is one she hopes will not occur again. And now for the weather—"*

She stared down at her lunch feeling as though her privacy had been invaded, but she realized it was her own fault for granting the Baytown Gazette an interview. Excusing herself, she left the lounge and hurried back to her classroom. Depressed, the afternoon did not provide the same energy she was used to, the minutes ticking by slowly.

While her students were at music class, she checked her email, seeing one from her mom. Fighting the desire to bang her head on her desk, she opened it. *Yep...just what I expected.* Sighing, she read as her mother berated her once more for working in the backwaters of the Eastern Shore where crime must be at an all-time high since she discovered a dead body. Did she not think how embarrassing it was for them to have her name to be in the news? God only knows how many of their friends would see it. She should leave immediately and her father would arrange for her position to be opened at the private school near them.

*Not asking if I'm okay...just worried about their reputation...still. Even after our phone call.*

Clicking delete, she decided to reply would only make a bad day worse. When the school day was finally over, she bolted to her car, one destination in mind.

Pulling out of the school's parking lot, she drove toward town before turning onto Turner's Lane, the road that would take her to Lance's house. She had no idea if he was home, but the desire to see him was overwhelming.

Slowing down to make a sharp turn in the road, she noticed a dark pick-up in her rearview mirror, traveling too close to her back bumper. Unable to view the driver's hair color with a cap pulled low over his head and his face was obscured with sunglasses. Observing how close he came to her bumper, made her angry.

"Back off, buddy," she grumbled out loud, tapping her brakes a few times. Suddenly the truck whipped into the other lane to pass. "Fine, fine. Just go on."

The truck pulled alongside her and then slowed to her speed. She turned her head to look at the driver, but the side windows were tinted dark. Suddenly the truck swerved back into her lane, sideswiping her vehicle and running her off the road. Slamming her foot on the brake, her scream mixed with squealing tires as she lost control of her car and collided into a tree.

---

The sound of glass shattering and metal crunching was drowned out by the airbag hitting her full force, knocking the breath out of her. Gasping as the pain across her chest intensified, she sat motionless for a few seconds. White powder had billowed out, causing confusion as she continued to fight to breathe. Her lungs burned but as she coughed, the pain in her chest was so intense that she lifted a hand to her mouth in an effort to quell the spasm.

Looking up, she watched the truck as it careened down the road until out of sight. Anger and fear mixed with shock.

"Oh, God, oh, God," she whispered, barely able to catch her breath.

As she glanced downward, she realized the seat belt still held her tightly in place. Good, but painful. Lifting her gaze again, she observed the hood and front driver's side of her car was crumpled and shards of glass were covering the insides.

Her purse was on the passenger floor and, as she lifted her hand to unsnap her buckle, shaking ensued, making the simple task almost impossible. Finally free, she tried to lean forward to grab her purse, but the sharp pain in her chest had her quickly moving back to a seated position.

Adrenaline coursed through her veins causing her stomach to churn. *I've got to get out!* Another sharp pain, this time from her left foot, jolted through her as she attempted to move in that direction. Blinking against the sting in her eyes from the airbag powder, she could see her foot was caught in tangled metal. Feeling faint, she closed her eyes, fighting tears.

"Miss, miss, are you all right?"

Vision blurry, she saw an older man rapping on the passenger window. Tears began to flow as the enormity of the situation struck her.

"I need...someone hit me...I need to call..."

The man reached into his pocket and placed a call to 9-1-1. She listened as he gave the information to the dispatcher, a sob hitching from deep inside, the movement causing pain. She covered her mouth with one hand, trying to stop the wail from bubbling forth. The man hustled around her car and reached in to unlock her passenger door.

"Do you think you can get out, ma'am?"

She jerked her head, too afraid to move any further, when she heard the siren. Thankful she was just a mile from the main center of town, she winced, each breath hurting her chest. Looking up, just as another tear slid down her cheek, she watched as Zac alighted from the ambulance, directing the volunteer firefighters in the firetruck.

Hurrying over, he peered through the passenger door. "Jade, honey. We'll get you out." Barking orders over his shoulder, he turned back to her. "We're gonna have to take you out from this side, but we're gonna make it safe first, okay?"

More sirens filled the air, soon followed by shouts, before Mitch's face appeared where Zac's had been. She stared, numb, trying to focus on his words.

Mitch stepped back, allowing Zac to move in again as they covered the passenger seat with thick blankets so she could be maneuvered out with a lessened chance of more cuts. He stalked over to Ginny, who was on the phone. Looking down, he asked, "Lance?"

She nodded and he moved to Grant, who was standing on the street looking at the tire marks.

Zac climbed into the passenger seat and fastened a neck brace, stabilizing her head. Then he tried to gently shift Jade so that she could be pulled from the open door.

"My foot is stuck. The metal is all crushed."

"One second, I got you." Zac slowly moved her leg until he was able to get her free, working carefully so that he caused little additional pain. Just as he and the other firefighters slid her body from the car onto a waiting gurney, she heard another vehicle squealing around the corner.

Mitch looked to the side, seeing Lance's SUV come to a stop, seconds before he jumped out, rushing over. Stepping up quickly, Mitch grabbed him by the shoulders. "Easy man, she's gonna be okay. Has some injuries, but she was wearing her seatbelt and the airbags deployed."

"What happened?" he asked, voice hoarse as he moved closer to the crumpled car.

"Don't know. She might have taken the curve too fast," Ginny said.

As Lance moved to the stretcher, Grant approached Mitch, and said, "Chief, you need to take a look at this."

Moving to follow Grant, Mitch and Ginny halted in their steps as Lance reached Jade and she tried to rise from the stretcher, clutching his arm, crying, "I was hit. They followed. They hit me. Ran me off." Her eyes implored him to listen as Zac gently forced her back on the gurney. "Lance…someone did this to me."

Jaw tight, he wanted to cup her face, but the slivers of glass embedded there kept his hand on her side. "Just breathe. Breathe with me, honey. Calm down and breathe. We'll talk as soon as we know you're all right." He shifted his gaze to her left foot, seeing one of the rescue workers putting an air brace there for stabilization.

Lying on her back, Jade looked up with watery eyes. The breeze blowing the trees above was calm, while all around people hurried to take care of her. Another tear slid down her cheek, but she felt it being wiped away as Lance leaned over, filling her line of vision. His face was ragged with concern as his eyes pierced deep inside her.

Zac looked over to Mitch. "We're ready to take her to the hospital. You need anything?"

He patted Lance's shoulder, reminding him he needed to talk to Jade. Leaning over, Mitch asked, "Is there anything you can tell us now, Jade? Anything at all?"

Swallowing, she nodded. "Dark, truck. Dark tinted windows. Driver had a ball cap on his head. Wore sunglasses. Big guy. Followed too close and then tried to pass. At my side, he swerved to hit me and forced me to wreck."

"Did you see any part of the license tag?" Lance asked, already fearing the answer. As she nodded, his eyes widened, impressed that she was able to catch anything with everything that was going on.

"The first three letters were C.A.B. I didn't get the numbers, but I just remember thinking he drove like cab drivers in some big cities." Lance's smile was still worried, but it warmed Jade's heart as she lifted a hand, clutching his.

He looked up at Zac as they loaded her into the back of the ambulance and said, "I'm coming with you." As Zac nodded, he tossed his keys to Grant and asked, "Can someone get my SUV to the hospital?"

"No problem. If not one of us, Jillian and Katelyn will take care of it."

With that, he climbed into the ambulance, taking her pale hand in his.

Lance kept his eyes on Jade for the entire thirty minute ride to the hospital. Originally located in North Heron County, it had since moved slightly north to Accawmacke County. Zac worked efficiently on her, keeping her smiling with some of his corny jokes, but he still caught the pain in her eyes.

Pulling up to the emergency room, Lance hopped out, assisting as her gurney was taken from the ambulance, before stepping back to let the hospital personnel complete their tasks. He and Zac stayed outside the ER bay as a nurse assisted her into a hospital gown.

"I'm sorry, sir," the efficient nurse said as she left the room, "only family is allowed back with her."

"I'm her..." he hesitated a second, about to identify himself as her brother, when Zac interrupted.

"It's okay," he said with a grin. "He's her fiancé."

Both Jade and his eyes widened at the lie, but the nurse nodded and allowed him access behind the curtain.

Zac leaned over and kissed her forehead, saying, "I'll check on you later, sweetheart, but I gotta get back to Baytown now." Turning to leave, he slapped Lance on the back and, with a wink, said, "You can thank me later, fiancé."

After a chin lift thrown Zac's way, his gaze immediately shot back to Jade as the hospital personnel began their procedures. When they reached the part of her information concerning emergency contacts, she hesitated.

"Um…I guess you can put my mom down…but only in an emergency." She rattled off the name and phone number, along with a Virginia address.

As the nurse finished, a fresh-faced doctor entered the room and Lance looked over at him with suspicion, wondering if the kid was old enough to have completed medical school. The doctor smiled widely at Jade, introducing himself.

Knowing he should step out of the room to give them privacy, he nonetheless stayed standing nearby, fighting the desire to punch the overly friendly doctor.

The doctor took stock of all of her injuries, from her swollen wrist, injured foot, and glass cuts on her cheek, to the dark bruising on her shoulder, collarbone and chest.

"I want to send you to x-ray. We want to check out your wrist and foot, and also your neck, spine, and ribs. We'll check for a concussion as well. I'll be back once we have those and then we can see to your injuries."

With a parting smile, the doctor was out the door, unaware of Lance's glare on his back. Immediately, he swung his gaze back to Jade. Pulling up a plastic chair, he sat next to her bed, reaching out to hold her hand.

"How are you feeling?"

Blowing out a huge sigh, she admitted, "Like I was hit by a truck."

Chuckling, despite his concern, he shook his head. "That is so not funny, Jade."

She offered a small smile and quipped, "Well, *fiancé*, you're supposed to love me in sickness and in health."

Now a full laugh escaped from him, as he rubbed circles on her palm.

"I know why Zac did that, but I was going to say I was your brother. Of course," he said hesitantly, "I like what he chose instead."

Before she had a chance to respond, hospital personnel came to whisk her off to x-ray, leaving him sitting in her room, wondering what was coming over him.

*Why did I admit that I liked being called her fiancé? Way to scare someone off!* Deciding that when she came back, he would move into professional mode to make sure she was comfortable with his presence, he sucked in a deep breath, knowing she was so much more to him than a victim in need of comfort.

Down the hall, Jade moved onto the x-ray table, pain lancing through her back, shoulders, foot, arm...*damn, is there anywhere that doesn't hurt?* Trying to stay positive, she focused on Lance's words. *He liked that Zac declared him as my fiancé.* Knowing her feelings for him were growing, it was nice to hear that he felt the same.

"Okay, Ms. Lyons, we're all finished. We'll take you

back to your ER bay and the attending physician will be in to talk to you as soon as he's had a chance to look at all the radiographs. We'll confirm with him and then start you on some pain meds that we can put in your IV as well."

Within a few minutes, she was ensconced back in her ER bay, Lance hopping up from his chair to observe her as they hooked her back to the various machines.

She smiled, her eyes searching his, and greeted, "Hey. I'm so glad you're here with me." A curt nod was his only response, and she wondered why he was not reaching out to hold her hand anymore. "Are you okay?"

"Absolutely," he replied, his voice no longer warm. "I was wondering what else you could tell me about the accident," he said, taking out a pad of paper from his back pocket, along with a pen.

Sucking in her lips, she stared at him, uncertain of the change that had come over him while she had been in x-ray. She left with him saying he was glad Zac referred to him as her fiancé and now he was acting like a cop on patrol. Sighing heavily, she replied, "I left school as usual and was actually driving out to your house. I didn't know if you were home, but I...well...I just wanted to see you, that's all. I've had a crappy day—"

"Why crappy?" he asked, his voice now laced with concern.

"Lance, what's going on? I'm going to get whiplash from your mood changes and, honestly, the way I feel right now, I don't need that!"

Lance opened his mouth, then snapped it shut, uncertain how to respond.

Huffing, Jade leaned back on the uncomfortable bed, "Fine. Professional it is. I had a bad day because my students knew about the body on the beach and the local story was picked up by a TV station in Virginia Beach this weekend, which my mom so graciously continues to remind me of. By the time I left school, I simply thought I would spend some time with you. Obviously, a dumb idea, but there it is. A black pickup truck, with a big grill on the front, came very close to me. I couldn't see the driver clearly. A ball cap covered his hair and he wore sunglasses. I saw no one in the passenger side. They swung to the other lane and I thought they were going to pass. As they pulled along-side me, I glanced over, but the passenger window was tinted so I could see nothing. He jerked his truck into the side of me. I ran off the road and into a copse of trees. I looked up as the airbag deflated, and I might have been disoriented and terrified, but I still saw him driving down the road, leaving me wrecked against the trees." Letting out a sigh, then wincing when the movement hurt her bruised chest, she clamped her mouth shut. Tired, grumpy, and in pain.

He looked down at his feet for a moment, the silence in the room deafening. Shaking his head, he admitted, "I'm sorry, Jade. I didn't mean...I just don't know...oh, fuck."

Her eyes lifted to him, leaning against the wall, and her heart melted again. "Look, Lance. I don't know what's going on with you, but even if it's all pretend, I really need someone to just hold my hand." The last word was said on a sob, causing another grimace to cross her face.

Dropping into the chair, he grabbed her uninjured hand, squeezing it tight. "I'm so sorry, really I am." He gazed into her eyes, quickly developing dark circles around them, and saw fatigue and pain. Interrupted by another nurse, he watched as she gave Jade a painkiller through her IV.

"Now, this'll make you sleepy," the nurse warned, "so, if you have to get out of bed, make sure your handsome fiancé helps."

With a smile, the nurse left, and he observed Jade's face relax as the medicine took effect.

She rolled her head to the side, and said, "What were you saying?"

"I was admitting that I suck at letting people in, and sometimes completely forget how to be a friend, much less anything else."

"Why?" she asked, her voice whisper soft.

"Too many reasons to burden you with right now, but I promise, I'm getting help. I really want to be able to be a better man...like the man I used to be, but it'll take some time."

She grinned a wobbly smile, her eyes brighter now that the pain had receded. "I can wait," she confessed. Her smile slid off her face as her eyes began to close, "I liked it when you said you liked what Zac said. That was nice," her voice slurred. Her brow furrowed as she continued, "Not all, Mr. Big Bad Cop."

He grinned as her eyes closed completely, knowing she was not in pain and, if he was honest, happy that she admitted she felt the same as he did. Breathing a sigh of relief, he watched her rest, still holding her hand.

A few minutes later, his phone vibrated and, seeing it was Mitch, he slipped out of the room and into the hall. "Yeah?"

"How's she doing?"

"Doc's been in, checked her out, then they took her to x-ray. Got her on pain meds now, so she's sleeping. Doc's supposed to come back in when he looks at everything."

"She tell you any more?"

"Not really. She was definitely run off the road—"

"Yeah, Jason has looked at her car and has corroborated that the truck that hit her was painted black."

"Anything on the license plate?"

"Grant's running it now."

"I want the bastard, Mitch."

"I know you do and I know you'll do everything by the book, no matter how badly you want to go after him." After a moment of silence, he asked, "You bringing her home?"

"As soon as they release her."

"Lance, I gotta warn you, the women are gearing up to swoop in and take care of her. I know you like privacy, but you may have to kiss that goodbye."

Still holding the phone to his ear, he dropped his head to stare at his shoes. Waiting for the tell-tale signs of panic, instead his chest was filled with warmth. "It's all good, Mitch. But tell them to give her a day or so. She's banged up."

He chuckled, "You got it. See you when you get back." With that, he disconnected.

Observing the doctor walk back into Jade's room, he hustled in as well. A droopy smile crossed her face again and the doctor laughed.

"I see the pain medicine has made you more comfortable. Good, good," the doctor declared before turning toward Lance, speaking more to him than her. "She's suffered a hairline fracture of her wrist and has a severely bruised collarbone and chest from the seat belt. We'll splint her wrist and give her a sling to keep her arm from moving too much as it heals. Her ankle is not broken, but has severe contusions, so we'll have it in a boot, just to help with the swelling. She should stay off her left foot for several days to give it a chance to heal. She can't use crutches with her injured wrist, but with the boot, she can walk on it as soon as it is strong enough. As far as her lacerations, the nurse removed the pieces of glass that were embedded, and an antiseptic cream applied twice a day should take care of the small cuts."

His mind reeled as he listened to the doctor's list of injuries, but he was thankful her seatbelt and airbag kept her as safe as it did.

"So, we'll also prescribe a pain medication that she can take if necessary, but if over-the-counter pain medicine works, she can just use those. Any questions?"

Jade's nose scrunched as she said, "He talks a lot. Too many words."

Grinning, Lance nodded toward the doctor, saying, "I've got it."

As the doctor left, he leaned over and kissed her forehead. "And I've got you too, sweetheart," he said, the endearment falling easily from his lips.

---

## 18

Jade leaned her head back against the headrest of Lance's SUV. Grant and Jillian made the trip to the hospital and dropped his vehicle off after checking on her. She rolled her head toward him, the movement causing her to wince.

He noticed and reached over, squeezing her thigh while avoiding her sling and wrist. "I'm so sorry. I know every time you move it hurts like hell."

Deciding not to move again, she kept her eyes on his profile. Sighing, she asked, "Do you think Jillian is upset with me?"

"No way, Jade. She and the others just want to help, but I know you didn't want to stay with her. Or Katelyn when she called. Or Tori. Or Belle—"

Grinning, she said, "I've got good friends, but by the time Belle called, I was exhausted. I'll call them back when I feel a little better."

Squeezing her leg again, he turned onto the road

leading into Baytown. "Is there anything I need to get from your place before we head to mine?"

She blinked in confusion. "I really just want to lay down, Lance."

"Okay, then we can head to my place first and, if need be, I can get someone to grab things from your apartment."

"Why are we going to your place?"

He looked sharply over at her, saying, "Because I'm taking you home with me and I'm taking care of you."

"That's sweet, but I just want to go to my home," she persisted. "I don't need anyone to take care of me. I'll be fine."

Frowning, Lance glanced over, understanding filling him as he observed her closed eyes. He knew the pain meds she had been given in the hospital made it harder for her to concentrate and think things through. She would never make it up the three flights of stairs and, while the idea of carrying her in his arms held appeal, he refused to make things more difficult for her in the long run.

Continuing to his house, he parked as close as he could to the front door. He hesitated before getting out, just as her sleepy eyes blinked open. "Look, Jade, I don't want to upset you, but you're not supposed to put weight on your foot so I had to bring you here. There's no way you could handle your stairs."

Expecting her to be stubborn, her lips curved into a slightly lopsided smile. "M'kay."

Moving to her side of the vehicle, he scooped her into his arms, holding her good side next to his body. At the door, he managed to get it unlocked and then moved them inside, kicking the door shut with his boot.

By the time they made it to Lance's living room, Jade recognized that he was right—going to her apartment would have been a huge mistake. She would never be able to traverse the stairs by herself, even with her foot in a boot. As he set her gently down on the sofa, a tear slid down her cheek.

"Are you in pain," he asked, squatting at her feet. "What can I get for you?"

"I'm just tired," she said, trying not to cry, but the day's events overwhelmed her and the tears began to flow.

"Tell me what you need and I'll get it," he promised, his voice anguished as he gently wiped her tears.

"I just wanted to be in my own bed and now I'm making things hard for you."

Sighing, he pushed her hair back from her face and said, "Don't you understand? By allowing me to take care of you, I get the peace of mind knowing you are safe."

Swallowing audibly, she offered a short nod. "You're right, and I'm being silly. I'm fine, really, I am. And thank you so much for everything you did for me today. I really appreciate it."

Cocking his head, Lance stared at her, listening to her apparent dismissal of him. "I'm not sure what you think is happening here, Jade, but I'm not leaving your side."

Blinking again, she said, "But—

"No buts," he interrupted. "I'm going to get some

food in you, get you in bed, and give you the meds to make you rest easy tonight."

As she opened her mouth to speak he jumped in again. "Think about it, honey. Doesn't it make sense?"

Jade had to admit it did, and nodded. "If you're sure...I don't want you to feel obligated."

Standing, he scooped her up once more and this time stalked into his bedroom, sitting her on the edge of the bed. Kissing the top of her head, he smiled, "No obligation. Jade, I get to have you right by my side. This is no hardship, babe. This is me, joining the living again. I'm just glad you want me here. Now, let's get you settled."

He stood back, observing the contraptions she had on. Sling. Wrist brace. Foot brace.

"What?" she asked as his gaze moved over her.

"Trying to figure out what to do first," he confessed, then seeming to make up his mind, he leaned over and unfastened the sling, deftly sliding it off. Eyeing her blouse, he said, "I think we can get that over the wrist brace," and bent to unbutton the tiny buttons down the front.

She felt the heat of blush rush to her face but knew there was no other way to get out of her clothes, other than to call one of the girls over and she hated to do that. Keeping her eyes locked on his chest, she felt the cool air of her blouse being pulled off her injured arm and then quickly dropped to the floor.

Lance felt her embarrassment and determined to keep his eyes off her bra as he turned toward his dresser, but the sight of her bruises caused him to gasp.

Jerking her gaze up, Jade could tell he was looking at the bruises. "Does it look bad?" She knew the answer to her question by the look on his face. Standing, she hobbled over to the mirror, clutching his arm. Her eyes landed on a dark, black stripe from her neck extending between her breasts. Sighing heavily, she allowed him to help her back to bed. "I need something to wear," she replied, her voice numb.

Deciding a t-shirt would hurt her trying to get her injured arm through the sleeve, Lance moved to his closet, choosing a soft, flannel shirt instead. The button front made it a good choice since it did not have to pull over her head. Turning around, he stopped in his tracks.

Jade was attempting to unsnap her bra with her good hand, but looked up, her eyes filling with tears again. "This sucks but, I can't do it."

Walking around to the other side of the bed, he crawled behind her and unsnapped her bra, saying, "Sweetheart, I can't see anything, so don't be embarrassed. Just slide it off your arms and then reach your good arm back and I'll get this top on you."

She followed his instructions and found the soft, cotton material soothing against her skin. As he rounded her front again, she clutched the material together at first, but then decided that her modesty no longer mattered. Lowering her arm, she watched as he buttoned the shirt, his touch comforting.

"Let's do the pants," he said, bending to take the boot off her foot. Helping her to stand, and then unbuttoning and unzipping her pants, he slid them down her legs. Efficiently, he replaced them with a pair of cut-off sweats. Large, but they covered her enough to keep her warm. "We've got to get the boot back on, but I'm afraid it will hurt," he confessed.

"Honestly, I'm not feeling much of anything."

Nodding, he managed to brace her foot once more. Fluffing the pillows, he pulled the covers down and, once she was lying in bed with her back against the pillowed headboard, he kissed her forehead, careful of her facial lacerations.

"Gonna get your pills," he said, before leaving the room.

Lifting her eyes to the ceiling, she fought a tired grin. *Wow, I'm in Lance's house, in his bedroom, and he's just stripped me. And this is so not how I would've liked that to happen.*

Once the pills were down, he headed back into the kitchen to make soup and sandwiches. Placing the food on a tray, he went back into the bedroom, seeing her eyes peering up sleepily at him.

"Let's get food down you before you fall asleep, babe."

With encouragement, Jade ate everything he brought before sliding down under the covers. With her wrist propped on a pillow near her head and her foot carefully tucked underneath the covers, she felt her body growing warm and beginning to drift.

"Lance," she said, barely above a whisper.

Leaning over, he said, "Right here."

"Please stay. Stay with me all night," she begged in a sleepy voice. "Here with me. I don't want to be alone."

"I promise," Lance replied, knowing nothing could make him leave her side.

Taking her tray back to the kitchen, he fixed a sandwich for himself, eating it quickly. After making sure the doors were locked, he moved through his room and into the bathroom. Hurrying through a shower, he was back out within a few minutes, drying off. Pulling on his boxers, he walked back into the bedroom, staring down at the banged-up beauty. Knowing someone ran her off the road, on purpose, made his blood boil, but he tamped down those emotions as she moved and moaned in pain.

Slipping under the covers, he curled his large body into hers, hoping to keep her steady through the night. As his eyes closed he could not help but think, *She's in my room, in my bed, but not how I would have liked it to happen.*

---

Waking the next morning, Lance opened his eyes just in time to see Jade blinking awake also. He observed the confusion on her face as she tried to move before realizing his body was helping to keep her still.

"Hey," he greeted. "Don't move too fast. Give your body a chance to wake up and take stock of how you are."

She rolled onto her back, keeping her wrist supported as she stretched her legs, wincing at the pain in her neck and chest. Breathing gingerly, she nodded as she said, "My wrist and ankle ache, but it's the seatbelt bruise that makes it hard to breathe sometimes."

He rolled out of the bed and padded around to her injured side, pulling the comforter down. Placing his hands under her neck and back, he assisted her to a seated position before brushing her hair back from her face. "Okay?"

"Yeah," she smiled up at him. Taking a slow, deep breath, she lifted her arms to him and allowed him to pull her to a standing position. Blushing, she said, "First stop, bathroom."

He nodded and steadied her with his hand at her back until she disappeared behind the door. Sliding on his jeans, he left off his shirt and moved into the kitchen, pulling out his frying pan to begin breakfast.

A moment later, Jade hobbled into the kitchen, the scent of bacon and eggs calling to her. The sight of Lance's naked, muscular chest had her mouth watering for a taste of him more than for the food.

He looked over his shoulder and grinned. "I cooked the bacon in the microwave and just scrambled some eggs. Is that okay?"

"More than okay," she said, eyeing the plate he placed on the table. She attempted to maneuver into the seat, but he stepped behind her, his long arm snatching the plate.

"Let's get you settled where you won't topple over." Lance moved toward the living room and, once she was comfortable on the sofa, placed the plate on her lap and coffee on the end table within reach. "It's good you're right handed," he commented, pleased to see her digging into her breakfast with gusto.

"I'm starving this morning," she said, looking up. "Are you eating?"

Chuckling, he nodded and moved back to the kitchen to get his plate and coffee, before returning to join her on the sofa. After breakfast, he took the plates and rinsed them before leaving them in the sink. "Do you need a pain pill, sweetheart?"

"No," she replied in haste, scrunching her nose. "I hate the way they make me feel. But I'll take some Aleve in a little bit."

As he settled into the deep cushions of the sofa, he twisted his body so that he was close and facing her. "Jade, we need to talk."

Sighing, she nodded. "Maybe I do need a pain pill," she joked, her voice tinged with sadness. "I know what you're going to ask, but Lance, I have no idea why someone ran me off the road. Maybe it was just a teenager being stupid with a dare or something. Maybe I was just in the wrong place at the wrong time."

He thought about her stumbling onto the body on the beach, but could not connect the two at all. *Maybe she's right and it's just dumb, bad luck.* "You did not recognize him or the truck?"

"No, although I didn't get a good look and he wore sunglasses." Closing her eyes, Jade sighed heavily, causing pain in her chest. "Damn, I've got to stop breathing."

"Oh, no. Don't stop breathing," he responded, leaning over, placing a soft kiss on her lips. Standing, he stared down at her. "I need to go into the station, but I don't want to leave you here alone."

She peered up at him. "I don't know what to do. If you take me to my house, I'll be stuck up all those steps. Jillian, Katelyn, and Belle are all working. Before I came to breakfast, I called my principal and told her that I would need the next two days off. That should give me time to heal so I can get back to work."

Pulling out his phone, Lance dialed Mitch. "Hey, we need a favor. Can I bring Jade to your house to visit with Tori today? Everyone else is working and her third floor apartment is a nightmare 'cause she can't get up and down the stairs. My house is not close to anything—"

Pausing as he listened, he grinned. "Good. I'll bring her in a little bit." Disconnecting, he said, "Mitch said we didn't need to convince him you needed to be somewhere safe. He said Tori would be angry if you went anywhere else."

Laughing gently, while holding her hand against her chest, she nodded. "Maybe I can shower at Tori's house...she can help if needed."

His eyes darkened as he sucked in a quick breath. "I'd be glad to help you shower...but I guess Tori is a safer choice."

"Safer?"

Pulling her to a stand, he wrapped his arms around her back and held her close. "Jade, I love taking care of you but, gotta admit, in the shower, it would be hard not to stare at your beautiful body. And right now, you need to heal."

Leaning her head back, she smiled. "Okay. Heal first…and then?"

Bending to kiss her lips, Lance began slowly before he angled his head to take her mouth fully. Moving his lips over her soft flesh, he slid his tongue in…slowly at first in a gentle exploration. Her moan inflamed his senses and he began to take the kiss deeper. One hand glided up her back, cupping her head and her silky tresses flowed through his fingers like silk.

Jade, lost in the kiss, forgot about her injuries, and her fears, thinking only of the feel of his mouth on hers. Strong and soft. Steel and satin. His tongue searched her mouth, tangling with her tongue, and she felt the electricity zip straight to her core. Eyes closed, she barely noticed when he lifted his head, his warm breath wash against her face.

"Damn, babe. I'd rather stay here all day and do nothing but kiss you."

"Why don't you," she breathed, opening her eyes to see his hazel ones piercing her.

" 'Cause I'd never be able to stop at just a kiss," Lance confessed, pulling her head to his chest, afraid that if he continued to look into her eyes, she might see deeper into him than he was willing to let her at this moment. He knew he wanted her. Desired her. And more than just for sex or even friendship. He wanted her in a way he had not allowed himself to want in a very long time. Swallowing, he whispered to the top of her head, "We'll get there. I'll get there. You need to heal. I just need… some…time."

Her cheek pressed against his heartbeat, she held

tight, her arms wrapped around his waist. "I'll give you all the time you want, Lance. All the time you need. Just know that I want you too."

As those words filled his ears, he sighed in relief before pressing his lips against her silky hair.

## 19

"Glad Jade's doing okay, even though I know she feels like shit this morning," Grant said, his eyes full of concern.

Lance cast his gaze around the table in the police workroom, seeing the same expression on everyone's face. Nodding, he said, "Thanks. I'll tell her you all asked about her."

"She taking some time off?" Sam asked.

"Hell yeah. The ER doctor said she couldn't go back until Monday, so with the next two days off and then the weekend she'll have four days to recuperate."

"Even so, she'll need to take it easy with a bunch of second graders and all the activity they require," Burt added. "My six-year-old runs me and the wife ragged."

"She's with Tori right now," Lance said, with a nod toward Mitch, "so that'll help."

Grant piped up, "Jillian and Katelyn'll be over this afternoon to help as well. You'll need it as much as she does."

"I'll check in on her too," Ginny added, her face turned toward him with a smile.

A strange feeling slid over Lance as the words from his co-workers—*and friends*—hit him. A warmth spread from his chest outward. The realization that not only were these good people friends of Jade's, but that they were friends of his as well. Nodding was the only response he was able to offer, as his voice caught in his throat.

Mitch, stepping in, said, "Okay, we need to get to the body investigation, but also the truck that ran into Jade."

"I'm running the plates, but—"

Mildred interrupted as she hurried into the room. "Sorry, Chief, but I was looking at the report Grant asked for and this just came in."

Looking at the paper she handed to him, Mitch's jaw tightened. "Seems a truck matching the description Jade gave us has just been reported stolen. It belongs to Donald Haskins. He's got a farm in North Heron county about five miles from here.

"He's just reporting it stolen?" Ginny bit out.

"You and Lance head out to talk to him. When you get back, we will hopefully have more identification on the body. The first of the State lab reports come back today." Looking at Lance, Mitch added, "Check with Mildred when you get back. She's ordered more BPD polos and I'm sure they came yesterday." Grinning, he said, "Approval for you to be the new part-time detective for Baytown came through at last night's town meeting. Congratulations."

Lance met his grin as he accepted the congratulations from the others around the table. Nodding, he said, "Guess I've got paperwork to sign?"

"Yeah, Mildred'll take care of you and then we'll get your badge and firearm. For this trip, Ginny'll take the lead."

With a nod, Lance and Ginny left the room and headed out to one of the BPD vehicles.

---

"Thank you so much for letting me be here today," Jade gushed, her smile on Tori. "I know you're supposed to take it easy."

"Oh, pooh," Tori waved Jade's concerns away with a toss of her hand. "I'm good. I just need to watch that I don't overeat at one time and I really have to stay away from spicy food. I'm fine and so is the baby, so the doctor has me on no restrictions at all."

Smiling, Jade watched as Tori's hand sought her stomach as she spoke. "I hate being out of school today," she confessed. "My kids are so good, but I know it would be hard to move around the classroom."

"You think you could handle it, but I think you'd hurt a lot more just having to keep up with the kids. You're much better off having these days to rest your body."

"I know," Jade sighed gingerly, "but it's so inconvenient." Blushing, she added, "Thanks for the help with the shower earlier."

Smiling, Tori moved back into the kitchen and fixed

an easy lunch. Calling out a few minutes later, she asked, "I hope homemade tuna salad is okay?"

"Absolutely!" came the reply from Jillian.

Tori stepped into the hall, grinning as Jillian and Katelyn came through her door. "I should have known you'd come for lunch," she laughed.

"I brought dessert," Jillian said, holding out a pie from her coffee shop.

"And I've got a pasta salad I made last night," Katelyn offered.

"Yum," Jade grinned as she accepted gentle hugs from her friends.

"So," Katelyn began as they piled their plates full and handed one to , "tell us everything."

Swallowing, she asked, "About the accident?"

"Well, of course, but also about Lance. How he ended up with you last night and how you managed to get the town hermit to come out of his shell. See what I did there? Hermit, shell, get it?"

Frowning, Jade said, "He's not a hermit! He just prefers…privacy."

Katelyn quickly set her plate on the coffee table and rushed over to her, taking her hands in her own. "Oh, Jade, I'm so sorry. I truly meant no offense."

Jade's frown relaxed as she held her hands. "It's okay…really, it is. I've just gotten to know him and keep hearing him referred to as a hermit or a recluse. They're such negative terms. Although," she admitted, "when I first had a run-in with him, I called him worse things than that!" Giving Katelyn's hands a squeeze, she added,

"I should apologize to you for being oversensitive. But he truly is a good man."

Katelyn returned to her seat, smiling as she said, "Then tell us about that good man."

Laughing, she acquiesced. "I have no idea what has happened to him, or why he is such a private person, or anything about his past at all. We definitely haven't gotten to the place where he confides anything in me and I know he needs more time to be able to do that. But," she shrugged, "that's okay. He will when he's ready."

"Oh, Jade," Tori said, setting her plate in her lap, her eyes as warm as her smile. "You are so good for him. Mitch knew him, of course, back when they were overseas in the military. Even Mitch doesn't know what happened that changed him so much, but he said last night that Lance is so much more like his old self since you came along."

Tori's words warmed her heart and she smiled genuinely toward her friends.

"So, any word on the bastard that ran you off the road?" Jillian asked, breaking the nice bubble she had settled around her.

"Nothing yet."

"Well, what can we do to help for today?"

She thought for a second before saying, "I hate to ask, because there are a ton of stairs involved, but I thought maybe this afternoon, I could get back to my apartment. I've got a few things to do and I might as well get to them before Lance comes over this evening."

"Things we can help with?"

"Oh no. I've got a few bills to pay online, need to look over my lesson plans for the sub for tomorrow. Just easy things like that."

"That's simple enough," Katelyn agreed. "We can also do a quick grocery run for you, so you'll have food for the weekend."

Plans made, they finished lunch as they settled into easy conversation.

---

Driving along the dusty driveway of the Haskin's farm, Ginny started to park outside the house when Lance pointed toward the barn where he saw a man enter. Nodding, she pulled down the drive a little further, parking where he indicated.

An older man looked out, his eyes narrowing for a moment before he threw his hand up in greeting. As they approached, he called out, "Couldn't see who was coming down the lane. Glad to see it's you. Got any news about my truck?"

Lance stood back as Ginny introduced them and watched Mr. Haskins carefully as he answered Ginny's questions.

"Mr. Haskins, can you tell us when you discovered your truck had been stolen?"

"Wasn't until the misses and me got back this morning."

"Back, sir?"

"We went to Virginia Beach two days ago to visit with our new grandson. Margery hates to ride in the farm truck, so we took her little car. Got back this morning and the first thing I noticed was my truck wasn't parked at the house. I looked around and then called the police. It was here when we left, so I have no idea when it was taken."

"We have a report of a black pick-up truck with tinted windows, the first three letters of the license number as C A B, and it had a metal grill on the front—"

"That sounds just like mine," Mr. Haskins said, excitedly. "Has it been found?"

"No, sir," she continued. "If that was your truck, it was involved in an accident where the driver purposefully ran another car off the road."

Mr. Haskins opened his mouth several times but no words came forth. Finally, sputtering, he said, "Someone stole my truck and was involved in an accident?"

"We are uncertain, at this time, if it was your truck that was involved. The paint on the other car is being analyzed, but we need to investigate on the assumption that, very likely, it was your truck."

"Ran someone off the road?" Suddenly, eyes wide, he asked, "Oh, Lordy. Is the other person all right?"

"Minor injuries—"

"Oh, sweet Jesus," he cried then looked over as a woman approached from the house. "Margery! Someone done stole the truck and used it to hurt someone!"

Margery's steps became hurried as she made her way to her husband, her eyes first on him and then swinging to Ginny and Lance. "What?"

"Ma'am, we believe your truck was used to create an accident in which someone was injured. Any information you might have would be useful."

"I don't know...I just don't know," she said, her hand grasping her husband's.

"Who locally knew you were going to be gone?" he queried.

Shaking her head, she suddenly looked at him, her eyes wide as she sucked in a gasp of air. "I'm on Facebook. I put out a status that we were going to see the grandbaby in Virginia Beach. I'm friends with most of Baytown...lordy, lots of people would've seen it."

"Dang it, Margery, honey," Donald said, "I told you that Facebookie thing was gonna be gettin' too many people in our business."

A tear ran down her cheek as her husband wrapped his arm around her, pulling her in for a hug. "Now, now, don't fret. Hell, I told the workers we'd be gone as well, so it coulda come from me."

"Can I get a list of your workers?" Ginny asked.

"Sure, but I got some migrant workers that just come in seasonally, and sometimes they change daily. But, I'll give you my lead assistant and he can give you the rest of the information, if that's okay."

Nodding, they walked with him back to the barn where they got the information needed. As they drove back into town, he glanced at his watch.

"You need to be somewhere?" Ginny asked. "You need to get to Jade? 'Cause you're only part-time, so you're off the clock right now."

"I've got an appointment, if you wouldn't mind dropping me off."

"Sure thing. Where're we heading?"

Hesitating, he wished he had just told her to drop him off at the station and he could have walked. Sucking in a breath, he answered, "The Eastern Shore Mental Health building."

With a nod, she simply said, "No problem."

Appreciating her discretion, he waved a few minutes later as she drove away after dropping him off, before he turned and walked through the doors.

---

More comfortable with his counselor than previously, Lance held Charles' eyes as they began. "A lot's happened in the past week," he acknowledged. "Mostly good, some not good but, all in all, it's pushed me out of my shell."

"Gotta say you've captured my attention," Charles admitted. "We'll start with whatever you want to start with."

Rubbing the back of his neck, he thought for a moment. "Hell, I'm not sure where to begin." Sucking in a deep breath, he said, "I guess the most important news is that I've met someone who makes me want to be with her...you know, really get to know her, but that's fuckin' scary."

"Do you know why?"

"Yeah, 'cause if I get to know her then it's only right that she'll get to know me too. And laying myself bare to anyone scares the hell outta me." After a moment of silence, he looked up to see Charles was waiting patiently. Chuckling, he continued, "Okay, and you're wondering why?"

Charles grinned in return.

"Scary because my family is fucked up and she probably comes from a picture-perfect family and wouldn't understand why I'm estranged from my parents."

"That's an assumption you're making. First, you're assuming her family is close and second, you're assuming she will reject you based on your family situation. Sounds to me like you aren't really giving her a chance...or a choice."

Lance sat quietly for a moment, thinking that over. He realized that by holding himself back, he was keeping from learning more about Jade and not letting her know more about him. He then remembered her statement in the hospital about her mother. *Only call her in an emergency.*

"What are you thinking?" Charles asked, interrupting his musings.

"Sorry, I was actually thinking that you're right. I really want to get to know this woman better, so I'm gonna have to force myself to get past my hang-ups and go out on a limb with her."

"So, the not so good news?" Charles prompted.

"She was involved in an accident and, well, you might have heard, she was also the one who discovered the body on the beach—"

"Jade Lyons?"

"Yeah, unfortunately she's becoming well known for

it, since the paper and a TV station in Virginia Beach picked up the story..." His words trailed off as he began to think of the timeline of Jade's notoriety and the truck running her off the road. Jolting as he heard his name called, he looked up quickly, shaking his head. "Sorry," he mumbled, "my mind was engaged for a moment."

"You're a man with a great many things on his mind nowadays," Charles laughed. Sobering, he added, "For someone who values their privacy, how are you doing with these changes?"

He held back for a second before responding, "Well, I haven't told you about all the changes yet." Seeing the counselor's lifted brow, he said, "I've decided to continue my law enforcement career again. I'm the new part-time detective for Baytown."

Unable to hide his surprise, Charles shook his head, exclaiming, "You have had a busy week." Holding his gaze, he said, "Change in relationship status and a new job are two very stressful, albeit good, changes in your life. I'm glad but, concerned...are you ready for such big changes all at once?"

"I sure as hell hope so," he answered honestly. "Jade? Yeah. I really like this woman and, while it's been a long time since I had any kind of romantic relationship, I'm ready to take the plunge with her. And, God knows, my protective nature has reared its head with her."

"And the job?"

"Right now, it's only part-time, which is fine with me. I've still got some things to work on...with you... with myself, and figure this just forces me to face them a little sooner than I might have."

"All right," Charles smiled. "Then I suggest we face some of those fears."

Lance nodded, ready to talk. It was time to let the fears go.

———

His phone vibrated in his pocket, but with others around, the man did not answer. Sweat broke out on his forehead and he pulled off his cap, wiping the drops away with the back of his hand. As soon as he was alone, he slid his hand into his pocket, his fingers twitching as they closed around the phone.

Pulling it out with trepidation, he viewed the screen. His heart pounded as he listened to the voice mail, the threats renewing.

*I tried. I looked. Who knows where it was hidden?* He was running out of time. The problem was, he had no idea what to do about it. Hearing his name called, he waved and plastered a smile on his face, moving on about his job.

## 20

"You guys are the best," Jade enthused, as Katelyn pulled into the driveway of her apartment.

"Can I just pull all the way toward the back so you don't have so far to walk?" Katelyn asked.

"Oh, yeah. My landlords are away this week so I've got the whole driveway...well, if I had a car, I would. Damn! My car. I have no idea what I'm going to do. I need to add calling Jason on my list of things to take care of and see if my insurance agent has come out yet to see it."

"Don't worry about anything now, sweetie," Tori said. "Just take one thing at a time."

Jillian assisted her out of the back seat and steadied her until she could stand on her own. Moving to her outside door, she stopped suddenly, Jillian almost running into the back of her.

"My door," she gasped.

The other women leaned around to see what she was staring at and instantly Tori was on her phone.

"Mitch, get to Jade's house quickly. Someone's tried to break in...or maybe they're still up there. Right... right." She looked up and said, "Mitch says to get back and stay away. He's heading straight over."

"I need to see—" she started, but Jillian pulled her back carefully.

"No, honey. We've got no idea if someone is still up there."

"But...but..." she protested feebly, allowing her friends to turn her as they hurried back to the car. "I don't want to leave."

"We need to get back until the police get here," Katelyn said.

The sound of sirens filled the air, and within a minute three BPD police SUVs pulled into the driveway. Mitch jumped out, racing toward them as they backed away from the house. Ginny and Grant bolted from another SUV, Burt and Sam from yet another, and Lance screeched to a halt right behind them.

Having heard the call while he was in with Mildred, signing his official paperwork, Lance ran toward Jade and, as their eyes met, she lifted her arms, accepting his as he swooped in, holding her close.

"My lock's been busted," she said, her voice registering her disbelief.

"Babe, I need you to stay back." Looking at the other women, he said, "All of you, get inside your vehicle and stay there until we come back."

Running to her apartment door, he and the other officers drew their weapons, entering the narrow staircase.

"Jesus, is this the only entrance?" Ginny asked. "What happens in case of a fire?"

"There's a door in her apartment that leads to the upstairs hall of the owners. Jade's got a key."

Mitch ordered, "Ginny, Grant, Burt, get the key from her and take the house entrance. Sam, guard out here. Lance, you're with me."

As everyone dispersed, he and Mitch carefully ascended the staircase. Calling out their identification as they arrived at the top, noting Jade's door had been pried open, they threw it wide, hurrying inside.

"Fuck," Lance cursed, seeing the trashed rooms.

Ascertaining that there was no one in her apartment and the door leading to the lower floor had not been disturbed, Mitch unlocked it, allowing the others access.

"Shit," Grant said under his breath. Looking up, he directed at him, "Lance, you were just here. Do you know what they were looking for?"

He cast an appraising eye around the living room, but with the vast destruction, it was hard to tell if there was anything specific the perpetrators were looking for or if it was just vandalism. Shaking his head, he said, "No, but I gotta tell you that I was starting to connect the dots between Jade being in the news and someone running her off the road."

"You think it was more than just kids?" Burt asked.

"I sure as shit do now," he responded, barely containing his anger.

"Sam," Mitch called down on his radio, "we need Jade to come up here. Lance is coming down to assist."

He nodded, knowing she was needed to identify

what might have been taken, but his heart jolted at the idea of her seeing her beloved apartment. He started down the stairs, hating what he had to do.

A moment later, he re-entered, carrying her in his arms, feeling her body jerk as her gaze landed on the mess.

"Oh, my God!" Katelyn yelled, entering right behind, with Jillian and Tori on her heels.

"Tori," Mitch barked, moving to her side, "you can't be here."

"But Mitch," she protested.

"Honey, this is a crime scene. I know you and the girls want to support Jade, but right now, you three have to go."

Grant moved to Jillian and talked to her quietly. After a moment, she nodded and Jillian said to Katelyn and Tori, "Come on, ladies. Let's get some help for Jade so that when she's finished with this, we can take care of her."

Lance set Jade down on the floor, keeping a steadying hand on her waist. Peering around to observe her face, he saw the instant it hit her—the violation of her home.

"Oh, God," she cried, her voice shaky.

Cursing once more, he pulled her into his chest, rocking her back and forth as his hand moved along her back in circles.

"Okay, we don't need to do this now," Mitch said comfortingly, but his words jolted through Jade.

"Yes, we do," she said, pulling her tearful face from Lance's shirt. Lifting her good hand, she wiped her eyes and nose. She shook with anger, adding, "I need to do this. Whoever did this to me, I want them caught!"

Sucking in a cleansing breath, she turned toward the kitchen, and viewed the mess. Drawers were pulled out, even the items in the refrigerator and freezer had been rifled through. "It doesn't look like anything was taken," she said, still wiping her nose. "It's just been tossed around."

Taking the proffered tissue from Ginny, she blew her nose before moving into the living room. Cushions cut open. Books pulled down from shelves. Shaking her head, she hobbled into the bedroom, where the same treatment had been applied to her bed. Her dresser drawers were pulled out but, like in the kitchen, they appeared to be tossed with nothing stolen.

Sighing heavily, she said, "Maybe this won't be too much to clean up. I'll have to replace the mattress and sofa, but it really looks like just teens or someone wanting to cause a mess."

Turning back to the officers following her, she looked up into Lance's eyes and said, "Why? Why would teenagers try to run me off the road and then trash my place?"

He shared a glance with the others before saying, "Jade, honey, I don't think it was teenagers."

Her brow furrowed as his words sunk in, and she shook her head slightly. "I don't understand, Lance. Who would do this?"

"Jade, can you check the bathroom...any drugs...or anything, missing?" Mitch prompted.

With Lance's assistance, she stepped over the

bedroom mess into the bathroom but found more of the same. Nothing missing, just a mess. *Jesus, even my tampons were dumped onto the floor.* Feeling violated, she moved back into the living room, looking around again. "Nothing was taken. Not my TV, not my laptop...nothing."

Looking at the floor, she shook her head. "All my things...even my jars of sea glass were dumped onto the floor. It's all just a mess."

A sudden movement behind Burt had them all turning around. Sam appeared, his face red from climbing the stairs, but he looked right at Mitch, saying, "Sorry, Chief. But Mildred just called. The body's been identified...it's George Caday...the fisherman."

At that pronouncement, she collapsed.

The sun painted the sky in pink and orange before the blue slipped in, reflecting on the rippling bay. Lance turned his head on his pillow, grateful to see Jade still sleeping. He rolled onto his back, his ritual of staring at the circling ceiling fan bringing him a sense of calm for the moment.

His thoughts slid to the previous day, when he thought the sight of Jade's still bruised face as she viewed the destruction of her apartment was as bad as it could be, but then discovered just how much worse it was when Sam revealed that the body she had found was someone she knew. Watching her collapse in a dead faint had caused his heart to jolt and his arms reached out to grab her, barely keeping her from falling to the floor.

The others had rushed forward, Grant calling for an ambulance, which brought not only Zac and his partner up the stairs, but the girls as well. Jade's small attic apartment was not made to hold four officers, three friends, two EMTs, and one pissed off boyfriend holding one terrified victim.

Jade, once revived, was torn between embarrassment and horror. "I'm so ashamed," she had whispered to him. "I was upset over my apartment, which is nothing compared to poor George." As she remembered the state the body was in, she had fought back a gag, her body shaking.

Mitch, with his hands on his hips, had rubbed his forehead, ordering, "Okay, Burt, I need you and Ginny to stay here and dust for fingerprints...anything you can find. Sam, you head back to the station and cover the patrol before your shift ends. Grant, you and I'll go back to the office to see the report from the state, now that we know who the victim was." Looking down at Lance, with Jade still in his arms being checked out by Zac, he had leaned down, gaining his attention, asking, "Is she with you?"

He had nodded, glad her focus was elsewhere so she would not overthink where he wanted her to stay —with him.

Mitch had nodded, before turning to Jillian, Katelyn, and Tori, whom he told, "Ladies, I don't want anything removed from here as it is still a crime scene. Can you gather toiletries and some of your clothes for Jade to borrow and get them to Lance?"

Worried expression had crossed their faces as the three glanced toward Jade still sitting on the floor, as well as their own shock at the news about the body. They had hurried out of her apartment to take care of what their friend would need.

Lance had gotten Jade back to his place and settled on the sofa, just as the women, now with Belle in tow, had shown up, their arms full of bags. They had gathered toiletries and a few clothes for her to borrow until she could get back into her apartment. They even dominated his kitchen, filling the refrigerator and cabinets with food for more than two. He had hated to leave her, but Jade insisted he go back and meet with the other officers.

By the time he arrived back home, she was tucked onto his sofa, girlfriends around, and her smile, while small, was aimed at him. The women had left soon after, and he sat on the sofa, curling his body around hers, offering her warmth and comfort. They did not talk about her apartment, nor about George. He sensed she wanted to avoid the topics and that was fine with him.

After an easy supper the women had prepared and left to warm in the oven, she swallowed a pain pill and he tucked her into his bed. She fell asleep almost instantly. He had debated for only a moment as to where he should sleep—in bed with her or in the guest room. Actually, the debate was only a few seconds long, because he soon shucked his clothes, after making sure the house was secure, and climbed into bed with her.

Now, the next morning, he turned his head again, assuring himself she was still asleep. Quietly, he shifted the covers as he slipped from his bed and padded into the kitchen. A few minutes later, taking his cup of strong coffee with him, he stepped onto his screened porch, his mind now on the case.

George Caday. For him to be the murder victim

made no sense. When they met in the BPD workroom, they added the information to the case board on the wall.

George was sixty-three years old. Widower. One son —in prison for drugs, but not connected to any gangs. Son's prison record is clean. Grant and Mitch were going to go out to George's house immediately, but most of the gathering of new information would take place on the next day—today. Having already worked over his allotted part-time status, Mitch had sent him home to check on Jade.

His mind pored over the information involving her. She found George Caday's body. After her identity was blasted over the news, someone ran her off the road, possibly trying to kill her, and her apartment was ransacked. All related, but none of it made any sense.

Walking back through the house, he stopped in the hall, glancing into his studio. His latest sea glass mosaic, half-finished, tempted him. He had not worked on it for days. Standing there, he waited for the anxiety to begin, but it had dissipated. Right now, he did not need the solitude of his art to calm his nerves. Instead, across the hall, in his bed, lay the object of his need.

Moving into the bedroom, he quietly slid back under the covers. Jade blinked a few times as she began to wake.

Seeing him in bed, her lips curved into a slight smile as she reached out her good hand and cupped his face. "How is it that everything is so topsy-turvy and yet, right now, I'm just happy to be here with you?"

"Sleep good?" he asked, tucking a strand of hair behind her ear.

"Those pain pills knocked me out, but I'd rather not have to take them anymore."

"Hungry?"

She grinned again, as she answered, "Yeah."

"I'll fix something for us while you get ready." Seeing her eyes widen slightly, he said, "You've got to come into the station with me this morning. We need to find out everything we can about the connection between you and George."

The light left her eyes, dulling the green to a dark color. Pulling in a breath through her nose, she nodded wordlessly. He watched as she put slight pressure on her injured foot as she made her way into the bathroom. The cuts on her face were still visible, but would fade soon. The bruise on her neck from the seatbelt was darker and angrier looking than the day before, but he knew that was normal and would fade as well. Hearing the water run, he shook his head and walked into the kitchen, pulling out the ingredients for an omelet, knowing it was going to be a difficult day so they might as well face it with a full stomach.

———

Jade sat in the BPD workroom, her gaze darting around, feeling as though she were in a detective TV show. And just like on TV, she was saying, *"I don't know anything"*, when the viewers always knew they really did know something that would crack the case. *But I don't.*

The whole force was there, including Mildred and Mable clucking over her, plying her with pastries and coffee from Jillian's shop. She looked up as another man walked in, his crisp, tan uniform drawing her eye as the handsome man greeted the others.

Introduced to Colt Hudson, the North Heron Sheriff, she swallowed her pastry bite in haste. The confection suddenly tasted like cardboard, as she no longer felt as though she were just among friends. The reality she had tried to keep at bay up until that point, crashed down on her.

Lance noticed her shaking hands and reached over, taking them in his own, steadying her nerves.

As Mitch settled in with the others, he smiled at her, saying, "We need to determine if there is a tie between George's murder and you, as much as you hate that thought. You ready for this?"

Knowing it was a lie, she nodded.

"Let's start with your relationship with George Caday, and by relationship, I mean any communication you had with him at any time."

Taking a deep breath, she cast her mind to the past. "I first met George not long after I moved to town, when Tori introduced us. I was living in the Sea Glass Inn and she was taking me all around town to meet people. We went to the harbor one morning when the fishing boats arrived from their first early run. She explained to me that the local fishermen sell to individuals before most of their catch fills up the waiting trucks of the restaurants. I met George, the Taylors, the Carsons, and a few of the others that came in."

"Okay, how did your relationship progress?"

"I stop by the harbor about every other week, usually on Saturdays, and buy from George and the Carsons. I usually skip the Taylors, other than greeting them, 'cause I'm not really into cooking crabs myself. I just buy a couple of fish from George...uh, bought, I guess... and the Carsons...uh...they filet it for me and wrap it up and I pop them in the freezer when I get home."

"What did you talk about with George?" Ginny asked, her eyes sympathetic. "Anything at all, no matter how innocuous it might seem."

Biting her lips, she forced her mind back over her conversations. "Uh...the weather...he'd always comment on how the weather affected his fishing. Sometimes I asked about how he was feeling...he once told me that his arthritis was worse in the cold." Sighing, she shook her head slowly, "I don't know...we never had any in-depth conversations about anything." Looking up quickly, she amended, "Oh, once he told me his wife died from cancer and that he has a son in prison...um...for drugs, I think."

Lance gave her hand a reassuring squeeze, as he asked, "Anything else? Anything at all?"

She felt choked from the pressure of so many pairs of eyes centered on her, dissecting her every word. Looking up at him, she confessed, "I can't think with everyone staring."

"Close your eyes," he instructed gently. "Just close your eyes and let your mind wander back to the times you talked to him."

Trusting him to keep her safe, she nodded and

leaned back in the chair, closing her eyes. Without any visual stimulation, she cast her mind back to the harbor. "George's boat was older...the Carson's bought a new boat when they increased their fleet, and I think it made George a little sad that his boat was so old...and stinky." A slight laugh escaped as she remembered, "I could never figure out why his vessel was so much smellier than the Carson's. It never bothered the restaurant vendors who came...they climbed on board George's boat to buy from him."

"And did George ever ask you anything personal?" Lance prodded, his voice soft.

Shaking her head, with her eyes still closed, she said, "No, we didn't talk about my family, but then...oh, wait. He knew I was a teacher. We talked about my classroom kids some. I talked with the Carsons also, because I have the grandson...well, son also, in my class. But George always asked how my week had gone. He would ask if I liked Baytown...just stuff like that."

"Did you find you had anything in common with George?" Lance continued.

"In common?" she scrunched her nose, then winced as her cheek hurt. She lifted her hand and touched her small lacerations with her fingertips. Her eyes still closed, she missed Lance's narrowed-eye look of anger.

"Well, um...we both liked flounder—" she jerked her eyes open, a blush creeping up her face, and said, "I feel dumb...I can't...think of anything."

"Shh," he shushed gently, ordering once more, "Close your eyes and don't worry about what you say or how it sounds. We're trying to look for any possible clue and sometimes they come in the tiniest thing."

Pressing her lips together again, she again closed her eyes. "I once told him that I'd love to go out on his boat to see how he caught the fish and he said that he would like that, but we never did. When I got Ricky Carson in my class, the Carsons asked if I would like to go out with them and I was going to make arrangements one Saturday when Ricky was out with his dad and grand-dad. But I also wanted to talk to George about going out with him, since I kinda felt like he was a little jealous of the other boat."

"Jealous?"

"Well, George would look over at the Carson boat with a wistful expression on his face and he admitted he needed a new boat to stay competitive in the business."

"Did you get the feeling that there was a competition between the two fishing businesses?" Mitch prodded, his eyes catching Lance's.

"Sure, there was an implied competition, but there was no animosity there. I mean, when they arrived at the harbor, both of them had restaurants and seafood trucks ready to buy their catch. The owner of the Sunset View Restaurant was often there and he always boarded George's boat first before going over to the Carson's...at least when I was there. That's not to say that on other days he didn't go to the Carson's first."

Lance watched as Burt and Ginny scribbled down everything Jade was saying, knowing she was providing a lot of information without realizing it. Nodding toward them, he squeezed her hand. "You're doing great, Jade. Keep going...anything else you can think of."

Smiling at the memory, she said, "He once asked me why I was up so early on the weekends, saying most people came to the harbor in the evenings after their second run. I told him that I liked to get up early and walk on the beach. He asked if I looked for shells and I told him I looked for sea glass. Oh, yeah...he liked that and said his wife was a sea glass collector. I thought that was sweet and he even said he would give me some of her collection since he had no use for it, other than to keep a few pieces for sentimental value."

Her brow lowered in concentration as she remembered, "He did give me some one time...when I bought some fish. I took it into the school for an art project with the kids."

"When was that?"

"In the spring. So about six months ago."

"And none since then?"

Shaking her head, she said, "No, but he did mention it again the last time I saw him. But then one of the restaurant owners came by and I headed on to the Carson's boat."

"Anything else?"

"I told him once that I would see his boat out on the bay when I was on the beach and that even though I knew he couldn't see me, I would always wave." Her chin trembled slightly with sadness. "He seemed really touched by that...said it made him feel like someone was looking out for him."

Jade opened her eyes and looked around at the faces

all turned toward her. Shaking her head, she said, "No, I can't think of anything else." Sucking in her lips, "I don't understand what's happening. I discovered his...body, but that was by pure happenstance. As far as someone trying to hurt me, I can only imagine whoever murdered George thinks I know something or have something. But I don't."

Lance pulled her closer to him, kissing the top of her head, not caring if the gesture was unprofessional. "I'll make sure you're safe, Jade," he promised.

She smiled, but wondered if it was a promise he would be able to keep.

## 22

With Jade now safely ensconced in his office, Mitch began to assign duties. "Burt, I want you on the computer finding everything you can about George, the Carsons, their fishing business and bank accounts. Sam, while you're on patrol, talk to anyone who might have known him well. I've informed the mayor that our resources are spread thin, but we'll do the best we can. Lance, you and Grant head to George's house. Comb through it and see what you can find out." He looked over at him and, rubbing his chin, said, "Lance…I know you're supposed to be part-time right now, but we could really use your investigative skills in this case. Tell you what, Ginny, I'm reassigning you to go with Lance and Grant to George's house, but after he has a chance to look around I want Lance back here with me. He and I'll talk to Skip to find out why no one reported George missing. Then we'll talk to the Carsons and take a trip to visit George's son in the Indian Creek Correctional Center in Chesapeake."

"What about Jade?" he asked.

Mitch thought for a moment before shaking his head. "We don't have the personnel to give her full-time protection and haven't made a connection between her and George. The only thing I can think of is for her to stay here at the police station."

His heart plunged, knowing how she would hate that suggestion, but he was also unwilling to leave her unprotected.

"She can ride with me for part of the day," Sam suggested. "It'll get her out of the station and I can make sure she's protected."

"Can she be with others, as well?" Ginny asked. "If she's at the pub, I know Brogan and Aiden will protect her."

Lance nodded, saying, "Maybe a combination of those...part of the day with Sam and part of the day at the pub." Looking at Ginny, he asked, "Will you talk to Brogan? Let him know what's going on?"

"Done," she said, standing and leaving the room as she pulled her phone out.

"I agree," Mitch said. "As long as she's protected and moving around, she should be safe." Looking back at Lance, he added, "You good for working this case? I know we have to keep a check on your hours and not exceed what you're being paid for."

"I'm not going anywhere," he replied, receiving appreciative nods from all in the room.

Lance pulled up behind Ginny and Grant's SUV in the weed-infested, gravel driveway of George's house, set back from the road with few other houses visible. Climbing out of his vehicle, he stood for a moment, hands on his hips, surveying the area. Tall weeds in the yard, a sagging front porch, and a window shutter that hung at an awkward angle.

"Wow," Ginny said, as they approached the porch. "This looks terrible."

"I know he worked all day, only hired a few seasonal workers at a time on his boat, but still, I would have thought with his restaurant connections he would be doing better than this," Grant surmised.

Lance interjected, "We'll know more once Burt has a chance to look into his finances." They entered a hall that appeared to run the length of the house, beneficial for allowing a breeze to blow on hot days. He was halted by the sight of the living room, closely resembling Jade's in its destruction. The couch had been pulled from the wall and slashed with cushions tossed to the floor. The TV was left unmolested, but the easy chair had been destroyed.

"Fuckin' hell," Grant cursed, stepping into the room, snapping on his gloves.

Ginny walked in the opposite direction. He looked over his shoulder as she entered the dining room that appeared to not be used for eating, with its table scattered with bills, magazines, and newspapers.

The kitchen opened to the back of the dining area, exposing a sink, cluttered with a few dishes, and old appliances. The cabinets had been opened and the contents scattered all about. The refrigerator and freezer doors stood open but they were unable to ascertain if anything had been taken. Drawers had been emptied and the floor contained the remnants of the search.

He moved toward the back, entering a bedroom on the left that appeared to be the master. The mattress had been slashed, women's clothing scattered from the open dresser drawers. The musty scent made him wonder if George had slept in this room at all since his wife died. Moving to the closet, his thoughts were confirmed when he saw the only clothing was a woman's. The closet had been searched but, other than clothes off hangers, there was nothing else there.

Moving across the hall, into what may have at one time been the son's room, the bed was also slashed, but the room appeared to have been lived in recently. George's clothes were in the closet and on the floor.

As his appraisal moved over the house, he shook his head. *What would George have that someone was looking for and why would someone think Jade had it?*

---

Jade sat in Mitch's office, in the old, squeaky chair behind his desk, twirling out of boredom. Looking up as Lance came in, she smiled.

Lance had left Ginny and Grant to complete the sweep of George's house, and headed back to the station to report to Mitch and check on Jade. Finding her spinning, he met her smile. "Bored?"

"God, yes! I went out with Sam for a while and that was interesting...for about twenty minutes."

"Well, I'm taking you to the pub and leaving you there while Mitch and I make a run into Chesapeake to talk to George's son."

At the mention of George, Jade's smile left and she heaved a sigh. Not wanting to be a pest, she nodded and said, "That's fine. Whatever I need to do." Standing, she added, "But this can only continue for the next couple of days, you know. Monday morning I've got to be back at school."

Lance said nothing in return, but wondered how that would work, if they were no closer to finding George's murderer.

From the doorway, Lance observed the meeting room at the Indian Creek Correctional Center. He learned from Mitch that the ICCC was an intensive, long-term, institution based treatment program for incarcerated substance abusing offenders. George's son, Anthony, had been held in the medium security, dormitory designed facility for three years and was scheduled to be released in about six more months.

Walking in, they sat down at the table where Anthony was already sitting. The clean-cut young man reached his hand out in greeting as they were introduced.

"I know you've come about my father," Anthony said, his voice shaky. "I'll be able to attend his funeral, but…" sighing, "I can't believe I never had the chance to stay goodbye. I hate that the last thing he thought about me was that I was a still here and not out yet. Fuck…we had plans."

"When was the last time you spoke to your father?" Mitch asked.

Rubbing his forehead, Anthony replied, "I called him on his birthday, which was about two months ago. We chatted for the ten minutes I was allowed and I haven't talked to him since. I would've emailed, but he never got into computers, so that left us with just the phone calls."

Anthony shook his head, his lips pinched together.

"Did that bother you? About the computer?"

"Yeah, sure it did. I don't mean just so I could have talked to him more, but even for his business. Dad still used the phone to make calls, set up restaurant contracts…hell, everything. He could have done so much more with his business if he'd stayed up to date with technology."

"You mentioned plans earlier. Can you elaborate?"

"When I was growing up, the last thing I wanted to be was a fisherman like Dad. You know, typical teenage rebellion. I never wanted to go to college, but thought about working on cars or something like that. Hell, I even thought about joining the military at one time. Anything but smelling like fish all the time." Shrugging, he admitted, "But I got in with the proverbial wrong crowd. Started doing stupid shit like staying out half the night, smoking weed, then moved on to coke. Tried heroin, but coke was my drug of choice. I got my hands on it easily from a supplier and then started selling.

Hell, I thought I was the shit, man. I made more in a week than my dad made in a month or more out on his boat fishing from sunup to sundown."

Lance noted as Anthony grew introspective, a blanket of sadness settling over the young man. He had no idea if it was from past screw-ups or getting caught. "Something change with your dad in recent times?"

Anthony's gaze jumped to his before sliding over to Mitch. "Detox was a bitch and I hated the counseling at first, but I gotta tell you, I don't want to be back in here again. I also know that it'll be hard getting a decent job when I get out, so I got to thinking about my dad in a different light. He was his own boss. Worked hard but, at the end of the day, he got paid decently for what he did. He spent his days outdoors, not stuck in some cubicle somewhere." Sighing, he added, "After Mom died, Dad was lost, but seemed excited when I started talking about joining him when I got out. Said he had some plans for increasing the business. Said he wanted to buy a bigger boat. I remember he got kinda jealous when the Carsons bought a new boat."

"Was there competition between them?"

Chuckling, he nodded. "Sure…they worked in the same bay for their whole lives, competing for the fishing business and contracts. But the Carsons are up on technology while Dad was still in the dark ages."

Mitch explained, "When your father's house was entered by my officers this morning, it had been broken into and tossed. It appears someone was searching for something…drawers emptied, sofa and mattresses slashed."

Anthony leaned back, his eyes wide.

Continuing, Mitch asked, "Can you think what your father would have had that someone wanted?"

Shaking his head, Anthony replied, "Seriously? No. When Mom was alive, she kept a neat house, but neither of them liked a lot of stuff just sitting around, so it was kind of sparse. I wouldn't be surprised that Dad slacked off with just him there. But...but...fuck, man, that makes no sense. I know Dad said he was saving for a new boat, but he had his money in the bank. There's nothing there that anyone would have wanted." Squirming, he added, "Of course, I've been here a while and haven't been home, but I can't imagine Dad changing."

Lance observed Anthony carefully, "Can you think of a reason why someone would want to murder your dad?"

Anthony winced at the word *murder*, but shook his head. "Dad? Jesus, he wasn't hurting anybody. Never had...never would." He held Lance's gaze when he added, "I mean, who the hell would gain from Dad's death?"

As Mitch and Lance drove back across the long Chesapeake Bay Bridge Tunnel, he pondered the question he had asked Anthony. *Who would benefit from George's murder...and why would they think Jade was involved?*

## 23

Pulling up to the harbor, Lance and Mitch looked out at the activity. The fishing boats had returned. Thomas was on board talking to the Taylors. Skip was walking on the dock, several teenage boys wearing Harbor Helpers t-shirts following him around.

"God, I hate this," Mitch said. "Delivering bad news is the worst part of this job."

He nodded, knowing no verbal response was needed. They climbed from the police SUV and walked toward the boats, all eyes turning toward them as they approached.

Skip stopped, nodding his greeting, staring at them. Shifting to the side, he said, "Boys, y'all are done for the day. You can head on home." Waiting for the teens to hurry away, he came closer just as the Richard, Rick, and Harold came down from their boats. Thomas, right on their heels, filled the semi-circle in front of Mitch and him.

"With the look on your faces, I figured something

wasn't right," Skip offered. "That's why I sent the kids away."

"Good deal," Mitch acknowledged, looking at the small gathering. "No way to say this so it doesn't hurt, so I'm just gonna let you know up front. The body found on the shore recently was identified as George. George Caday."

Richard dropped his head, his chest heaving in a great sob and Rick grabbed his father. The two men held tightly to each other as Harold blinked rapidly, raising his gaze to the sky.

"Oh, Lord Jesus," Skip cried, pulling out a handkerchief from his pocket and wiping his eyes.

Thomas shook his head slowly, his eyes searching out Mitch's. "How...how?"

They gave the men a moment to let the news settle before Mitch said, "Skip, you got a private place where we can ask some questions? I know this is hard, but we need to get a handle on what he was doing and where he was."

Taking a shuddering breath, Skip nodded toward the Harbor Master office. "Let's head in there."

The gathering moved toward the building and into one of the equipment rooms where they pulled out folding chairs and sat around a small table.

"Skip, we notice George's boat isn't docked. Is this unusual? Did you hear from him?"

Rubbing his eyes, Skip replied, "Didn't happen often, but sometimes George would head out of the bay and he'd dock at the harbor up near Manteague. They got a harbor, but it's not near as big as us. If he had orders from one of the restaurants up there, he might just do sea fishing and dock there for a few days. 'Bout once a month he'd go there and we wouldn't see him for days." Lifting his blue eyes toward the others, he rasped, "I never guessed anything was wrong."

Thomas cleared his throat before asking, "Officers, can you tell us what happened?"

Mitch replied, "We don't know and the investigation is still ongoing, but it was a suspicious death. We haven't released any details at this time, but we will soon."

"I knew him far less than these men, but still…such a shock. Such a tragedy," Thomas murmured.

Richard swallowed audibly and blew his nose, before saying, "Knew George most of my life. We grew up here in this town together. Fished together and even talked about going into business together."

Rick looked at his father, his brows lifted. "I didn't know that, Dad. When was that?"

"Long before you were born. But, when it came right down to it, I was afraid of trusting George." Looking at the others, he hastened to add, "George was a good man, but he just wasn't interested in building anything big. His goal was to own a boat and fish every day. Me? I wanted a fleet of fishing boats…something I could grow and pass on to my heirs. I guess what I mean is that I didn't trust George and I to have the same business goals."

"Gentlemen, is there anything you can tell us that might be pertinent to the investigation, about George?

Where he might have gone? What he might have been doing?" he jumped in.

Sad expressions greeted them but no answers.

---

Walking into Finn's Pub, Lance's eyes adjusted from the bright sunshine to the darker interior of the comfortable bar and restaurant. His gaze immediately sought, and found, Jade. She was perched on a barstool at the far end of the bar, her smile infectious as she chatted with Brogan and Aiden. Inwardly pleased no other men were hanging around, he headed straight to her. As soon as her gaze landed on him, her smile widened, and he felt his heart tighten with emotion.

His thoughts shifted to the last counseling session with Charles and how unburdening himself made him feel as though he could breathe. As he walked closer, he knew he wanted this woman in his life—and not as just a friend. But to truly have her, he needed to open up to her as well, and he wondered if he could do that.

Jade watched as Lance approached, his expression morphing from a smile to a look of doubt. Tilting her head as he made it to her side, she reached out her hand, linking fingers with him, seeing his smile return. "Hey," she greeted softly.

"Hey, yourself," he replied, leaning over to kiss her forehead.

"Are you okay? You looked sort of…um…uncertain back there for a moment."

Lance peered into her deep green eyes, marveling

at how the color changed with the lighting or her mood. He appreciated her concern and squeezed her hand while reaching up with his other, tucking a stray lock of hair behind her ear. "I'm good. Honestly. Probably better than I've been in a long time."

Her smile returned, warming his heart. He lifted his eyes to Brogan and Aiden, noting both of them grinning at him.

Brogan nodded in greeting and said, "You gotta run or can I get you a beer?"

Seeing Jade still munching on a club sandwich and fries, he said, "I'll take a beer and a hamburger."

While he was waiting for his food, Ginny came in, sliding behind the bar and into Brogan's arms. Nodding toward Lance, she leaned forward, asking quietly, "How was your trip?"

"Not overly informative," he replied, cryptically, receiving another nod from her.

"I take it, things aren't going well?" Jade asked, her eyes searching his.

"It's early, sweetheart. We'll find out what's going on, but unlike TV, these things can take time." She pressed her lips together and he longed to kiss the tension from them. *Soon, hopefully soon.*

"You need anyone to keep an eye on her, man, you know she's welcome here anytime," Aiden said, his normally jovial manner set aside.

Brogan nodded, "Absolutely."

"Guys, I don't need to be babysat—"

"Jade," Lance interrupted, pressing a finger to her

lips, "we need to keep you safe...I want to keep you safe."

Holding his gaze, Jade felt the slight pressure from his finger on her lips, his touch warm. As he moved his hand away and turned to his food, which had just been delivered, she reached up and replaced his fingers with her own, her lips still tingling where his touch had been. Looking over, she noticed Ginny was staring at her, a smile on her face.

---

Lance assisted Jade down from his vehicle and escorted her into his house. Putting more weight on her booted foot, she reported to be in less pain. "I know you just ate, but do you want anything right now?"

Smiling, she replied, "I think I'll fix a cup of tea."

He started to tell her that he did not have any tea, but stopped when he saw her pull out a box from his cabinet before putting water on to boil.

She laughed, saying, "The girls brought some over for me. Would you like a cup?"

He declined, but grinned, loving the feel of having her things in his house. Shaking his head, he could not believe how much he had changed in a couple of weeks. "You know, I really like you being here," he blurted. Wincing at his words, he started to turn away.

"Oh, no you don't buddy," she said, grabbing his arm. "You can't tell me something so sweet and then turn away."

"You thought that was sweet? I thought it was kind of…sappy," he confessed, his gaze searching her face.

Jade placed her hand on Lance's chest, right over his heartbeat. "I thought it was beautiful. And for the record," she grabbed his shirt with her good hand and pulled slightly, "I like my things here too." He stayed upright, but his gaze dropped to her lips. Pulling again, she said, "Lance. Help a girl out. I want to kiss you but can't stand on my tiptoes."

Lance dropped his gaze from her eyes to her mouth, leaning down slowly until he was a whisper apart. Cupping the back of her head, he lowered his mouth over hers, the feel of her lips on his immediately sending his blood rushing to his cock and out of his brain.

Firm yet soft, her lips moved against his, taking his breath and stealing his wits. Banding her waist with his other arm, he pulled her gently against his body, the feel of her breasts against his chest making him dizzy with desire.

The sound of the kettle screaming pierced his lust and he lifted his head slightly. Reaching behind her, he slid the kettle from the eye of the stove, flipping off the heat, before smiling down at her again. Her dark hair flowed down her back and he brushed it away from her face, keeping his thumbs on her cheeks. "You are beautiful. The most beautiful woman I've ever laid eyes on."

Jade's gaze never left his as her voice, whisper soft, pleaded, "Please take me to bed, Lance. Please make love to me."

Picking her up into his arms, he carried her into his

bedroom before carefully setting her down on the edge of the bed. "I want to make love to you, Jade," his voice was rough with need, "but I don't want to hurt you. I never want to hurt you."

Swallowing deeply, she breathed, "The only thing you could do to hurt me would be to leave."

"Never," he vowed, leaning over her body and latching onto her lips. Sliding his tongue into her warmth, he explored slowly, teasing her tongue as his lips moved over hers, nipping and sucking.

Moaning, she reached up and tried to lift his polo, but with only one good hand, she was unable to pull it over his head.

Lance stood, hating to lose her lips for a second, but recognized her unspoken request to remove his clothes. Grabbing the bottom of his shirt, he jerked it up in a swift motion, tossing it to the floor. He toed off his shoes while his hands went to his khakis. In a movement, just as fast as the other, he divested himself of his pants and stood before her in just his boxers.

Biting her lip, Jade stared at the work of masculine perfection in front of her. From his head to his toes, she could not think of one thing she would change. Muscular, his chest tapered to a narrow waist and, if the bulge in his boxers was anything to go by, he was well endowed in every aspect. Suddenly nervous, she wondered about her battered body and how he would view her.

As if he could read her mind, he moved forward, kneeling at her feet. Reaching out, he undid the buttons on her blouse, making her think of the same action from last night, and yet it was so different right now. Sliding the material down her arms, he carefully moved it over her wrapped wrist. He hesitated and she knew the glaring, black bruise across her chest appeared painful.

"Sweetheart, I really don't want to hurt you."

Lifting her hand to his cheek, she shook her head. "Please don't stop, Lance. We can be careful."

Nodding, he reached behind her and unsnapped her bra, sliding the material down her arms and over her hand until it joined her blouse on the floor.

She blushed under his perusal, but as he lifted his hands to cup her breasts reverently, she leaned her head back, a groan of pleasure leaving her lips.

Lance marveled at the soft, pliant flesh, kneading her breasts gently while caressing her nipples with his thumbs. Leaning forward, he sucked one rosy nipple into his mouth, teasing the bud with his tongue. Moving between both breasts, he suckled, hearing her purr deep in her chest. Wanting to see her expression, he looked up just in time to catch her wince.

"Was that too rough?" he hesitated, suddenly worried.

"Huh? No, no! Keep going."

Moving his hands up and down her sides soothingly, he pressed, "You winced. I saw you."

She looked to the side and bit her lip, avoiding his eyes.

"Baby…"

"Okay, I breathed a little too deeply and maybe it hurt my chest…but just a little—"

"That's it. We definitely shouldn't be doing this now," he stated firmly, releasing her and sitting back.

"No! I really want to. I *need* to. I need you, Lance. "

At the look in her eyes, so open, honest, and passionate, he couldn't turn her down. Didn't want to turn her down. In all honesty, he needed this just as much as she did. "Okay, but you *have* to tell me if I'm hurting you. Deal?"

"Deal!" she returned eagerly, grabbing his face and kissing him.

Pulling his mouth away regretfully, his hands moved to her pants and, with assistance from her, he slid them down her legs, snagging her panties as he went. Finally removing the last item, he dropped his boxers, freeing his cock.

Moving her to lay on her back in the bed, naked for his perusal, he worshiped her body, first with his gaze and then with his hands.

"Relax, baby," he whispered. "Let me take care of you."

Obeying his gentle command, Jade felt her body relax, his caress making her feel beautiful in spite of her bruises. She watched as he snagged a pillow from the head of the bed and lifted her injured foot, placing the pillow underneath to give her added support. She held his eyes as he climbed onto the bed next to her, keeping his body close while avoiding her injuries.

Lance kissed her again, his tongue teasing as it tangled with hers. Gliding his hand down, his fingers felt her pulse beating wildly at her neck before he cupped her breasts again, gently rolling her nipple.

Swallowing her soft moan, he continued his exploration of her body as his hand slid over her tummy and between her legs.

Jade opened her legs wider, encouraging his access, jolting as his fingers slid through her slick folds. Entering her body slowly with one finger, his hand mimicked his kiss as both moved inside her warmth. The coil deep inside tightened as his fingers continued their ministrations and his kiss stole her breath.

Gasping, carefully this time, she clutched his shoulder with her good hand, her fingers digging into the muscles. Just when she did not think she could take the exquisite torture anymore, her orgasm rushed over her, sending tingles throughout her body as her core tightened on his fingers.

Lance felt her body respond and he lifted from her lips only long enough to observe her beautiful face, flush with pleasure, not an ounce of pain showing in her exquisite expression. Moving back in, he continued to move his mouth over hers in worship as his finger slid from her folds reverently.

Opening her eyes, Jade stared into his hazel ones, so close she could distinguish between the shards of gold mixing with the brown, mesmerizing her. "Wow," she whispered her confession, feeling her face burn with a blush. "It's been a while."

"It's probably been longer for me, sweetheart," Lance said, his eyes never leaving hers. Seeing the slight widening in them, he nodded, "Yeah, seriously. I haven't wanted anyone for a while and sex, just for sex's sake, wasn't anything I was interested in."

Sliding her hand from his shoulder to cup his strong jaw, she smiled. "Me either. So, you don't have to worry about running into any past lovers here in town."

Surprised at how good that declaration felt, his lips curved into a full grin.

She watched as the smile changed his handsome, but usually austere, face into one of absolute beauty. "So, uh…are we going to…finish what we started?"

"I don't want to hurt you and, like I said, it's been a while, so…I'm good if we stopped right now," he said, still lying to her side, his hand trailing patterns on her skin.

"But I want more, and as long as your weight isn't on my chest, we should be perfect." Her eyes begged him to not leave her side and as he moved off the bed, her heart plunged at the thought of his refusal. Closing her eyes for a moment to block out the sight of his magnificent body walking away, they popped open again at the sound of a condom wrapper being ripped.

"Last chance, baby. Full disclosure, I can't be held responsible for making you moan so hard your chest twinges a little," he warned her, face full of mischief.

Reaching to the side to snag a pillow, she launched it at him, laughing. "That a promise?"

Wriggling his eyebrows, Lance rolled the condom onto his aching cock before looking back at his beauty, beaming, her green eyes piercing his. Her arms raised, beckoning him to her, he couldn't remember the last time he ever felt this…free…happy. And it was all because of her.

Crawling back over her, he carefully settled his body

between her open legs, making sure her foot was still supported on the pillow. With his arms on either side of her, he propped his weight on his forearms, leaning down to capture her lips in a scorching kiss.

Placing his cock at her entrance, he felt her legs shift wider and halted, making sure she was comfortable.

Jade felt his hesitation and whispered against his lips, "I'm not made of glass. I promise I'll let you know." Twisting her head, she angled her mouth, her tongue teasing his, and swallowed his groan with a smile on her lips.

Easing his cock into her warmth, Lance fought to last, afraid he would unman himself and come immediately. Inch by glorious inch, he pressed inward until he was balls deep and the ecstasy was almost more than he could bear. Moving slowly at first, and then with greater urgency as he felt her heel pressing into his ass and her hand clutching his back, he thrust harder and harder until he was mindless with any thought other than her luscious body welcoming his.

With his balls tightening, he knew he would not last much longer. Wanting to take her with him, he balanced his weight on one arm and slid his other hand to her clit. Circling the swollen nub, he pressed gently, feeling her abdomen clench and her inner walls grab his dick.

Groaning through his clenched teeth, he poured himself into her, pumping until his cock was drained, feeling her orgasm rushing through her at the same time. He caught himself just before he crashed onto her chest, pulling out and rolling to her right side away from her injured left wrist and foot.

Jade, her sex still quivering, looked to the side at his panting body, his chest moving up and down with each ragged breath. "Wow," she said again, unable to think of anything else to say when her body was sated and her mind was too full of emotions to make sensible conversation.

He turned his head her way and grinned. "Yeah...wow."

"Does it make me sound stupid to say that I'm glad I was the first one in a while? Because I don't want to scare you away, and I know we got to it pretty quickly considering how long we've known each other, but sex means something to me, Lance. It's okay if it doesn't mean everything...but for me, it at least means something."

Rolling toward her, Lance leaned up on one elbow and peered down into the depths of green now holding his heart. He tucked a damp strand of hair behind her ear and said, "Jade, baby...it means the world to me... and so do you." He had more he wanted to say, but for now, he just let his heart speak.

24

---

After dealing with the condom, Lance headed to the kitchen, telling Jade to stay in bed. Eschewing the tray, he loaded plates high with some of the food the ladies brought over. Grapes, cheese, cold cuts, and crackers piled alongside hummus and chips. Snagging two bottles of water, he hurried back into the bedroom, hating to be away from her side.

Hobbling out of the bathroom wearing a light robe, Jade's eyes widened as she crawled back into bed and watched Lance carry plates of food over to her. Grinning, she settled against the headboard, making her lap available for a plate. The cold food was perfect and she popped a couple of grapes into her mouth.

"This is such a good idea," she said, reaching for the cheese and crackers.

Lance arranged himself on the bed, his back against several pillows, and faced her with the plates close by. They were silent for a few minutes, each busy nibbling. Finding he wanted to learn more about her, he hesitated, acknowledging that if he asked her questions it would open himself up to the same. Sucking in a deep breath, he realized his desire to truly know Jade outweighed his desire for privacy.

"Can I ask you a question? It's personal and I don't want you to feel like you have to answer," he began.

Jerking her eyes to his, she smiled. "Honey, you can ask anything you want. We just made love and confessed that it meant something to both of us. As far as I'm concerned, you can ask anything you want."

Nodding slowly, he said, "Well, I noticed you gave your mom's phone number as the emergency contact at the hospital, but you didn't seem to want to talk to her."

Shaking her head, she lifted a napkin to wipe her mouth, and said, "I'm afraid I'm a huge disappointment to my parents...so much so, we are not currently speaking much. Well, I suppose that's not entirely true...they speak, saying the same thing over and over. I think that my mom is sure if she berates me enough, I'll come running back home."

Not the answer he expected, his brow furrowed in unspoken curiosity.

Licking her lips, she continued, "I guess you might as well know, my parents have money...quite a bit of money. As a child, I never thought about it. You know how, as a kid, normal is what you are exposed to? Well, I had an exclusive private school education, horseback riding lessons, and even learned to play the violin... although not well," she added with a laugh. "But as part of our high school's community service project, I went with my grandfather to work at a homeless shelter and,

I'm embarrassed to admit, I was stunned. Somehow, I saw homelessness as a problem of adults and not of children. When I saw the children in line for food, it broke my heart." Cocking her head to the side, she amended, "No...not broke my heart...it gave me my heart. It was a pivotal moment because I knew I wanted to work with children who needed me."

"So, is that why you went into education?"

Nodding, she smiled. "I went to college here in Virginia and, while it was a major battle with my parents, they finally accepted that I had no interest in a business major, majoring in education instead."

"If they accepted the college major, then why are you not speaking?"

Popping another grape into her mouth, she chewed thoughtfully for a moment before answering. Sighing, she said, "My father, unbeknownst to me, arranged a teaching position at a private school. I should say, an expensive, exclusive, best-of-the-best kind of school. But, I had already been in search of a system that was desperate for teachers."

Jade became distracted by Lance's lips closing over a cracker piled high with hummus and the way his mouth worked as he chewed.

He swallowed and looked at her, prompting, "Jade?"

Blinking rapidly, she blushed as she shook her head slightly. "Sorry, but you eating is so sexy."

Barking out a laugh, he leaned forward and placed a swift kiss on her lips. "Go on, I want to hear more."

"Okay, well, I investigated the school systems in North Carolina and Virginia and looked for the poorest counties. In Virginia, I discovered North Heron is the poorest, or almost the poorest. I also checked out the public schools here and found there was a huge need for qualified teachers. The pay isn't great but there are grants available. So, I came out to visit. Stayed at the Sea Glass Inn. Met Tori. Visited the school and checked out Baytown. That was it...I knew I had found home."

Lance watched her animated face as she spoke of moving to Baytown and thought of the similarities in their backgrounds. *Well, up to a point.* She embraced life and her new environment, while he used it as a place to hide.

"And your parents? I take it they aren't happy with the choice you made?"

Rolling her eyes, she shook her head. "Hardly. As far as they're concerned, I am wasting my life here and can't stand that I am doing my own thing and doing it my way."

He noted her faraway expression and stayed quiet, letting her gather her thoughts.

"You know," she finally said, "it really bothers me that they act like I'm being a rebellious child. My decision was well thought out, planned, executed, and more importantly...I'm happy. But that's not important to them. They are more worried with how my career choice reflects on them and, as far as they're concerned, it does not reflect well."

"So, do you have any contact with them at all?" he asked, thinking of the similarities in their families.

"We call and email occasionally...most recently because my mom saw me on the news. That was a mess.

But, usually, it's just them asking when I'm going to stop working in the backwaters of Virginia and come back to Northern Virginia." Seeing his brows lift, she quickly added, "But I'm not. I'm happy here. I plan on making my home permanently in Baytown."

"You said the pay isn't good? Will that make a difference?"

Scrunching her nose, she said, "It's not so good. But, my car is paid for and I got a great deal on my attic apartment."

They fell silent for another moment, still snacking on the food he brought in. Chewing a cube of cheese, she lifted her gaze to his and said, "I want to ask you about how you ended up here, but I feel like that would be intrusive. I just want you to know that you can tell me anything, but you don't have to. I respect your desire for privacy."

"I want to tell you," he rushed, thinking if he spoke quickly it might make the punch to his gut easier.

Peering at him closely, Jade observed the panic in his eyes and began to shake her head. "Lance, no...this night was too special to ruin it by too much talking—"

"No, don't you see?" he asked, sitting up straighter, so that his body was facing hers, close enough their legs touched. "Tonight is the perfect time because of what we shared."

Worrying her bottom lip between her teeth, she nodded slowly, allowing him to say whatever he wanted to say.

Dropping his gaze to their plates for a moment, he sucked in a deep breath before letting it out in a long sigh. With a rueful chuckle, he said, "The truth is that our families seem to be somewhat alike. My parents are also wealthy. My dad cares more about his next portfolio conquest than he does about being an honest businessman. My mom is too used to the cocktail hour at the country club to be involved in anything else. Oh, she likes charities...as long as all she has to do is write a check so her name is on the donor list for everyone to see."

Lifting his eyes, he admitted, "Me telling you this has a déjà vu feeling. I just told Mitch this story the other day. Anyway, Dad always planned for me to graduate from high school, attend his former university, and join his investing firm. But in ninth grade, I watched the Twin Towers fall and knew I was destined for another calling. Dad hated it, but as soon as I turned eighteen years old, I joined the Army. I went into the military police and eventually attended the Criminal Special Agent school. Was assigned to the Criminal Investigative team. Not only did I find my calling as an investigator, but doing it for the Army was everything to me."

"And your family?" she asked softly.

Shaking his head, he said, "Dad cut me off completely, thinking that if I didn't have his money I'd come running back. Instead, it just solidified my resolve." Shrugging, he added, "I've got some money from a trust my grandfather left me. I don't need it, but it's there...just to keep my dad pissed probably. Anyway, his firm expanded and he and my mom moved to Florida before I got out of the Army. Which was for the best, really. Distance. I got a job in Richland working Vice for a few years, then came here."

Jade's face had relaxed, watching the animation in his expression as he told her about his early years, but after relaying his history with his parents his face closed off. "Why Baytown? How did you end up here?"

"Mitch invited me," came his instinctive, short response. Lance jerked his eyes to her face and shook his head. "Sorry," he mumbled.

She reached out her hand and placed it on his arm, her touch gentling him.

"Jade, this is the part that I've told no one but my counselor." Seeing her eyes widen, he hastened to add, "Yes, I finally went to talk to someone...mostly to get Ginny off my back."

Smiling slightly at the idea of Ginny hounding him, Jade said, "Then you know you don't have to share with me. We're good, no matter what."

Shaking his head, he replied, "That's just it though. Keeping it to myself hasn't made it any better. Hasn't kept the nightmares away. Hasn't given me peace. Sure as hell hasn't made me a better man." Struggling to find the right words, he added, "I think that maybe that's what this comes down to. I want to be the man I was before everything went to hell. And becoming a recluse didn't do that." She flinched at his choice of words but, holding her gaze for a moment, the current zipping between them, he lifted his hand and cupped her cheek. "Meeting you...coming to care for you...it's made me want to find who I am again."

Nodding, she simply leaned her head into his hand,

loving the feel of his fingers caressing her cheek. She closed her eyes, only for a moment, as she reveled in his warmth against her skin. Slowly he slid his hand from her face and she opened her eyes once more, steeling herself for whatever he was going to confess.

"As CID...we investigated criminal activities. Sometimes...well, often...we worked in less than optimum conditions." Sighing, he said, "It's hard to explain and I know you probably don't—"

"Stop," she ordered gently. "Don't think about what you think I do or don't want to hear. Just talk...just let it out."

Puffing out his cheeks as he blew out a breath of air, he nodded. "When you think of police here in the states, you think in terms of them investigating crimes and having the upper hand. But in the military, we had a job where we were dedicated to investigating crimes but our hands were tied. They shouldn't have been," he added quickly, "but it was murky waters we had to wade through. We were mostly enlisted personnel and sometimes had to investigate officers, who hated like hell to answer questions from us. When we went into a camp we weren't exactly greeted as friends...it was as though we were the enemy. And the fact that we wore the same uniform as the people we were investigating didn't matter. It was them against us."

"Can I ask what kind of crimes were happening? I guess I've always had such a red-white-and-blue image of our soldiers in war times."

He held her eyes for a moment and said, "A lot of times, that's exactly the image that fits. But, sweetheart, there are all kinds of people. Some who should never have taken the uniform to begin with. Some who were just opportunistic. And others who were lured into criminal activities by stronger personalities."

"I know Ginny had problems that she told us about. Problems with sexual harassment and even a whole investigation into soldiers who hid cameras in the women soldiers' showers."

Nodding, he said, "Exactly. That's exactly the kind of thing we investigated. Also, there's a lot of buying and selling on the black market. A shit ton of our weapons ended up in the hands of the enemy 'cause some soldier wanted to make some money. Drugs. Stealing. Sexual assault. Whatever you find in the worst of society in the civilian world, you have it in the military. Thank God, that's not most...but enough that I always had a job to do."

"And you loved that job," she stated, already knowing it was fact.

"Hell, yeah. I loved the military. Considered those men and women to be my family. And that's why I worked to weed out the bad apples, 'cause the good service men and women deserved the best. We weren't always popular when we went into a place, because when you're investigating, you have to prod, pry, and turn over every stone. But my squad was the best. We set record after record for cases solved." Smiling, he added, "Jose was my best friend...right hand on all the investigations. Married, with two kids. Best of the best. Chuck, Matt, Dominic, Rusty...all the best."

She watched his face, so full of pride, the creases

from his eyes softening for a moment as the good memories slid over him. But something happened... something that changed him. Both scared to find out what it was and desperately wanting him to unburden himself, she waited patiently until he was ready.

"My team and I were sent to one of the outer camps in Afghanistan to investigate a report of stolen weapons being sold to locals who had the backing of the rebels. We helicoptered into the area and, of course, were greeted like we carried the plague—"

"Why? I don't understand," she interrupted, her forehead furrowed in question.

"Money to be made. And, even if you're not the one doing it, there's a natural desire to protect your mates. So, someone reported it anonymously and we showed up, ready to find out everyone involved. The investigation was going, but it was really hard to get the ringleaders of the black market sales to crack. We finally got intel about who was buying the weapons and a group of us went out in armored vehicles to find out what we could."

Shaking his head, Lance's memories moved into the dark, murky waters he so tried to keep at bay.

Jade swallowed deeply, her heart pounding as she watched his hazel eyes morph into darkness. He moved his arm away from hers as he told his story, but she reached out to his leg, still stretched near hers on the bed, and placed her hand on him.

"We were set up. Our driver veered off the road at a strange point and jumped out. I was right next to him and tried to grab him as soon as the door opened. I fell out and rolled several feet, just as the transport ran over an IED. Fucking thing exploded right under us. Blew fire and metal in all directions, the noise deafening. I covered my head, still trying to keep the driver in my sights, knowing he had been part of the ambush. But there was no way…too much smoke…too much destruction. Jesus, the screams of my men."

Lance jumped up from the bed, breath catching in his throat, his nakedness no longer comfortable. Stalking to the dresser, he pulled out a pair of cut-off sweat pants, jerking them over his legs before walking into the bathroom and closing the door.

Jade sat on the bed, the barely heard whir of the overhead fan circling the only noise in the room, besides her ragged breathing. Suddenly uncomfortable with her state of undress as well, she climbed off the bed and found her clothes lying on the floor. She managed, with difficulty, to get her panties and bra on, but her wrist hurt trying to do the buttons on the shirt. Seeing his drawer still open, she found a large t-shirt of his and pulled it over her head. Sucking her lips between her teeth, she stood for a long moment of indecision. She could not leave because she had no car, but then she realized she did not want to leave. She wanted to comfort him, but had no idea how he would respond, and did not want to make things worse.

Her gaze drifted from the closed bathroom door and back to the bed. She now hated that they had started the conversation there. What should have been nothing but an incredible memory of lovemaking in his comfortable bed, was now tainted by the horrible memories he dredged up there...*at my suggestion*. With a heavy sigh leaving her lungs, she winced and hobbled to the bed, picking up the plates, most of the food eaten. Making her way to the kitchen, she discarded the scraps and washed the plates in the sink.

The moon was hanging over the bay, visible from his screened porch. Pulled by some unknown force, she walked onto the porch, the sound of the gentle surf easing the pain in her chest. Standing, with her hand on the screen, she felt the breeze blow off the bay as the moon's reflection painted the water's surface with glittering diamonds. In the distance, she could see the lights from the cargo ships anchored in the bay and thought about the men and women who spent their careers on them. Sailing from shore to shore, country to country. Closing her eyes, she knew she was just trying to keep from thinking of Lance, the man who held her heart. The man whose pain was real and keeping him from moving forward.

Feeling a tear escape, she wiped the moisture from her cheek.

"Don't cry for me," came a rough voice from behind her.

Whirling around, she looked into Lance's face, her heart now in her throat. "I'm so sorry, honey."

He stepped closer, encircling her with his arms as she rested her cheek on his chest. "You've got nothing to be sorry for."

"But I brought up all this terrible past for you and—"

"And nothing," he shushed. "Babe, this past is always there. It's been right there first thing every morning.

And right there as I lay in bed at night, staring at the damn ceiling fan. It never leaves me. But, what I realized standing in the fucking bathroom, staring into the mirror, was that I'm sick and tired of carrying it by myself. Tired of letting it define who I am and what I do."

She pulled back slightly to peer into his eyes, now hazel again in the moonlight, warm as they stared back at her. His gaze roamed over her face as his sigh washed over her skin.

"I love seeing you in my shirt, babe, but you shouldn't be out here in the cold. Come on, let's go back inside."

She allowed him to lead her in, his arm supporting her as they walked. She hesitated in the living room, but he continued to guide her back toward the bedroom.

"Honey, maybe we should sit out here for a while."

He looked down, his head tilted as he considered her words. "Any reason why?"

"I just thought maybe it would be better to talk out here...not on the bed."

Another heavy sigh escaped his lips. "Shit."

Eyes wide, she startled. "What?"

"Baby, we started talking in the place where we made love...the perfect place to learn more about each other. But when I got overwhelmed and afraid you would see things on my face I wasn't ready for you to see, I fucked up that place." Seeing her about to protest, he placed his fingers over her lips. "Don't deny it, sweetheart. I can hear it in your voice."

Turning his body so they were facing each other in

the hall, he said, "Come on." This time, he led her into the studio, flipping on a small light that gently illuminated the room, allowing the sea glass to sparkle all around. "This is where I need to finish my story. In here, where it will make sense."

## 25

Jade sat, perched on the stool near Lance's work table, her eyes on the man standing in front of her.

Taking her cold hands in his, he said, "The scene was utter destruction. The vehicle was smoking, torn, scrap metal. I jumped up and ran as close as I could, my eyes taking in what my mind did not want to accept. Most of my team were inside, already dead. I ran around the perimeter, but all I saw was..." he sucked in a deep breath through his nose before letting it out slowly. "But all I saw were pieces. Body parts. My men were gone. Nothing left. As I stood there, my lungs burning, my heart ripping to shreds, I heard new screaming over the roar of the fires. Racing back to what had been the passenger side, I saw Jose."

Bending slightly, his chest tight, Lance sucked in more air, the room feeling small...choking. Jade, squeezing his hands in hers, uttered soft words of comfort as she watched him struggled with the memories.

Finally, standing back up, he continued, "Jose was alive. Barely, but alive. I ran over, dropped to his side and pulled him further away from the vehicle. And that's when we both saw."

Afraid to speak, Jade sat, unmoving, willing her strength to pass through to his body.

"Jose's legs were mostly gone. The blast took part of his legs and...and...even higher. I had a medical kit in my pack and I grabbed it to try to get some pain meds in him while I called for help. I only turned my back for a few seconds but it was too much. He looked down, realizing his legs, as well as his manhood, were gone and he fuckin' couldn't deal. I turned back with the syringe in my hand and he had his gun in his hand, the barrel right against his head."

Her eyes were now huge, her breath catching in her throat as well. Her mouth opened, but no words came out.

Nodding, his eyes now full of sadness, he let go of one of her hands to run his fingers over his face as he sighed. "Yeah. My best friend, who in that moment of painful agony could not face the idea of life with what had happened, pulled the trigger."

"Oh, Lance," she gasped, tears now streaming down her face. "I'm so sorry...so sorry," she cried over and over, her voice barely above a whisper.

Standing, Lance looked over her head for a moment before lowering his gaze back to hers, his thumbs wiping away her tears. "I was never the same after that. I came back to the states, off the assignment. I suppose I should have wanted revenge and to go after the fuckers who set us up, but to keep going, with my team all dead...just couldn't do it."

"The driver...what about him?"

His heart turned cold as he replied, "I staggered over to where he had crawled, my weapon out, ready to do to him what Jose had just done to himself, but I didn't have to. A large piece of metal was embedded in his chest, but he was still alive. Fucker was still alive. Barely. He looked up, his eyes wide as death clawed at him. And I just stared. Watched him die and did nothing to ease his pain. Just watched him die." Looking at her, he said, "And now you know. You know what haunted me for so long and what kind of man I am."

"Oh, honey, I think you are the best of men," Jade vowed. Her eyes left his face as they moved around the room, the perfectly balanced mobiles of glittering sea glass twinkling around. "Your art. The mobiles...the mosaics. You put the pieces together to make beautiful objects."

Nodding, he agreed. "I told you I'm not a trained artist. Never thought of art. Hell, if my team even thought I was creating artwork they'd laugh their asses off." His fingers trailed through a plastic tub of beautiful green pieces of sea glass. Picking a dark green piece out of the bin, he continued, "But somehow, working with these made me feel a little better. I had no idea until recently of the healing psychology behind it, but creating something whole out of the pieces gave me a sense of peace."

He brought the deep green piece toward her face and offered a small smile. "My favorite color was always the green ones…they look like beautiful jade." Chuckling, he said, "Guess I should have realized I was a goner the first time I looked into your green eyes. And then your name? Yeah, I might have roared and growled, but I was a goner for you."

"And now?" Her soft voice soothed him, but Lance knew what she was asking in just those two words.

"Now? I'm working on becoming the whole man I once was. One who wants to make things right…work at putting my own pieces together again. One who is willing to use his skills as an investigator. And one who wants to protect the people he loves."

Wordlessly, she stood from the stool, taking his hand in hers and leading him out of the studio and back to his bedroom, ready to claim it as their place of love once more. Smiling, Lance went willingly.

---

Hours later, lying in bed watching the ceiling fan turn, Lance recognized that everything was different now. Jade, her head on his shoulder, her wrapped wrist propped on his chest and her legs carefully tangled with his, slept in his arms. His thoughts moved over his Army buddies, but instead of horror, he thought of how they were before the mission. Laughing, joking, talking. Jose liked to share the letters, pictures, and care packages his wife sent. A smile curved his lips as he thought of Jose's barking laughter making every joke even funnier. The blades of the fan turned overhead and he knew it was time to let go.

*Man, you gotta know, I carry you in my heart. But now, I gotta make room for someone else...someone who's right here, right now. Hell, buddy, someone's after her and I gotta give this all I've got to keep her safe.*

An image of Jose grinning back, throwing a thumbs up as he walked away, filled his mind and for the first time in years, he fell into a peaceful slumber of a night with no nightmares.

———

Standing on the screened porch the next morning, Jade watched the day dawning as Lance brought coffee to her. Taking a grateful sip, she nodded toward the cargo ships in the bay, and said, "Looks like a few more have joined the wait to get into the Chesapeake ports."

Lance smiled, tucking a wayward strand of hair behind her ear, loving the silky feeling. "So, are you sure you want to go to your apartment today?"

"I know you're worried, but I really need to. My foot is much better...honestly just a dull ache now. The girls will be with me and I know Gareth has already changed the locks. Mr. and Mrs. Poletta called and said that I was not to worry. They were more upset that someone wanted to harm me than they were about the apartment."

"I'd really like you to stay with me," he said, his voice caressing her ear as he leaned over, placing a kiss on her neck.

Giggling, she said, "I'm just going over to do some cleaning and to make sure everything is in place."

Turning in his arms, she peered up into his face, seeing sincerity. "To be truthful, I'd like to be here too, but let's give us a chance. A lot has happened and I don't want to rush things too fast."

"I know and, normally, I'm a cautious man, but sweetheart, I want you with someone during the day and with me at night. Whether here or there, I don't want you left alone." He hesitated before adding, "And Jade...right now you don't have a bed to sleep in at your place."

Lance watched her face fall and he pulled her tighter. "The sooner we can find out who murdered George and why they think you have something, the sooner your life can move forward."

Pulling back, she offered a little smile. "Okay, then... I agree."

"Good, now let's get you to your apartment and then I'll head to the station."

---

Assisting Jade into her apartment, searching it carefully before welcoming Jillian and Katelyn inside, Lance kissed her soundly before heading back down the stairs. After making sure everything was fine with Gareth, who was outside installing a security system, he drove to the station.

Once inside the police workroom, he poured another cup of coffee before sitting down to see what progress had been made.

Mitch entered, asking, "So, what have we got?"

Burt pulled up his laptop and began his report. "George was not a wealthy man, generally pouring most of what he earned back into his business…gasoline, new nets and traps, paying the workers on his boats, repairs, insurance. Now, that's not unusual for someone who owns their own business, but what is unusual is the amount of money he'd been putting into his bank account in the last six months. He went from a bank balance of about eight thousand dollars to over fifty thousand dollars."

Grant whistled at the increase while the others had similar expressions of surprise.

Mitch inquired, "Any idea where the money was coming from?"

"He made cash deposits of about five grand every other week for about the last five months."

"Cash?" Ginny asked, her eyes wide. "What was he involved in that gave him that kind of money?"

"Something worth murdering for."

The other officer's eyes jumped to Lance, his face hard and unreadable as he scanned the report from Burt. He looked up at Mitch and said, "George was doing something and somehow he involved Jade. She has no knowledge of why, but there's got to be a tie-in. Something he said to her, gave to her…something, Goddamnit!" His fist landed on the table, slamming home the point of his frustration. "What are we missing?"

"Stay objective," Mitch ordered. Turning to Ginny, he said, "Pull up the notes from Jade's interview. Let's look at what she said again."

As Ginny scrolled on her laptop, Callan walked in. "Sorry, late night. Had to rescue a few drunk businessmen out on a boat, thinking they knew how to handle their vessel when all they managed to do was get lost. Floated too close to one of the cargo ships in the bay. It should have had alarms that sounded when the smaller boat got close but, like a bunch of the ships in the bay, half its equipment probably didn't work."

Lance's head swiveled around to Callan and he repeated, "Its equipment probably didn't work?"

Callan nodded, "Just like trucks on the highways, some of those big, old cargo ships, especially ones that come from other countries where regulations might be slack, have things on them that don't work worth shit."

"They're supposed to have equipment that alerts them to other ships in the area?"

"Absolutely. They should know the location of all other watercraft in the area. When you look out on the bay and see them anchored, awaiting permission to enter the port area, they are anchored well away from each other."

"And small boats nearby...they know when one is near?"

"Absolutely. Even at night."

"So, what happened last night?"

"We got a call from the small boat when they sobered up enough to realize they had no idea where they were or how to get back to the harbor. When we finally got to them, they were perilously close to one of the large ships. We contacted the ship and ended up having a very one-sided conversation with some

Russian crewmembers." Rolling his eyes, he added, "Bet a paycheck, the guy knew more English than he was letting on."

Mitch observed Lance closely, before asking, "What are you thinking, 'cause I know you don't give a shit about the ships in the bay?"

"I kept focusing on what George may have given or said to Jade. Maybe that's not it at all. Maybe it's something that she was doing that had nothing to do with George."

---

Jade stood in her apartment, staring at the empty space where her sofa had sat. Trying to make herself feel better, she remembered she bought it on Craig's List, though she had paid extra for them to deliver it to her third floor home. The mattress had been bought new, but it was low quality, all she could afford at the time.

Arms wrapped around her from behind and she smiled at Katelyn's voice near her ear. "It's gonna be fine, sweetie."

"I know...really I do."

"You know what we need? A bridesmaid party!" Jillian's arms came from the front and the three of them stood hugging for a moment.

"To go along with all the wedding-planning meetings we had!" Katelyn agreed.

"Well, I get married just after Thanksgiving, which is, wow, in just about a week actually, and I think it's the perfect time for another girl's only party," Jillian laughed.

"Sounds good to me," she nodded. "Just let me know when and where."

As they surveyed the apartment now that the furniture was put right, the clothes were washed, and the kitchen items were out of the dishwasher, she tried to look at it as fresh and new. But all she could see was some unknown person rifling through her belongings, slashing her sofa and bed, and searching for God knows what.

"Have you decided what you're going to do? Where you're going to stay?" Katelyn asked.

Sucking in her lips, she replied, "Belle invited me to stay with her, but I don't want to bring any danger to her. Lance wants me with him and as much as I want that too, I hate to rush things. We're so new…new to each other as friends, new to each other in a relationship. What if by moving in, things go badly—"

"Honey," Jillian interrupted, holding her arms as she moved in close. "You can't worry too much now about a bunch of *what ifs*. You've got someone after you. The police don't know why now, but I promise they will. And in the meantime, you've got a hot detective who's broken down his barriers to take care of you. I say, go for it!"

"Well, when you put it like that, I guess I will!" she grinned, her heart finally lifting.

"So, what the hell was Jade doing?" Grant asked, staring at Lance.

"She goes out and searches for sea glass every chance she gets." Seeing the other officers about to protest, he threw his hand up. "But that's not all. She catalogs the information on the ships in the bay."

Mitch's eyes narrowed as he asked Lance the question he figured everyone was asking themselves. "Why?"

"She uses the information in her classroom. She said that she finds where the ships come from and then teaches the kids about geography when they find the countries on their maps."

Callan leaned back, rubbing his chin, shaking his head slightly. "I'm just not connecting the dots here, Lance. I still don't see a connection."

"To be honest, I don't either," he admitted. "But when the news picked up on the little article about Jade, declaring she was the one who found George's body, that's when someone ran her off the road and then trashed her place. There's got to be a thread that ties together George, something he had, and someone thinking that Jade's got it or saw something."

"But she claims he gave her nothing...well, other than a flounder," Ginny quipped.

"Just because he didn't give her anything, doesn't mean he didn't have something to give," he argued.

Mitch agreed with him, "He's right. If someone was after something George had, then they only have to have a suspicion of where it might be to go after it. After trashing his place, they must have tried her place."

He looked at Callan, asking, "What do those ships contain? Or more to the point, what could they be smuggling in?"

"Smuggling? Hell, could be just about anything contraband. But, if you want specifics, it could be human trafficking, money, drugs, diamonds, guns, weapons, hell, even fish."

Eyebrows raised, he repeated, "Fish?"

Chuckling, Callan said, "I know you might not realize it, but there's a huge market for contraband fish. They call them Aquatic Cocaine."

"Fuckin' hell," Sam moaned, scrubbing his hand over his face as he leaned heavily back in his chair, "now I know it's time to retire."

"So, you want to tell us what the hell Aquatic Cocaine is?" Lance prodded, his curiosity at war with his frustration.

"There's more than one type of fish that can bring in big money, but the Totoaba is worth the most. The bladder of this large fish can be worth thirty thousand dollars."

Stunned, they all stared at Callan, but Lance's mind raced with possibilities. "Keep going," he encouraged.

"The ships containing the illegal fish can come from Mexico, Hong Kong, China, Russia, or Thailand. It's hard for us to catch the smugglers, especially since these huge ships don't have to contain much to be profitable. And honestly, it doesn't have to be the whole ship involved. Could be just a few men on board."

"Just someone on board who has the fish or the fish bladders and can sell them—" Grant began.

"But you told us that sailors from other countries can't leave the ship even when they are in port," Ginny reminded.

"Yeah, but if a boat made contact at night and the ship's alarms were disabled, then a deal could be struck. And the local dealer could make enough cash to add fifty thousand dollars to their bank account," he surmised.

"You think that Jade may have seen something or someone thinks she did, and that's why they're after her?" Burt asked him.

"I still say that doesn't make sense," Ginny refuted. "Even if George was dealing in smuggling, he didn't give her anything. She'd have known if she had a huge fish bladder instead of a flounder!"

"I agree, but I still think that George was involved in something with the cargo ships in the harbor, but what he was after or given, I don't know," he argued.

"We searched his place and came up with nothing,"

Burt reminded, "but then, if he was getting something illegal, he probably didn't want it at his house."

Pulling out his phone, Lance dialed Jade. "Hey," he greeted, concern in his voice. "The girls still with you? Good. Listen, sweetheart, I need you to check something for me and I'll explain later. Did you cook the fish you last bought from George?" Listening to her answer, he confirmed, "It's still in the freezer? I need you to unwrap it and tell me if it's the flounder you bought." After she responded, he said, "Really? You're sure? Okay, thanks. I'll see you this afternoon."

Disconnecting, he explained, "What's in her freezer is really a flounder filet, but..." capturing their attention, "she said the original brown wrapper that he had placed it in had been taken off and re-wrapped in a different way. Which means someone—"

"Thinks George gave her something," Grant jumped in, leaning forward.

"And that tells us that George did have something he probably needed to get rid of," Callan finished.

Mitch, his sharp eyes moving around the table, said, "We focused in on the possibility of illegal fish, because George was a fisherman. But the reality is that his involvement could have been simply because he had a boat. Therefore, if he were involved in moving stolen goods, it could have been drugs or any of the other things Callan mentioned. We still need to work the problem."

"Think Jade would mind if you got her phone and we looked at the ships she was identifying right before George was found? I could cross-reference them with the information I can gather from the ships' GPS and Harbor Masters," Callan requested.

"No problem. And I'd like to talk to some of the other local fishermen," he agreed. "See if Skip, the Carsons, or the Taylors can tell us anything, before George's funeral tomorrow."

Just then, Callan's phone vibrated. Taking the call, his lips tightened as he listened before disconnecting. Looking at the others, he declared, "George's boat has been found. Scuttled in an inlet in the county, north of Baytown.

Mitch nodded sharply and said, "I'll get Colt to let us work the scene with his deputies. Lance, you can talk to the fishermen later. I want you with us, gathering evidence at George's boat."

---

Jade stood, the flounder still in her hands, as Jillian came up behind her.

"Was that Lance?"

Nodding, she said, "Yeah, and he asked me the strangest thing. He wanted to know if the flounder George gave me was truly a flounder. So, I checked and it is."

"So, what's got you spooked?" Katelyn asked.

"When George handed this to me, it was carefully wrapped in the brown paper, with a strip of masking tape holding it together. But, when I just pulled it out of the freezer to unwrap it, the tape was undone and the wrapping paper looks like it was removed and then folded back around the fish in a different way. Not folded the same way George had it."

"That's weird," Jillian said, staring at the wrapping paper, now flat on the counter with the filet of flounder laying on top."

She started to throw the fish away, not wanting to eat something that whoever had been in her apartment had touched, but hesitated. "I know this sounds crazy, but I'm putting this back into the freezer just in case Lance needs to look at it later."

"I wonder what on earth they're uncovering about George," Katelyn pondered aloud. "I can't imagine the flounder business being very clandestine."

Unable to hold back a giggle, she and Jillian both laughed, Katelyn joining in. Sobering, she said, "I feel so bad laughing under the circumstances...it must be my nerves."

"Hey, am I missing the party?" Belle asked, walking through the door. "Gareth was just finishing, so he let me in."

"Come on in," she invited. "We've about got the place put back together, although I won't be spending the nights here for a while. I still have the creeps about people being in my space...well, and I also don't have a bed."

Before the women could respond, Gareth appeared in the doorway. "Hey, ladies," he greeted. "Jade, let me walk you through the security system."

Allowing him to assist her down the stairs, she quickly learned how it worked and her new codes.

Scooping her up in his arms for the ascent, they heard a deep throat clearing behind them.

"You wanna tell me what you're doing with my girl in your arms?"

Gareth turned around and grinned. "Your girl? Well, seeing how my own girl is upstairs, I guess I won't pretend that Jade is mine," he joked.

Lance returned his grin and walked forward, his arms out, taking Jade from him, Gareth settling her into his embrace.

"I was just showing her the new system," Gareth greeted. "It's good security, but I hope like hell she won't need it."

Nodding, he and Jade both agreed. Heading back up the stairs, he looked around at her cleaned apartment, sans sofa and bed. Thanking the others, they said goodbye before she showed him the new system.

"I'm glad it's in, but I still want you with me even when you get a new bed. Or if you're here, I want to be here with you," he said.

"Because you think I'm unsafe?" she asked, peering up at him, her eyes wide.

"As a precaution, sweetheart," he said, then leaned in for a kiss before adding, "but mostly because I want you next to me when I sleep and next to me when I wake."

Grinning, she agreed, "That sounds perfect."

---

Pulling up to the harbor, Lance looked over at Jade.

"Hope you don't mind, but while you're buying some fish, I'll talk to the Carsons and Taylors."

Her gaze dropped to the BPD logo on his long-sleeved shirt and sucked in her lips. Shifting her eyes back to his, she nodded slowly.

He noted the specter of sadness in her eyes, turning them a darker green. "Are you okay, sweetheart?"

Swallowing deeply, she looked out the front window at the harbor. "It's strange being here, knowing I'll never see George again." Sighing, she added, "And I know you're not just here with me, but here as an officer. And that's a good thing...but also a reminder of what's happened." Turning back to hold his gaze, she asked, "Why would anyone want to hurt that sweet, old man?"

"I don't know...but I promise to find out," he replied, reaching his hand out to cup her face.

After he assisted her down from his vehicle, they walked toward the boats. Stopping suddenly, she placed her hand on his arm, capturing his attention. Twisting his head, he looked down at her, his brows lowered in concern.

"I haven't bought fish here since all of this happened. I'm not sure I'm ready," she confessed. "You go on and I'll just sit on the bench over there and take in the view of the harbor."

Nodding, he watched her move over to one of the wooden benches on the harbor, overlooking the many docks where a few sailboats were moored. Turning his attention toward the Carson's boat, he headed that way.

Richard nodded as he climbed aboard, his gaze

dropping to his shirt. "Howdy, Officer. How can I help you?"

Shaking the older man's hand, he replied, "I'm Lance Greene, a detective with the Baytown Police. I'd like to talk to you about George, if you don't mind."

"Damn shame," he said, pushing his cap up as he shook his head. "Known George for a long time."

Rick walked up as well and with quick introductions, he agreed with his dad. "Hell, Dad and George have been fishing this bay for my whole life. I remember going out with him a few times as a teenager. Dad always said it was good to get a feel for different boats and ways of doing things."

"I was wondering if you could shed any light on his business for me?" he asked, noting the look shared between father and son at his question.

Richard jerked his head toward a couple of benches built into the side of the boat and they moved over to sit. Sighing heavily, he began, "Fishin's a hard living. Up early, home late. Long hours in rough weather. Gotta know the territory, the environment, the business. It's not just fishin', you gotta deal with the mechanics of the boat...hell, repairs alone will drive you batty. To stay competitive, you gotta stay up on the marketing. We've even got a website now thanks to Rick's wife." Chuckling, he added, "Sometimes I wonder if I'm getting too old but, then, it's the only life I know."

"And George?" he prompted. "Would you say he was up on everything?"

Richard looked at his son before shifting his gaze back to him. "Hate to talk poorly of the dead...and fuck,

I can't believe that George is dead. But, to be honest, George was old school. Nothing wrong with that, but he was feeling the pinch. His boat needed repairs. Instead of gaining new contracts, he tended to just keep the ones he had."

"George changed after his wife died," Rick added. "His son's in jail for drugs and when his wife died, I got the feeling George thought life had kicked him."

"Did he change any of his habits lately? Or in the last year or so?"

"Habits?" Richard asked, the lines in his face deepening.

"Fishing habits…or personality changes? Anything that seemed out of the ordinary for him?" he explained.

Knuckling his cap back further on his head, Richard heaved a deep sigh. "He missed a few more days fishing than he used to. In this business, if we don't fish, we don't earn. But, for the last year, he'd skip a day a week. I just figured he might be ready to hang it up. You know, he must have had some savings over the years, but I had offered a time or two, that if he got ready to give it up full time and wanted to work for us occasionally, I'd let him."

"Work for the competition?" he asked.

"Hell, Officer, we might be competitors in the sense of us both fishing in the same area, but this ain't exactly a big harbor. Me and George weren't no hard-ass competitors. My business was growing and his wasn't. I had a son to help and George didn't. He'd hire a couple of guys occasionally, but never seemed to keep 'em very long. I knew he couldn't keep going forever and thought that maybe he'd like to just fish and not be worried about the business end of things."

"He ever act like he wanted to take you up on the offer?"

"Hard to tell about George," Richard replied. "He'd hem and haw about, but just kept doing the same things."

"He and Thomas got all cozy as soon as the restaurant in town changed hands. It didn't bother me none, 'cause I knew Thomas would buy from both of us, but they got real chummy."

He cast his eyes over the vessel and said, "Your boat looks much better than George's."

Rick grinned widely as he nodded. "Me and Dad got this one rehauled and then bought the new one as well."

"Business must be good."

"We got several new restaurant contracts," Rick added proudly. "You might have seen some of the trucks that were here earlier. They meet us when we come in almost every day." Looking over where George's boat used to be moored, the smile left his face. "But ol' George just never seemed inclined to fix his up. Or, maybe, he just didn't have the money."

"Can you think of anyone who would want to harm him?"

"George?" Richard asked, his eyes wide. "Hell, George never bothered no one and never acted like anyone bothered him either. Can't imagine anyone would have a grudge against him."

Rick nodded along with his father. "George never had an enemy, far's I know."

Completing his questions, Lance stood and shook hands with both men. "I'll let you get back to work, but thanks for talking to me. If you think of anything that might help us understand what happened to George, please give us a call."

As he made his way over to the Taylor's crab boat, he noted the Harbor Master sitting on the bench with Jade. Reminded that he needed to talk to Skip as well, he hustled over to the next boat.

"His biggest problem was that he just got lazy…least-wise, that's what I thought," Harold Taylor said, taking off his cap and wiping his brow. "I told George over and over that he needed to keep his boat in better condition, but…well, to be honest, it was my wife that finally got me to understand that after Sylvia died, George just wasn't the same."

Shifting his stance slightly, Lance prodded, "The same?"

"Yeah…without his wife or his son, George just seemed to not work as hard, and this isn't a business you can slack off with and expect to put money in the bank. He'd act like money didn't matter to him, but then I'd see him staring at Richard's new boat like he was jealous. I don't know…George just seemed to lose his direction."

He nodded, looking around at Harold's deckhands, standing around, their hands busy but their attention directed to the conversation about George. "Any of your men have dealings with George?"

Harold turned and looked at his small crew. "Any y'all ever work for George Caday?"

They all shook their heads before returning to their tasks. He turned back to Harold and asked, "Can you think of anything else about him that would help our investigation?"

Shifting on his feet, he replied, "I always liked George. Easy to get along with. He'd have your back if you needed him." Sighing heavily, he said, "Gonna miss him."

Back on the dock, Lance walked toward the bench occupied by Jade and Skip. Nodding to the pair, he sat next to Jade, wrapping his arm around her. "You okay?" he whispered.

She turned her sad gaze up to him and nodded. "Yeah. Skip and I were just reminiscing about George. Of course, he knew him for years and I only recently met him, but the harbor just doesn't seem the same without George's smile."

Turning toward Skip, he studied the weather worn face of the Harbor Master. Up close, it was easier to see that he was younger than first expected. His ring finger was bare, but the indentation from a former ring was visible. Shifting his gaze to his face, he asked, "What can you tell me about George?"

Heaving a sigh, Skip replied with a nod out toward the boats, "Probably not as much as the two you've been talking to. I've been Harbor Master here for about eight years. Came from a much bigger harbor...I worked out of Norfolk for the first part of my career, but after coming here to do some fishing, I fell in love with the place. Decided that I'd rather be the head person at a small harbor than just one of many in a much larger place." He leaned forward, resting his forearms on his knees as he dropped his head, staring at his boots. "Me and George hit it off. He'd let me go out on his boat some and then, when I applied for the position, he backed me all the way. Our wives became friends and they'd come out early in the morning to look for sea glass together."

"It sounds like me," Jade smiled. "I go out almost every morning I can when school's not in session."

"Bet you give some of it to Lance to use for his art."

Slipping Lance a sly grin at the memory of their first encounters, she replied, "I take it to my students. In fact, I've recently taken a bunch there for them to create sea glass picture frames for their art projects."

Nodding, Skip said, "My wife wasn't artistic but she and George's wife would save the glass in big jars." Sobering for a moment, he added, "Hell, me and George ended up having more in common than we should have." He twisted his head around as he explained, "My wife got cancer about the same time as Sylvia. Both good women, but the disease took its toll on all of us."

She reached out, resting her hand on his arm. "Oh, I'm so sorry. I had no idea."

"George's wife actually died first. My Anne lasted almost another year, but it was hard and she finally denied the last of the treatments. George was a good friend then, even though he was dealing with his own grief."

"I know you've already thought of all of this, but do you know of anyone who would want to harm George?" Lance asked.

"That's what makes no sense," Skip said, leaning back suddenly, his voice harsher. "Old man...not much money...didn't have the new, shiny boat or equipment... didn't have a lot of business. Hell, there was nothing for anyone to be jealous of or want that he had."

"So, he didn't have much money?" Lance prodded, carefully watching Skip's response.

Snorting, he looked at him, shaking his head. "I figure you've seen his house. Sylvia kept it so nice, but after her death, George lived in a mess. I don't reckon he had much money to begin with, but in the past several years, he sure as hell didn't earn a lot."

Nodding, he gave Jade's shoulders a squeeze and said, "Thanks for keeping Jade company and answering my questions."

As they stood, they shook hands before Skip smiled at Jade. "Been a while since I had a pretty lady to just sit and enjoy the harbor with me. Thank you."

Smiling in return, she shifted into his embrace as they walked back to his vehicle. After settling her inside, he jogged around to the driver's side, noting the huddle of helpers from the Taylor's boat deep in conversation, before they turned and looked at him.

Another tear fell, but was quickly wiped away with a tissue pressed into her hand by Lance. She peered up at him, grateful for his presence, as well as his understanding.

The minister gave a beautiful, graveside service for George. The cemetery had placed chairs underneath a canopy for the townspeople to stand nearby, and Mayor Corwin Banks had taken his wife's arm and led her to the front, until he saw George's son sitting there. With a purple hue to his face, Corwin moved to the other side, sitting next to Silas Mills. After the minister's service, he called for a few of George's friends to speak.

First Richard walked to the front, his anecdotes bringing smiles to the large gathering. "We started out together as teens, fishing on the weekends for old Mr. MacGreggor and, damn, if George didn't fall into the fish tank the first time we went out by ourselves. It was raining and I was trying to figure out how to get him out. By the time we got back to the harbor, we had a few fish we'd caught, but stunk like ol' seaweed." He wiped his eyes at the memory, before heaving a sigh. "Hard to believe he's gone, but for anyone who knew him, he was not just an old salt o' the sea, but truly a good man." Looking at the picture sitting on the coffin at the front, he said, "I'll lift a glass to you in the pub, old friend."

Harold shook hands with Richard on his way to the pulpit, before facing the crowd. "When I think of George, I think of a man who loved his wife and son, and loved his job. For those of us who spend our lives out in the elements of the sea, we feel closer to God, out on the water, than anywhere else. George began to drift over the last few years, and I think that Sylvia was his anchor. So, George, my friend, you're with her now."

Lance shot a glance to the front, seeing Anthony wiping tears from his eyes. He was wearing an ill-fitting suit, sitting next to a suited, prison guard. He found it impossible to not analyze the case, even when at the funeral.

*Who gained from George's money? Obviously, Anthony, since George's Will only listed his son as beneficiary. But did he know how much money his father had in the bank? And did he know how his father was getting the extra cash? And where did the money come from?*

An elbow in the side sent his gaze darting back to Jade. Blushing, he faced the front again, now interested in Thomas Fedor. He approached the front from his seat next to the mayor, his expensive suit and polished shoes in stark contrast to Richard and Harold's clothing.

"As most of you know, I've only been in town a couple of years, but I got to know George before I arrived. I was interested in the restaurant for sale, but knew I wanted fresh, local fish, so I hung out at the harbor for several months beforehand. Got to know all the good fishermen there and George was always willing to get what I needed..."

He stopped listening as Thomas' words hit him —*always willing to get what I needed.* He narrowed his eyes as he stared at the man in front of the gathering. *Thomas is talking about seafood, but what if someone used*

*George to get something off the ships in the harbor? Not smuggling for himself, but as a means to an end for someone who was using him?*

Another elbow jab brought his mind back to the funeral and he caught Jade's lowered brow. "Sorry," he mumbled, pulling her in closer. Thomas was still speaking, so he tuned in once more.

"George will be missed and his place in the fishing community...as the whole community, will be hard to fill." Stepping down, Thomas walked back to his seat next to Corwin Banks and his wife, a smile on his face.

As the crowd dispersed, he kept his arm on Jade as they walked over the grassy terrain of the cemetery, making sure she did not fall. Assisting her into his SUV, he asked, "You want to go to the pub or go home, babe?"

"The pub," Jade replied without delay. Seeing his lifted eyebrow, she rushed, "I'm not tired, Lance. Well, I am...but that's from the emotions of the last week, not from my injuries. My foot is much stronger and my wrist will be back to normal soon." Placing her hand on his forearm, feeling the steel of muscles underneath, she added, "I'd like to spend some time with our friends for a little while. And I know the pub will be more of a celebration of George."

When they arrived, the pub was packed, Aiden and Brogan behind the bar pulling beers and keeping a practiced eye on the crowd. Katelyn assisted the servers as Gareth worked behind the bar as well. Ginny slid into the booth next to Grant and Jillian, facing Mitch, Tori, Jade, and Lance.

His gaze traveled around the crowded room, staring at the faces but unable to discern anyone who might know what George was involved in.

Jade eyed him and said, "I could see the wheels turning in your head all during the service." Looking at the other officers, she asked, "I suppose it was the same with you all?"

Ginny grinned, while shaking her head. "Yeah, it's hard to turn it off."

"Can't you talk about it a little?" Jillian said, tucking a wisp of hair behind her ear.

"Babe," Grant replied.

Jillian rolled her eyes and looked at Tori and her. "I swear, he says *babe*, and it's supposed to mean something different depending on how he says it. That was his *you know I can't talk about police business* babe." Smiling at Jade, she said, "Get used to it."

She nodded, happy that Lance seemed at ease with their friends and with his new police responsibilities.

As though Jillian could read her mind, she said, "I have a feeling I just gave up one of my favorite artists, Lance."

"It's my stress reliever, Jillian. I'm sure you'll still get some work from me."

Before anyone could respond, a loud whistle sounded throughout the bar. Aiden stood on a chair to get the crowd's attention and said, "Richard wants to offer a toast to George, so if everyone could listen up."

Aiden hopped down from his perch and the crowd quieted as Richard stood in front of the bar. Looking down at his boots for a moment, he said, "George was a sailor…a fisherman…a member of this community…a good husband and father…and to me, a good friend." Lifting his beer, he called out, "To George Caday."

The gathering lifted their glasses as well, repeating the toast as George's name rang out in the bar.

## 28

---

"Are you going home for Thanksgiving?" Jade's voice broke the peaceful silence.

Lance had been dragging his hand along her arm in slow movements, but stilled at her words. They returned from the wake after enjoying time with their friends, settling on his deck with glasses of wine to watch the sunset. Neither of them spoke for a long time as the sun slipped into the horizon, streaking the sky with hues of blue and orange. She sat between his legs, her back warm against his chest.

"Thanksgiving?"

"It's this week, you know. I...well, I wondered if you had plans?"

Shaking his head as his hand continued to glide over her petal skin, "Nah. Mom would be delighted if I came home, but she'd see it as my deciding to leave this place and returning to the fold."

Sitting quietly, she did not reply.

"What about you?"

Her chest heaved as she sighed. "No, I'm not going home either. I have a five-day weekend, since school is out on Wednesday. I'll try to visit my parents over the Christmas holiday, but I don't want a repeat of last year." Feeling a slight squeeze on her arm, she grinned at his nonverbal indication she should explain. "I went home last year for Thanksgiving, hoping to have a nice break from school, but all my parents did was bitch about me working in an impoverished area. They said they were embarrassed to tell their friends where I lived. So," she shrugged, "I ended up leaving a day early because I couldn't stand it anymore."

"So, what are your plans?" he asked, now curious as to how she was going to spend the days off work.

"I guess it depends on you…"

"Me?" he asked, his voice filled with surprise and pleasure.

Grinning, she twisted her head around and said, "Yeah, you. If you're going to be here, we could do our own Thanksgiving meal…something simple, and then maybe join some friends later in the afternoon."

Lance was quiet and Jade began to nervously fiddle with her wine glass. "Of course, we don't have to—"

"It's been a long time since anyone wanted to spend a holiday with me," he interrupted. "Or a long time since I wanted to spend it with someone else."

Her mouth opened but no words came forth, unable to think of what to say.

He leaned around, staring into her wide eyes, and said, "Can't think of anyone I'd rather be with on a day to give thanks."

Feeling a smile curve her lips, she faced forward once more, the ever-changing night sky filling her vision. Lance began rubbing her arm again, her soft skin smooth underneath his fingers.

"Has it only been a few weeks?"

"What's only been a few weeks, sweetheart?" he mumbled into her silky hair.

"Us knowing each other."

Smiling, he thought back to the first time he had seen her. Her beauty struck him, but he had forced himself to hang on to his irritation at her intrusion into his world. "I was an asshole when we first met," he reminded.

Snorting, she nodded, taking another sip. "Yeah, but I killed you with kindness...well, I tried."

"Such a pest," he joked.

Setting her wine glass down on the deck, she twisted in his arms, resting her hand on his chest, over his heart. Peering into his eyes, she said, "I have no idea what was going through my mind when I decided to return to sneak some sea glass onto your front porch. But, Lance...I'm so glad I did." Leaning forward, she softly touched her lips to his.

The kiss began slowly, the simple movement of silk against satin. Jade loved the feel of his lips. Strong, yet yielding. The rough stubble of his whiskers against her skin. His breath warm against her face, the scent of his masculinity mingling with the taste of the dark wine. Heady, yet addictive. *Addictive.* The thought that she needed him for more than protection, but for her heart too, settled into her mind as she allowed him to take over the kiss, falling under his spell.

Lance felt the instant she yielded to him, her trust hit his heart, while her lips on his communicated her need as well as her desire. Cupping her face with his large hands, he angled her as he took the kiss deeper. Sliding his tongue into her warmth, he tasted, tangled, and triumphed as she melted into him.

Shifting her body, he stood with her in his arms, their kiss proclaiming what their hearts silently acknowledged. Entering the house, he stalked toward the bedroom, their wine glasses forgotten on the deck.

---

Wrapping his arms tighter around her, Lance watched Jade sleep. The blades of the ceiling fan twirled slowly, but no longer held his attention. Smiling, he stared at her face as the sun hinted at rising, the faint illumination coming through the blinds in his bedroom. Her eyelashes lay in crescents on her cheeks as her deep breath passed her lips, her mouth open slightly.

Smiling, he thought of the previous evening and his cock, already awake and ready, nudged against her ass. She stirred, her eyelids fluttering before she stretched. Not wanting to wake her, he reluctantly moved back slightly but she grunted.

"Uh uh," she said, pushing her ass backward until his cock was once more pressed tightly against her.

"I wanted you to sleep, babe," he whispered, reluctant to move again.

"Sleep is overrated," she said, wiggling against his erection. "I'd rather have you."

Cupping her breast with the hand under her, he slid his free hand down her chest, over her tummy, chuckling as he skimmed over a ticklish spot and she wiggled more. His hand continued its path downward as she spread her legs, before sliding into her slick folds. Taking his time, he moved his fingers into her sex, the warmth holding him tight. She began to undulate as he gently plunged his fingers in and out, his thumb circling her clit. He felt her body stir to life, fine tuning a perfect instrument.

Jade shifted onto her back, desperate to see Lance's face in the morning light as his hands continued to work their magic. His face loomed over hers, filling her vision. Reaching up, she rubbed her fingers over his dark morning stubble, his eyes holding her captive. Emotions passed between them without words.

Suddenly, her inner core tightened and she sucked in a quick breath as his fingers found the place they had been seeking. With pressure on her clit, she fell apart.

Lance watched the blush rise from her tightly beaded nipples upward until her entire chest and face were a delectable, deep rose. Slowly withdrawing his fingers, he brought them upward, dragging them along her stomach and over her breasts, finally circling her lips.

Jade tasted herself on him and her chest heaved in desire. Her lips curved in delight as he shifted over her, his weight welcome as she wrapped her arms around his neck, smoothing them down his shoulders.

Lance's cock, eager to play, nudged her entrance. The thought of protection kicked in, barely moving aside the desire to plunge immediately. Balancing his weight on one arm, he snagged a condom from the nightstand before pushing back on his knees. Holding her eyes, he palmed his cock, teasing her with the pearl of pre-cum on the end. Slowly rolling on the condom, he grinned as her breathing increased.

"Want this, babe?"

Her breath caught in her throat as her head jerked up and down. "More than you can imagine, Lance. I want you...with me. All of you with me...no pieces left behind."

The smile stayed firmly on his face as her words penetrated. Leaning closer, he entered her slowly, fighting the urge to plunge even though her heels were on his ass urging him on. Gliding into her sex, inch by inch, he watched as her head pressed back against the pillow, her breasts pushing upward as her back arched. She bit her bottom lip and squeezed her eyes shut.

"If you want all of me, babe, you gotta open your eyes," he groaned, the sensation of her tight sex clutching his sensitive cock almost more than he could bear.

Her eyes popped open, the wide green pupils staring back at him as her teeth let her bottom lip go, curving instead into a smile.

Never taking their eyes off each other, he continued to thrust, slowly at first and then with more vigor, as the emotions collided with the physical need.

Jade slid her hand over his shoulders and down his

back, the play of his muscles underneath her fingertips capturing her fascination. The immense strength and power of his body as it moved over and into hers took her to new heights. "More," she begged. "I want all of you."

Close to his release, Lance wanted her to come with him. Once more balancing on one arm, he slid his other hand over her curves, finding her clit, swollen and ready for him. Circling the nub, he watched as her eyes closed again. Just as he was about to remind her to keep them open, her green eyes landed on him as her body quivered, her sex clutching his cock. With a moan, his neck muscles tightened and his orgasm pulsed from his body into hers. His whole body shuddered, but he forced his eyes to stay on hers as well.

As the last stream emptied from his cock, he fought to catch his breath, enjoying the rosy blush over her body again. Continuing to thrust gently as her orgasm milked him, he cupped her face. Falling forward slightly to the side so as to not crush her, with his cock still planted, his chest heaved in gasps.

*Powerful.* That was the only word Jade could come up with at the moment, as her inner muscles continued to quake with the shared orgasm. The tingles slowly subsided and she felt his cock ease from her body. A sad groan protested from her lips at the loss of the connection.

"Be right back...I need to deal with this," he mumbled as he sat up and tossed the condom in the trash can before immediately encircling his arms around her.

They lay entangled, bodies slowly cooling from their shared passion. Brushing back a damp tendril from her forehead, Lance stared at her heated beauty. She completed him, as though all the broken pieces fit back together—not in the same way he had been before, but as a new man.

## 29

Pulling into the parking lot of the elementary school, Lance parked in the front. "Got big plans today?"

Jade nodded, her eyes bright. "We're finishing our projects for Thanksgiving. They're creating sea glass picture frames for their class pictures. I thought about making that project for the Christmas holidays, but the art teacher has them doing other things then."

He observed her animated face and was unable to hold back a grin from reaching his lips.

"What?" she asked, her voice huffing playfully.

Leaning over, he gave her a quick kiss, wanting to take it deeper but mindful of their location. "You're just cute, babe," he murmured against her lips.

Shaking her head as she grinned back, he walked around to her side and assisted her down.

"Jade," he called as she began to walk away. As she turned and looked back, he reminded, "Don't go anywhere until I come pick you up."

Nodding, the light dimming in her eyes, she replied,

"I promise." With a little wave, she made her way into the building, unaware of the occupant of another car in the parking lot, staring at her.

---

"So far, what we've got is a whole lot of facts, but none of them connecting the dots," Grant grumbled to the group gathered around the BPD workroom.

Mitch walked in and quickly took a seat. "Got the preliminary report from Colt on the finding from George's boat. Not everything is in, but there was definitely blood on the deck. There was an attempt to clean it with bleach, but whoever was cleaning was not nearly thorough enough. Multiple samples were taken and they matched George."

"So, he was killed on his boat," Lance said, sighing heavily. "Fingerprints?"

"Colt said the boat was wiped down, but they did manage to lift some partial prints from the underside of the wheel."

"Whoa, that might have been a big error the killer made," Grant surmised, to the nods of the others.

Lance knew the puzzle pieces would eventually fall into place, but investigations took time to separate what was not needed from what would show them the way. "I listened to the speakers at the funeral and did some digging this morning into Thomas Fedor."

Seeing the raised eyebrows of some of the others, he continued, "This guy had everyone suspicious when he first came to buy out the Sunset View Restaurant, but has now integrated into the community and has the backing of Corwin and Silas."

At the mention of the mayor and town manager, eyes rolled, but he added, "He came from New York and his background is somewhat murky—"

"Murky?" Ginny asked, her sharp eyes on him.

Nodding, he said, "His full name is Thomas Fedorov, and it appears he has an uncle involved with some of the less savory, underground movers and shakers from the New York crime families. They're not at the top... hell, probably not even in the middle, but he definitely has some family members running with the mob crowd."

Shaking his head, Mitch asked, "How the hell did none of this show up when he was at the auction or when he started buying up property along the shore?"

"Don't know, but then, I suppose there wasn't much to check on at the time. He had the financial backing to make an offer on the auction and the sellers were just glad to get someone willing to pay millions."

"Anything else on him?" Mitch inquired.

"Yeah...his casino in New Jersey is having financial problems," he announced, drawing disbelieving looks from the others. "I know. You'd think that a casino would be doing fine, but for reasons I haven't been able to discern, he poured a lot of borrowed money into restructuring the casino and the bank is wanting their loan payments."

"You think this is tied into smuggling and possibly George?" Grant asked.

"I haven't got any evidence that Thomas was doing

anything wrong, but it makes him a person of interest. He certainly has the family connections to put a hit on someone."

Mitch rubbed his chin for a moment, his thoughtful gaze on the whiteboard with the list of possible scenarios. "George had to have been involved in something to have those large sums of cash deposited into his account. He never took trips anywhere away from the area...only had an old laptop in his house, which produced nothing more than an email account. But he went out in his boat every day and, according to the other fishermen, his catches were small, at best. Thomas continued to do business with him, but we have to wonder why, when it might be easier for him to just deal with the other fishermen who could manage his large seafood supply need."

"So, was George getting something from a ship in the bay for Thomas? Something that would help Thomas pay off his staggering debt and give George some money to retire on?"

Lance shook his head, saying, "It's a way to connect the dots, but we need more than supposition—"

Callan interrupted as he walked briskly into the room. "Sorry, everyone., but I just received the list of the ships that were anchored in the bay the days before George's body was discovered." Passing copies of the list to everyone, he continued, "We're in luck because there weren't as many as usual. We've got Dutch, Greek, United States, Belize, and Liberia." He looked at the group as he said, "My bet's on the Belize or Liberia."

"Why?" he asked, his head tilted in question.

"Flag of convenience," Callan stated before offering his explanation. "Our oceans are filled with ships that are not from the country whose flag they're flying. Take Liberia—the country is impoverished from years of war, famine, no tourism, no crops, and yet, because of their liberal use of flags, ships from other countries who would like to hide their origins will pay Liberia a fee to use their country's flag. It's a money-maker for Liberia...well, for the ones who pocket the money. Dare say the poor never see the benefit."

"What is the benefit?" Burt asked, leaning forward, his forearms resting on the table.

"Ships can reduce operating costs or avoid the regulations of the owner's country. They might be able to pay lower wages to the workers on board, get involved in criminal activities, illegal fishing, or polluting the waters. They operate under the regulations of the country they are flagged with. So, a shipowner finds a nation with an open registry to take advantages of reduced regulation, lower fees, and maybe friendlier ports."

Ginny, her head shaking, asked, "Is this legal?"

"Yeah. It's been going on for decades, but coming under a lot of criticism. Special enforcement is now taking a closer look when they make a call into various ports. That's been part of our job and why I was so interested in the ships Jade was taking pictures of."

"You can't stop them?"

"Only if they have been detained three times in a twelve-month period. We're doing what we can, but it's still like plugging the dam with our finger."

Bringing the conversation back to their case, he asked, "What has you looking at the ships from Belize or Liberia, besides the flag of convenience?"

"The cargo ship flying under the Dutch flag was carrying machinery and electrical equipment. The ship has a clean slate and no prior problems on record. The ship from Greece contained plastics. Also with a clean record. And neither ship has been to China, Russia, or anywhere in Asia for over a year."

"And the ships with the Belize and Liberia flags?" he prodded.

Callan grinned as he leaned forward. "The ship from Belize was recently in the waters off Russia. Their holding tanks are carrying fish. If George was after the Totoaba fish, they'd be my guess for ease in smuggling. The one from Liberia was also in Russian ports recently. Not fish, but still, I'm damn curious what George was getting that afforded him that much money. Drugs or weapons are a big possibility."

As Callan took a seat and the group began pouring over the new information about the ships, his thoughts roamed back to Jade. "Something's still not adding up," he said, his frustration palpable. "Why would the killer go after Jade? She took pictures that tell us nothing... Callan's given us more information about these ships than her pictures ever could. She even said she got the identifying information from the websites available."

"All George ever gave her was fish," Ginny protested.

"But, the killer must think there was something else she discovered." Rubbing the back of his neck, he battled the desire to see her against the desire to stay and keep working. As the others worked, he stepped out of the workroom, pulling out his phone, seeing a text from her.

**Faculty mtg after school. I can get a ride if you need me to.**

He quickly typed, **No. Wait for me and I'll be there.**

Waiting for a moment, he grinned as she replied, **I'll always wait for you. <3**

If the others observed his expression as he walked back into the room, no one said anything, but his heart was so full, he did not try to hide his smile.

---

"Tomorrow is the last day before our Thanksgiving break, everyone, so make sure to place your finished picture frames on the bookshelves so they will dry overnight. Tomorrow, we'll place your pictures in them and they'll be ready for you to take home."

Jade smiled as the students rushed around, excitement in the air as their voices reached a fevered pitch. Quieting them, she checked their work before lining them up at the door once their belongings were gathered. As they walked down the hall toward the door leading to the buses, she gave them a thumbs-up for their behavior. Waving as they headed to the bus monitors, she ran into Bill as she turned to go back into the school.

"Did you hear?" he asked excitedly, swiping his hand through his hair, his eyes twinkling.

"Hear what?"

"No faculty meeting!"

Her eyes widened as excitement raced through her. "Really? I thought the principal had the agenda all set?"

"Seems the superintendent called all the principals to a meeting at the School Board Office instead. And I'm sure she won't hold one tomorrow since it's the day we get out for Thanksgiving, so… no faculty meeting this week."

"I know we have things we need to go over, but I'm so glad," she gushed. "It was a little tough being back today and I'm tired."

His gaze dropped to her bandaged wrist and he asked, "How are you doing? I couldn't believe you were in a car accident."

"I'm lucky. My foot was banged up, but it's getting better. My wrist isn't badly broken…just a hairline. The kids were great, but after a couple of days with a substitute last week, they were a little rambunctious."

"I…uh…heard through the grapevine that you were run off the road…like, uh…on purpose?" he asked, his eyes searching her face, landing on the small cuts still visible.

Her gaze flashed fire as she nodded. "Yes, some bastard in a stolen, big, black truck hit me and then purposefully ran me into a bunch of trees before speeding away."

His forehead wrinkled as he pursed his lips. "That's horrible, Jade. Do the police know who did it?"

"No, not yet. But if they ever find out who did, I'd like to get hold of them first before they haul him off to jail!"

He chuckled, rubbing the back of his neck. "Wow, you sound ruthless, but then I guess you have a right to be."

As they reached her classroom, she said, "I've got to let Lance know he can pick me up earlier, so I'll see you tomorrow."

"I'll wait with you," he said. "I would offer you a ride, but I came on my bike this morning."

"I'm definitely too old to ride on your handlebars," she joked. "I'll send Lance a text and then meet you out front."

Ten minutes later, they sat on one of the benches in front of the elementary school. After several minutes of chatting, Bill looked down as his phone vibrated an incoming message. Sighing heavily, he looked at it before sliding it back into his pocket.

"You okay?" she asked, observing the deflated expression on his normally smiling face.

"Yeah," he said, his voice lacking conviction. After another moment, he asked, "Do you ever wonder about teaching? Like, is it enough?"

"Enough?"

"My mom was a teacher and my dad was a principal. My uncle was a coach at a high school. I've got two sisters and one is a school nurse and the other teaches special education. Hell, teaching was all I ever knew." Sighing again, he added, "But it sure as hell doesn't pay all the bills...or at least not very well. In the spring, I'll get to coach afterschool at the high school, so that'll bring in a little more money."

Nodding, she said, "We'll never get rich in this

career, but Bill, we get to touch the lives of so many children. Make a difference. Help them reach their potential. And hopefully, for some of them, help them rise out of poverty through education."

Chuckling, he said, "You sound like a commercial for teaching."

Nodding her head as she laughed, she agreed. After the mirth slowed, she asked, "What made you think of all of that?"

"Got a notice from the bank. I'm overdrawn again by about twenty dollars...but hey, payday is tomorrow. Normally, I don't cut it this close, but my second job had a little...uh...hiccup this month, so I was overly generous with my credit card payments."

"I didn't know you had a second job."

Shrugging, he looked into the distance before bringing his gaze back to her. "I do some work for Thomas Fedor...well, for the Sunset View Restaurant. Just some odd jobs when he needs me."

Before she had a chance to ask more about his work, an SUV pulled to the front and she smiled, seeing Lance's face. Turning to Bill, she said, "Thanks for waiting for me." Standing, she looked back at his boyish face. "Are you going to be all right?"

"Don't worry about me," he assured. "I'll be fine."

As Bill watched Jade reach the vehicle, he pulled his phone back out, texting Thomas, **I need more work. ASAP.**

## 30

Lance parked at the harbor, noting the fishing vessels were gone but there was still plenty of activity with a few sailboats and personal boats docked. As he climbed out of his SUV, he waved toward Skip, who was walking back to his office with a few young dock helpers.

Greeting him, Skip invited him into the messy office. Papers were scattered across the desk, along with an open laptop. Charts and maps lined the walls.

Skip shook his head. "I know this place is a mess. Lord only knows how I keep up with everything, but somehow I know where it all is."

"The building looks fairly new," he commented, his gaze roaming about the room.

Grinning, Skip said, "It's one of the changes I've finally been able to make. It's small, but we have bathrooms, including showers, for the people coming in to dock for a night or longer. With the Seafood Shack at the end of the parking lot, people have got a nice place to eat. In the busier season, I've got some teenagers who help me out on the docks as well." Motioning for him to take a seat, he added, "This harbor even won an award after I got a grant to fix the place up. We redid some of the harbor, replacing anything worn or rotten. We got the parking lot and loading ramps fixed, cleaned the whole area and lined with flowers beds. Been working here for a while, but damn if the town manager doesn't balk at everything I try to improve."

Chuckling, he said, "That's what I hear from everyone. Silas likes to have the last word on just about everything."

Skip's intelligent gaze landed on him. "Well, enough pleasantries. I figure you're here to talk about George."

Nodding, he replied, "George and anyone else you think might know something."

Blowing out a breath, he asked, "Anything in particular you're looking for besides what we've already discussed?"

"We're looking at the possibility that George might have gone out into the bay at night...not for fishing, but perhaps to meet up with someone. Any chance that could happen and, if so, could that be tracked?"

Skip rubbed his whiskers, a worried line creasing his brow as his chin dropped to his chest. "Well, obviously, he could go out at night and no one is here to monitor the harbor after hours. Granted, I'm usually here long after my stated hours, but once I'm gone, there aren't any watchman or guards here. 'Course the Coast Guard is right over there," he added, pointing out to the far side of the small harbor.

"Would they keep track of boats coming in and out of this harbor?"

Shaking his head, he admitted, "Nah. That's not their job. We got boats, commercial as well as personal ones, coming and going all hours. In fact, for personal boats, we have an honor system set up for the docking payment if they come at night when we aren't here."

"So, it's possible for George to have gone out at night, be gone a couple of hours, and return unnoticed?"

"But why? Why would he?"

Lance waited silently, giving Skip time to answer his question.

After a moment, the harbor master sighed heavily and said, "Yeah…it wouldn't be hard at all. Especially for him."

He tilted his head and Skip explained, "He knows… uh…knew…the harbor like the back of his hand. He could slip out and back in barely making a ripple. And while I never knew him to disable his marine GPS… well, it's possible he could have."

The men sat in silence for a moment before Skip added, "I get the feeling from this investigation that George was involved in something…something out in the bay that wasn't fishing." When Lance did not confirm, Skip continued, "George was a good man, but for the past six months or so, he seemed to not care as much about his business. His boat needed some repairs and the last time I was at his house, it needed work too. I thought maybe the bills from his wife's medical costs or his son's legal woes might have drained him. Offered him some help. Offered to let him work the docks at times when he wasn't out fishing. But, he always turned me down."

"Did you think he was making money somewhere else?"

Snorting, Skip shook his head. "That's just it...didn't look like he was getting much money. So, I figured he was just winding down his career and hoped like hell he had a backup plan. If he hadn't saved for retirement, things were going to get real tight for him."

"Anyone special come around to deal with George?"

"Just the regulars. As soon as Thomas Fedor got into town and re-opened the Sunset View Restaurant, he came most days. He would talk to George, usually first, and then make his way over to the Carsons and the Taylors."

"Was that odd? That the restaurant owner would come? Wouldn't it be a chef or manager?"

Skip shrugged, and said, "Baytown's small enough that eventually you see everyone doing all kinds of things. I just figured he liked checking out the local scenery or was a real hands-on kind of owner."

Shaking hands, Lance left the harbor and drove back to the office. Mildred and Mable were both in the reception area, greeting him as he walked by.

"Chief wanted to see you when you got in, Lance," Mildred said as Mable's head bobbed next to her.

Tucking away his smile at the two women, so alike in mannerisms, he walked to Mitch's office toward the back of the police station. Knocking on the door, he entered and Mitch nodded for him to take a seat. "You wanted to see me?"

Mitch eyed him for a moment before saying, "You were hired to be part-time, Lance. In the past week, you've put in full-time hours."

Tilting his head, he said, "I'm not asking for more money, Mitch. I'm only logging my part-time hours—"

Mitch's raised hand interrupted him, as he shook his head. "It's not your reporting that has me concerned. I know you're only turning in the agreed upon hours of contracted work, but that makes a lot of what you're doing for the town on your time."

"Are you telling me that you turn this job off when you leave the station?" he countered. Seeing Mitch's mouth snap shut, he nodded. "Thought so." Leaning forward, he heaved a sigh before continuing, "Mitch, you invited me to move here because I had no desire to go back home after I got out and working Vice was too much at the time. Nightmares were a bitch...my family was impossible to be around. I was one of the lucky ones though, 'cause I had some money and could disappear from society for a while. I never meant to become involved at all. Not with the town, not with friends, and sure as hell, not will someone I could fall for."

Mitch's lips twitched before he dropped his eyes to his desk. "I hear you. I never expected to find Tori back here in Baytown."

They sat in silence for a moment before Lance asked, "What's got you bothered? Me working here? Working over my hours? Being involved with Jade—"

"No to the first and last. You working here is great. You're a damn good investigator and I'm thankful you decided to join the living and help us out. And Jade?

Man, I couldn't be happier for both of you. But the hours? Yeah, we've got to keep an eye on that. I need to stay within budget, but I also need you to be careful with your time. We don't want a case compromised because you're involved with a possible witness, or that you're investigating on your own time."

He nodded, but he was not happy with the idea of cutting back. Looking at his watch, he said, "I want to interview Thomas Fedor...you want to take the lead?"

Grinning, Mitch nodded. "Oh, hell yeah, let's go."

Fifteen minutes later, they sat ensconced in Thomas' lavish office on the second floor of the Sunset View Restaurant. Lance's gaze was drawn to the large window facing the bay, the view creating a focal point for the room. The walls were painted a dark red, stark in contrast to the highly polished, light pine floor. The furniture was masculine and he recognized no expense had been spared.

"Chief Evans, how nice to have you visit. How is that lovely wife of yours?" Thomas greeted, his smile wide.

"She's fine, thank you. Officer Greene and I would like to ask you a few questions."

Lance, allowing Mitch to take the lead, settled into the plush, leather chair.

"Certainly, certainly," Thomas replied, his smile still firmly in place. "How can I be of assistance?"

"We're trying to understand George's movements and how he conducted his business," Mitch began. "It's our understanding that you would visit the harbor almost every day, overseeing the buying of the local fish?"

Nodding profusely, Thomas replied, "Yes, yes. I try to get out every day that I can. I find that it's important to remain on top of things in this business and there were some things I wasn't willing to take a chance on."

"Your chef isn't involved in that aspect of the restaurant?"

"Actually, yes, but we divide those duties. My head chef…have you met Chef Louis?" As they shook their heads, he continued, "Oh, you must the next time you're here. He is wonderful and I think will really put the Sunset View Restaurant on the map—"

"You were explaining the different duties?" he interrupted.

Chuckling, Thomas nodded, his smile still wide. "Oh, yes. I get carried away when I talk about the restaurant." Clearing his throat, he propped his elbows on his deeply padded, leather chair, his fingers in a steeple as he continued. "Chef Louis is sincere about using the freshly grown produce and he, along with some of the other cooks, scour the area for the produce. He is also particular about the oysters we serve because, as I'm sure you know, we offer a wide variety of oyster dishes. So," he spread his hands out wide, "the fresh fish fell to me to buy."

"Not another cook?"

Shrugging slightly, he lowered his brow, "I suppose I could have one of them take over that duty, but officers, I really enjoy taking care of it myself. I enjoy meeting the boats as they come in. Enjoy getting to know the fishermen. I find it to be a welcome break from some of the more tedious tasks in owning this business."

"You still have business dealings in New Jersey?"

A shadow crossed Thomas' face, fleeting, but not unnoticed.

"Yes...there are family businesses, but some are less profitable than others, so I'm focusing my attention on this one."

"A casino, I believe," Mitch pushed.

A mottled red rose over Thomas' face as his gaze shot between them, his Adam's Apple bobbing several times. "Yes." Hesitating only a second, he added, "A family business."

"It must be hard to run a casino in New Jersey and a restaurant in Virginia, as involved as you seem to be."

Thomas' intelligent eyes held Mitch's before sliding over to Lance's. "Officers, let's not sit here and beat around the bush. Since you know of my family's casino, then you know my real name. I assume you are here to see if I had anything to do with George Caday's death."

Thomas reached up with his hand to tug on the tie at this neck and squirmed slightly in his chair. Letting silence fill the room, Lance was not surprised when Thomas eventually continued to speak.

"While my name is on the casino as primary owner, my extended family actually owns the business, in that they put up the money for it and run it. It has not been as profitable as they had hoped. I...well, I wanted to move on to something of my own. Something away from the...uh...family business. So, when a friend told me this property was up for auction, I decided to go for it."

"Are the restaurant and adjoining marina all yours or is it also owned by the family?" Lance prompted.

"All mine. I assure you, officers, it is all mine."

"And has it been profitable?" Mitch queried.

Swallowing deeply, Thomas replied, "All businesses take a while to start running in the black. But I have every expectation that the Sunset View Restaurant, as well as the marina, and the wedding business we are creating, will soon show the profit needed."

He continued to prod. "Why did you want to separate yourself from your family's business interests?

Thomas looked out the large window, any telling expression safely hidden under a mask. Finally, sucking in a heavy breath, he replied, "We have no control over the family to which we are born."

For a second, Lance's mind flashed to his own family, Thomas' words hitting a little too close to home. Forcing his thoughts back to Thomas, he remained silent.

"I was only ten when I first realized that my family was not like other families. By that, I mean, my family appeared to not only have wealth, but power. I was sixteen when I first witnessed my family's power when they crushed a local business that did not pay money owed. That business was owned by the father of one of my good school friends. I saw what that did to their family and instead of being filled with pride, I was filled with shame.

"I belonged to a powerful family but felt powerless." Sucking in a deep breath, he continued, "I was taught what they wanted me to learn. Lived the way they wanted me to live. When I was twenty-five, I was told to sign for the purchase of the casino and I did. I hated the work...hated the business. But, I amassed a small fortune in my own name and was determined to use it to get out from under their thumb someday." With a rueful chuckle, he added, "Who would have guessed that it would come from a tiny town on the Eastern Shore?"

Turning his gaze back to them, he said, "I heard about an ad for the auction. Took a drive down and here I am. The sellers were thrilled to have a buyer and I was thrilled to have something of my own...something my family would not touch. I assure you, officers, I will have a successful business here and do it on my own, because I have no desire to go back to that way of life."

On the drive back to the BPD station, Mitch looked at Lance sitting quietly in the passenger seat. "What are you thinking?"

Rubbing his hand over the back of his neck, he replied, "As much as I like Thomas' story...it just makes it more obvious that he would do anything to keep his family out of this business. And that might include smuggling."

Stretching, Jade rolled over, smiling at Lance as he slept. She leaned on her bent arm, propping her head on her hand, and allowed her gaze to drift over his face. The lines from his eyes were relaxed. His dark lashes were thick, slightly curled, and she thought of how many women would love to have such perfect lashes. His eyes were closed, but she had the color memorized. *Hazel. Or hazel...ish.* It was hard to pinpoint their exact color. When angry, they appeared darker, the brown taking over. Other times, especially near the water, they appeared brown with blue flecks. And she remembered, when he detailed his time in the Army, they had shone golden.

Dark stubble covered his strong jaw and she longed to run her fingers over his face, feeling the contours and textures, committing them to memory as well. His shoulders were bare, his t-shirt still on the floor where it was tossed last night. She sucked in her lips as her gaze moved over his muscular arms. Arms that had held her as his body rocked hers in passion. Smiling, she memorized the corded muscles of his chest.

"Hey," he said, his voice rough in the early morning. "My face is up here."

"Busted," she laughed, blushing.

"Babe, you can look all you want. I know I stare at you every chance I get." Rolling toward her, he pulled her in for a kiss, his hand cupping her cheek.

"Mmmm," she moaned, "are you sure you have to go to work? This would be such a great day for you to work on your art here at home with me."

"Don't tempt me," Lance said, as he climbed from the bed, carefully maneuvering her along with him. "What are you doing today? I need you safe while I'm at work."

"If we're doing our own Thanksgiving meal here tomorrow, then I need to run to the grocery store and hope they still have some things on the shelves. Then I'll just be here cooking."

Brow lowered, he said, "How about if I run to the store with you this morning and then drop you off back here?"

Sitting up, she stared up at him, scrunching her nose. "Honey, do you really think that—"

Shifting his body so that he was leaning over her, he placed his hands on her cheeks, saying, "For now...yeah. We still don't know who tried to run you off the road."

"Okay," she agreed easily. "I hate the inconvenience, but I'll never fuss about you going to the store with me."

"Humph," he snorted. "You haven't seen me shopping yet."

Thirty minutes later, Jade stood with her hands on

the cart and glared at Lance. "Do you have to be in such a hurry? I need to see which yams are packed in syrup and which are in water. I don't want the extra calories."

"Jade, it doesn't matter. It's Thanksgiving...calories are not part of the equation."

"You can say that...the extra calories don't stick to your hips," she bit back, huffing as she picked up the can of yams again, reading the ingredients.

He grabbed the can and tossed it into the cart as he moved to her side, his other hand landing on her waist, fingers gently pressing into her hip as he bent close to her ear. "Sweetheart, there's not one inch of you I'd change. So just focus on the fact that we're here together...buying food for our first Thanksgiving."

Twisting her head around, his touch branded her skin through her clothes. Eyes wide, she whispered, "Our first..."

"No way this'll be the last holiday we spend together. Babe, I want you in my life for all the holidays...and for all the other days that we'll celebrate just because we're together."

Facing him fully, she placed her hands on his chest as she peered into his eyes, blinking her own as tears threatened. "That's the sweetest thing I've ever heard. I really want to take you home right now," she confessed.

Chuckling, he brushed her lips with his as he turned her back toward the cart. "Then let's get the yams and get out of here."

The small turkey was marinating and the yams were cooked and ready for Jade's special casserole. She remembered their cook, when she was young, did not create the usual dish with marshmallows on top but, instead, created a pecan, brown sugar crumble on the top of the yams. Shaking off the thought of the extra calories, she grinned, still remembering the feel of Lance's hands on her hips.

With some time on her hands, she moved to her school bag and pulled out her laptop, pushing a bowl of sea glass out of the way. Remembering she still had a bag of sea glass left in her classroom desk, she decided to bring home what the children did not use, and add it to Lance's collection.

Walking into his studio, she stood for a moment, letting the sun that flooded through the windows, warm her face before she moved slowly around the room, her eyes reverently taking in the beautiful work. Thoughts of all his sleepless nights bent over his work table, creating art from the many pieces of colored glass, filled her.

Moving to his current project, the large mosaic, she reached out, her fingers barely skimming over the fragments—individually broken but, together, creating a whole. She walked to the table on the side of the room where he had the colored glass sorted. The square, plastic containers appeared to hold glass that was sorted by not only color, but also size. Wanting to surprise him, she thought of the perfect pieces in the bag, still in her classroom. Pleased at the thought of more of her findings ending up in his mosaic, she made a mental note to bring that bag home. *Part of me joining with part of him.* That thought sent a smile across her face and she knew, his first mosaic would never end up on Jillian's galleria wall...*it'll always be a part of us.*

———

Walking into Ed and Nancy Evans' house two days later, Jade felt Lance tense at her back and she twisted around to see his jaw was set. "You okay?" she whispered.

With a curt nod, he dropped his eyes to her worried face, and said, "Sorry. Sometimes, I look at other families and can't help but wonder why my parents couldn't have gone for a simpler life. Less...and yet, more at the same time."

"I know what you mean," she said, her hand lying gently on his arm. "My parents had Thanksgiving prepared by the cook and then would invite some of my dad's cronies over. Mom tended to delve into the sherry by that time and I usually just escaped into my room, absconding with a plate of pie."

With a soft chuckle, he stared into her eyes, full of concern. "Sounds a lot like my family. All the right food, but none of the right emotions for the holidays."

"Welcome!" a voice cried out and the pair looked up to see Mitch's mom, Nancy, walking from the back. Offering a hug to Jade, she took the plate from Lance's hands. "I'm so glad you two could come!"

"Lance, Jade," Ed greeted, walking up behind his wife. Peeking into the dish of yam casserole, he grinned.

"Best tradition ever...the day after Thanksgiving, we host the *Bring Your Leftovers* meal and have the greatest time. Come on back."

As they entered the large den, they could see the backyard was covered with a mixture of picnic tables, card tables, Adirondack chairs, folding chairs, and a pop-up tent covering the food. Completely haphazard and completely comfortable.

Lance recognized everyone and, for the first time since moving to Baytown, he realized it felt like home. With his arm draped across Jade's shoulders, he glanced down at her smile aimed at their friends. She stood on her toes, offering her mouth—an offer he would never refuse. With a quick kiss, she headed toward the kitchen to join Jillian and Tori.

He watched her walk away, her graceful movements, in spite of her slight limp, holding his attention. He lifted his hand, unconsciously rubbing his chest where his heart beat steadily.

"It's hard and easy, isn't it?"

Jerking his head over toward the man next to him, he observed Brogan staring at Ginny. Lifting his brow, he waited for him to speak again.

"Easy to fall for someone, but hard to accept they've chosen us as well. Been with Ginny for a few months now, but I lost my heart to her a couple of years ago when she first came to town. Had no idea I might have a chance with her. And now? I can't fuckin' think of a day that I wouldn't have her by my side."

Nodding slowly, Lance shifted his gaze back to where Jade was moving through the sliding glass door, her hands wrapped around a platter. As he continued to stare, he observed her with a large group of women. Jillian and her mom, Claire, as well as Katelyn and her mom, Corrine, were arranging the sliced turkey and ham. Grant's mom, Marcia, poured glasses of tea. Tori and Belle walked over, pies in their hands.

"Never thought about finding someone," he said. "Figured it just wasn't for me."

"And now?"

Chuckling, Lance explained, "Just as you said…hard to believe I did and easy to love her."

*Love?* It was the first time he admitted to himself that he did love Jade. *Can someone fall so fast?* His lips curved slightly as he realized he did not care about the answer to that question. He just knew what his heart admitted.

Seeing Ed and Steve Evans, along with Eric MacFarlane, beginning to arrange the chairs outside, he and Brogan moved with the others to assist. Zac, Aiden, Mitch, Grant, Gareth, Jason, Callan, with a few of his single Coast Guard friends, made easy work of the furniture, allowing everyone to have a seat as soon as they filled their plates.

A short while later, stepping over the bench of the picnic table, he settled next to Jade, accepting her ready smile, touching his lips to hers. The gathering looked expectantly at Ed, as the host.

He stood, his eyes moving over the large group before landing on his wife with a loving twinkle. "I grew up in Baytown and have thanked God every day for the chance to live in a place that I can happily call home, in the truest sense of the word. This special tradition began when our children were small. First, it was just our extended family. Then we invited more of the Baytown Boys and their parents. And now, we've grown to include not only our children, but their significant others, as well as their friends. Life's not always easy...some years are better than others. I remember when you all were off to war...our Thanksgivings were smaller and our hearts ached to have you all return. But good friends, as well as family, now make Thanksgiving so much better."

He lifted his glass of tea, and said, "So here's to being thankful for Baytown, our family, and our friends."

The gathering lifted their glasses as well, cheers of, "Here, here," ringing out. Lance sipped to the toast, before smiling at Jade, his heart full as more pieces of himself fit together.

Lance eyed Callan walking in, a report in his hand. "You look like a man who's got something."

Callan nodded, saying, "Coast Guard hit pay dirt last night. The CG based out of Norfolk has been working on a smuggling case and boarded two ships that were in the bay and docked yesterday in Norfolk. The one from Belize, along with its regular fish tanks, was carrying a small container of smuggled fish, including Totoaba and Puffer. The one from Liberia is still being checked, but from what the Commander told me, they are expecting to find something there as well. As soon as I know, I'll give you a call."

The early morning fog rolled off the bay and blanketed the shore. Pulling into the empty parking lot on Saturday, Jade sat for a moment with a smile on her face as she peered through the windshield at the Baytown

Elementary School. The modern building, normally bright with the sun, was shrouded as the heavy fog cloaked it. Climbing out of her loaner car, she clicked the locks before walking toward the front door. Used to the noise of chattering children, the silence of the area was strange.

*How lucky I am*, she thought, recognizing once more how much she loved her job. *Job?* She chuckled, knowing that teaching children was not a job, but more of a vocation...a calling. With Lance working today, she emailed the principal, asking for permission to get some work done in her classroom. Agreeing, the principal gave her the access code, letting her know that the weekend cleaning staff would not be there over the holiday weekend.

Her smile remained, thinking of the children in her class. Reaching the door, she halted after placing the key into the lock, carefully reviewing the instructions the principal had given her, before starting the security sequence. Opening the front door, she hastily entered the main office and moved to the security panel. Lifting her hand to enter the code, she hesitated, the green light already lit, noting the silence in place of the beeping that she should hear. Wondering if someone else was in the building, she stood in indecision momentarily. When the alarm did not sound, she left the office and walked down the hall toward her classroom.

Hearing a noise from the right, she stopped, listening carefully. Glad for her rubber-soled sneakers, she tiptoed to the door of the gym. Turning the handle, she barely opened the door, breathing a sigh of relief when she spied Bill moving some boxes.

Throwing open the door, she called out. "Hey! I see I'm not the only one here today. I thought it might just be me and the ghosts of schoolyears past."

Startled, he jerked upward, but a smile quickly came across his face as he lifted his hand in a wave. "The principal said you might come today and figured I should be as dedicated as you."

Walking closer, she asked, "What are you working on?"

"Some equipment came in on Tuesday and I didn't have time to put it away, or even go through the purchase order to see if it was all here. Thought I'd take care of it this morning." He swiped at the blond hair falling into his eyes, his gaze pinning hers. "You?"

"Kind of the same. Ever since the accident, I've felt disorganized and lost. Lance is working today, so I thought I'd spend a little time in my room since this is a long weekend. Next weekend is taken up with Jillian's wedding, so I feel the need to get my lessons planned for the next couple of weeks."

He nodded, but she noted his eyes darting to the side toward the gym's outside door. "You okay?" she asked.

"Yeah…just…uh…need to get this finished so I can get to my other job."

"How's that going with Mr. Fedor?"

Shuffling his feet, he shrugged. "It's good. Money's good. Nothing permanent, you know, but it helps cover some of my bills. Almost got my truck paid off, so that'll make the teaching salary go further."

Eyes wide, she smiled. "Wow, you made enough to pay off your truck? That's amazing! I was still driving my old car that I had in college. I can't get something new until my insurance claim goes through!" Turning, she waved over her shoulder, saying, "I'm heading to my room now. See you around."

Walking back through the door, she missed the way his eyes darted from her retreating form to the outside door of the gym.

Once inside, she scanned the room for a few seconds, allowing the familiar scene to fill her vision. Little chairs, all scooted up under little tables. Her functional desk stood neat and orderly in a corner. She walked by the large map on the wall, the colored push-pins marking the ship origins. Bookshelves under the row of windows in the back were filled. The children's sea glass frames were still resting on top, the glue now firmly set.

Out of habit, she hung her coat in the tall cabinet to the left of the door before sitting and opening her laptop. It did not take long to complete another week's worth of lesson plans, since she stayed organized and had some from last year that just needed updating for second grade.

Remembering the unused sea glass, she pulled open her desk drawer, searching for the bag. Picking it up, she held it up to the sunlight, admiring the colored and clear pieces catching the rays. Her lips curved at the idea of giving it to Lance.

*He can add it to his mosaic and then it will have bits of both of us captured in his art.*

Thinking of him, she took out her phone, sending a text to him. **At school to get some work done.**

After a moment, her phone vibrated with an incoming message. **Are you there by yourself?**

She grimaced, knowing he worried about her. **I have the security code and I'm fine. Bill is working in the gym, so I'm good.**

It only took a few seconds for the reply to come in. **I still don't want you there without others around. Stay locked in. I'll be there soon.**

Smiling, she sat at her desk with her laptop opened and continued working on her lesson plans.

---

Lance stood from the table, his face grim. Seeing the questioning expressions from the other officers, he said, "Jade's gone to the school to get some work done."

"Alone?" Mitch asked.

Nodding as he closed his laptop, he said, "She said Bill was there in the gym, but after seeing him working for Thomas, I don't trust him. I'm heading over there to pick her up."

As he offered a chin lift and turned to walk out of the room, Mildred rushed in, barely skidding to a stop. His hands shot out to steady her, his gaze dropping to her face.

"The fingerprints from George's boat just came in," she rushed. "I've got the report loaded to your notes."

Shooting his gaze up to the whiteboard where the computer image of the report was projected, his jaw tightened. "Fucking hell," he ground out, as Mitch and the others stood quickly.

The officers piled into three SUVs as Mildred placed the call to Sheriff Hudson, letting him in on the situation. The drive to the harbor only took a minute, and Lance was pleased to see both the Carson and the Taylor boats docked.

After Mitch parked, he jumped out, heading straight into Skip's office with him, while Ginny and Grant stayed outside. Thrusting the door open, a quick glance proved the office was empty. Turning around, he headed back outside, his eyes focused on the Carsons' boat.

Jade's stomach growled and she glanced up at the clock on the wall. Knowing Lance was on his way, she thought of stopping by the diner on the way home and getting hamburgers and fries to go. As her stomach grumbled again, she saved her work and closed her laptop.

Shaking her head, she tossed her phone and the bag of sea glass into her purse. Standing, she opened the cabinet door to grab her coat, but a soft click caused her to halt her movements. Hearing the footsteps of someone in the room, she peered around the cabinet door. Her brow knit in confusion as she watched Skip stalk over to the window, staring down at the children's artwork. He appeared to be searching for something as he moved along the bookshelf, body bent over each frame.

"What are you doing?" she asked, her mind unable to catch up with the bizarre scene playing out in front of her.

Startled, he turned suddenly, his hard, unsmiling gaze landing on her. "Where is it?"

"What?" she asked, placing her hands on her hips, exasperation in her voice. "Skip, what are you looking for?"

He dragged his hand through his hair, grimacing as his eyes darted around the room before landing back on hers. "The sea glass. Where's the sea glass you said was here at school?"

"Sea glass?" she repeated.

"Yes," he barked. "You said the other day that you found a bag of sea glass on the beach. A plastic bag. Then you said it was here and I want to know where it is." His voice became deeper, more strident with each word.

"Why?" she asked, a trickle of fear covering her body. Her gaze moved toward the shut door, but before she could move, he stepped forward, effectively cutting off any escape. Snapping her eyes back to him, she observed the sweat on his brow in spite of the coolness of the room.

"Skip," she began, softening her voice, hoping it would be effective in calming him. "I don't know what you're looking for. Why don't we go outside and you can let me know what you need—"

Shaking his head, he said, "No, Ms. Lyons. We're not

going outside. We're not going anywhere together." Sticking his hand in his large coat pocket, he continued, "You're going to get my bag of sea glass. And then I'm leaving. By myself."

Keeping her eyes on him, she said, "You still haven't told me why."

"Because it's not sea glass."

Blinking hard as her head gave a little shake, she repeated, "It's not sea glass?"

"No." His voice cracking, he said, "You have a quarter of a million dollars in your possession and had no idea."

"Quarter of a million…"

"Diamonds, Ms. Lyons. You have my bag of uncut diamonds."

Lance's footsteps pounded up the metal plank before he jumped the last few feet to the deck. Richard and Rick stopped in their tracks, their eyes wide as they watched the Baytown Police swarm the dock.

"Officer—"

"Where's Skip?" he shouted, his steps not halting until he reached the two men. "When did you last see him?"

"Uh…uh…" Rick stammered, shaking his head in uncertainty, his eyes darting between him, his father, and the other officers.

Richard stepped up to him, a grimace firmly in place. "Fuckin' hell." Sighing heavily, he said, "Skip—"

"What? What about Skip?" Rick blurted, his brows lowered as he looked at his dad, confusion marring his expression.

"Boy, if the police are investigating a murder and they come hauling ass in here looking for someone, don't you think they got a reason?" Richard bit out, staring at Rick. Turning back to him, he answered, "We got back to dock about an hour ago. Ain't seen hide nor hair of Skip. He's usually here this time of day, but not always." Rubbing his calloused hand over his face, he said, "I'm sorry as hell, but I got no idea where he's at."

Lance turned around and shouted, "Burt, get in Skip's office and check his computer."

Mitch hurried up the plank as well and said, "Fastest search warrant I've ever seen. Judge Harris just sent the word to Mildred."

Standing on the deck of the boat, feet apart and hands on his hips, Lance cast his eyes toward the bay. *Would he have gone out on a boat?* Hearing a noise behind him, he turned to see Harold Taylor walking toward the Carson boat.

"What's goin' on?" he yelled up.

"You see Skip leave this morning?"

Nodding, Harold replied, "He was here as I readied my boat, but I saw him get in his ol' truck and leave real early. There was still a heavy fog out and he usually stays around in case he's needed in the harbor, so it was strange."

His gaze shot to Richard, still standing next to him, and he asked, "Old truck? What does it look like?"

"He's got an old Ford...dark blue with some scratches on it. Had it for years, but figure it's good to have around here for hauling all kinds of equipment—"

Calling into his radio, Mitch ordered, "Mable, get the license number of Skip Morton's truck. Put out a BOLO and call it into Colt."

"I'm going to the school to get Jade. I don't want her

unprotected," he barked, jogging down the plank to the dock. Looking over at Ginny, he nodded as she called out she would ride with him. Hearing footsteps behind him, he glanced over his shoulder and heard Mitch order Grant to follow.

---

Blinking again, Jade gasped, "Diamonds? Di...what?"

"I don't have time to waste time with you...just give them to me," Skip said through gritted teeth. His eyes darted around again before he swung them back to her. "I don't want to hurt you, but I've got to get those diamonds."

Swallowing deeply, her chest heaved as he pulled a gun out of his deep coat pocket. "No..." she whispered, her mind racing to find an escape but seeing none. Her purse, with the bag of sea glass mixed with what she now knew were diamonds, lay on the desk.

"I need those diamonds," he reiterated, his eyes shooting back to the children's frames, before he moved slightly toward the windows. "Did they use them? Are they mixed in over here?"

"Yes," she lied, desperate to keep him away from her and on the other side of the room. "They used all the sea glass I brought."

He swung his gaze around before grabbing a canvas bag full of books from the floor, dumping the contents. "Put 'em in here. Now."

Not seeing a choice, with the gun waving toward her, she walked over on quivering legs, her hand shaking as she lifted it to take the bag. Following his instructions, she picked up the first frame and placed it in. The cold barrel of the gun jabbed her between her shoulder blades.

"Hurry," he growled. "You don't gotta be careful. Just dump 'em in the bag."

"Why? I don't understand?" she said, trying to get the frames in and praying he did not notice that all of them were just covered in sea glass. "Did you kill George? Were you the one?"

"He messed things up...for both of us," Skip replied. "If he had kept doing what he needed to, we'd both be rich."

"On stolen diamonds?"

"This was just part of it. Hell, we had it made—"

Hearing a noise at the door, they both turned around, but with the door closed and no one visible through the narrow window, she had no idea if someone was there or not.

*Bill's in the building...please let him come looking for me.*

Poking her again, Skip ordered, "Hurry. Get 'em all in."

The canvas bag was full as she placed the last frame into the top, gasping as he jerked it out of her hands.

"Come on," he said, waving to the door with his gun.

"What are we going to do?"

"I'm not going to hurt you, but I gotta take you with me. You'll be my insurance for making sure I get out of here."

"I won't tell—"

"Shut up." Cocking his head to the side, he said, "Did you hear something?"

Shaking her head jerkily, she said, "No. There's no one here but me."

"Bill's here…that's how I got in."

Heart pounding, her breath caught in her throat. *Oh, God…Bill let him in!*

---

Lance, listening to Mitch on the radio, drove past the Baytown Elementary School's parking lot first, looking over to see Jade's loaner car in the lot and an old, dark blue, pickup truck parked to the side of the building.

"Son of a bitch," he growled, still listening to Mitch's instructions.

"There's a side road that the buses use…turn down there and we'll come up behind the gym where there won't be any windows."

Following the road around the curve, he pulled behind the school and parked just as Mitch arrived as well. Seeing another truck, the bed partially filled with boxes, he alighted from his vehicle with Mitch, Ginny, and Grant on his heels.

"Colt and some of his deputies are on their way," Mitch said, "since the school is part of Baytown but also the county of North Heron."

"That's Bill's truck," Ginny said, jerking her head toward the red pick-up.

Mildred's voice came over their radios. "10-24, 10-

29. Reported intruder at the Baytown Elementary School."

His brows lowered as he looked at Mitch, who spoke into his radio. "Who called it in?"

"Bill…said he saw Skip inside the school and he's got a gun."

"Shit," he cursed. Staring at the large, one-story building, he knew it would be a labyrinth. Grimacing, he looked at Mitch. "You know the layout?"

"For emergency purposes, we have the area school buildings coded and the floorplans memorized. Stay with one of us."

With a nod toward him, they drew their weapons and slipped through the door.

---

Opening the door with a shaky hand, Jade stepped into the quiet hall. The peaceful school, normally so full of children's voices and the excitement of the day, now lay eerily silent. The bright halls covered with children's art were now dimly lit, the shadows casting fear through her.

A nudge from behind caused her to stumble slightly, and she was surprised when Skip mumbled, "Sorry."

As he stepped into the hall behind her, he instructed, "Go left. Don't know if Bill's still here, so we'll take the long way around to the back door."

With hesitation in her step, she moved forward, eyes shifting right and left, wishing some idea of escape would suddenly occur to her. Turning the corner, she gasped at the sight of Bill as he jumped behind another corner.

Skip looked over his shoulder at the empty hall behind him as he dragged her along with him. "Where does this lead?" he whispered hoarsely.

"Pods...first grade...pod," she stammered, as she tried to not think about the weapon in his hands while refusing to take her eyes off it.

"Pod? Jesus, this place is a maze."

It was on the tip of her tongue to explain the concept of pods for organizing an elementary school before realizing how ridiculous that would sound. His fingers, wrapped around her upper arm, tightened as she stumbled. The heavy bag of sea glass frames banged against her leg as they moved around another corner.

A fire exit door was in the middle of the hall and Skip pushed it open, dragging her along, his gun now facing forward. "Fuck," he muttered, when they entered a center courtyard. Sweat poured from his brow despite the cool weather.

A shiver ran over her as the breeze hit her. He turned his glazed eyes to her, his chest heaving.

"How do we get out?" he growled.

Realizing he assumed the fire door led to the outside, she looked around the school's garden courtyard and shook her head. "We have to go back inside the school," she said slowly, forcing her voice to stay soft.

Turning, he grabbed her injured wrist as he headed back toward the door they just came through.

She cried out as the sharp pain stabbed her wrist. Tripping, the canvas bag hit the back of her legs and she stumbled through the door, Skip falling forward as well. She tumbled on top of his body. Before she could react, hands grabbed her waist and lifted her upright while Skip attempted to scramble to his feet.

"Come on," a voice yelled behind her and, twisting her head around, she peered into Bill's eyes. Trying to back away, he held onto her arm.

"But you're with him. You let him in!" she said, struggling.

"No, I'm not!" he cried. "I saw you in the classroom and called the police. I've been following, trying to figure out how to help."

Accepting his answer, they darted around a corner just as a gunshot rang out in the hall. Instinctively throwing her hands up over her head, she felt a chip of cinderblock slice her arm as the bullet slammed into the wall.

"Shit!" Bill cursed. "What the hell is he doing?"

"He wants the diamonds," she replied, barely able to hear her words over the pounding of her heart.

"What diamonds?"

Giving her head a shaky jerk, she whispered, "I don't know."

Grabbing her hand again, Bill ordered, "Come on," as he ran across the short pod to the next hall. Rounding the corner, she gasped at the sight of Lance and Mitch, guns drawn, as they moved down the side of the hall toward them.

"Lance," she breathed, her body moving forward.

"Stop!" Skip yelled from behind, causing her to skid to a halt, Bill right next to her.

Lance's heart pounded as he viewed Jade and Bill trapped in the middle of the long hall, Skip right behind them.

"Skip," Mitch called. "It's over. You need to drop your weapon and let them go."

"Not happening, Chief," Skip yelled back. "I want what's mine and she's gonna make sure I get outta here."

Jade's gaze stayed plastered on Lance, seeing not only anger in his tight jaw, but fear sliding through his eyes. Like a punch to the gut, she understood what he had said all along. *To care is to risk losing. It can all fall to pieces.* Staring at the face she had come to love, she whispered, "Lance…it's okay. I'll be fine."

His expression morphed into anguish as he stared at the unfolding scene in front of him. Lance caught Mitch's subtle movement to the left, knowing he hoped to get a better angle at Skip. Hoping Grant and Ginny were coming up behind Skip, he forced his thoughts to calm. With a nod Jade's way, he watched as a sad smile barely curved her trembling lips.

Skip moved forward, his gun steady in his hand, still pointing at her back. "You," he said to Bill. "Move back with us. You're my insurance that they won't shoot me now."

Jade felt Bill shift to her side and, with Skip's hand on her shoulder, he pulled her back down the hall toward another corner.

Desperate to keep Skip from getting Jade out of his sight, Lance called out, "Skip, when did George decide he wanted out? That he no longer wanted to help you?"

"George was worthless," Skip growled, wiping his brow with his free hand before reaching down to jerk the canvas bag back into his hand. "He wanted what these could bring but decided to take the moral high road and stop."

Grant called into the BPD earpiece his location. "Backup from Colt is here. Pod one and two are clear. Blue hall and green hall are clear. Moving toward yellow."

Lance's eyes shifted upward to the colored paint strip at the top of the hall, understanding the code. With Jade working here, he vowed to have the layout memorized as soon as possible. *But, Jesus, I hope I never need it again.*

Determined to keep Skip talking, so they knew his location, he called out, "George took the moral high road?"

"The asshole didn't mind working for me as long as we were dealing in smuggled diamonds, but he balked at fish."

Another radio call came through. "Colt and deputy are approaching the orange hall, past the fourth pod." He inwardly cursed again at not knowing the building's emergency plan. Looking over at Mitch, he caught his nod and moved forward toward the corner. From the new angle, he saw that the hall Skip took Jade and Bill down had an orange stripe at the top.

Approaching the corner, he received the signal from Grant that Colt was at the other end of the orange hall. Steeling his nerves, he held his weapon steady. Nodding toward Mitch, they rounded the corner but only saw Colt and his deputy. "Shit, he moved into another pod," he growled.

---

"Fish? What is he talking about?" Bill whispered, turning to look at Jade. She shrugged, her eyes moving toward Skip, who had taken them away from the police and into the fourth-grade pod. This area contained an exit that was used for fire drills and emergencies only.

"Perfect," Skip said. Waving the gun, he indicated for her to move through the door.

As she put her hand on the push bar, she hesitated for a second, knowing a shrill alarm would go off. Before she could warn the others, she was pushed from the back, Skip's hand between her shoulder blades. Slamming into the door as it gave way, the exit alarm began to shriek.

Skip startled, his eyes shooting upward toward the alarm over the door, allowing Bill to take the advantage. Flinging his arm out toward Skip's gun hand, the two men grappled for the weapon. Righting herself, she turned quickly but Skip tripped into her, sending them both to the concrete pad outside the door.

The gun went off, the sound reverberating throughout the building.

Lance, Mitch, Colt, Grant, and Ginny had just met outside the pod when a deputy from outside called over the radio that he had visual contact with the trio coming through the emergency door. As Lance readied himself to move around the corner, he jolted at the blast of a gun being fired.

The sound of Jade's scream pierced his heart and his knees threatened to buckle. As Mitch surge forward, Lance bolted into action along with the others, his pulse racing. Seeing a tangle of bodies at the door, his mind shut down when he saw Jade lying on her back, eyes closed and blood splatters across her face, Skip and Bill laying sprawled over her.

"Fuck," he roared, charging to her body, dropping to

the sidewalk. Rolling Skip's body from hers, he looked at her bloodstained shirt. "Jade," he moaned, ripping her shirt open, but only seeing pale skin beneath. "Oh, Jesus, oh, thank Jesus." Cupping her face as she blinked her eyes open, he bent, kissing her lips gently. "I've got you. I've got you, baby."

Hearing his vow, Jade inhaled a shuddering breath, her voice ragged, "Bill? Skip?"

Lance looked over as Zac and another EMT approached the scene while Grant put pressure on Bill's bleeding arm. Skip, appearing dazed, sat with his hands behind his back as Mitch cuffed him.

"My bag...that's my bag," Skip groaned, seeing Ginny pick up the canvas bag.

"They're not there," Jade said, sitting up with Lance's assistance. Seeing Skip's gaze jump to hers, she drew another ragged breath and reiterated, "The frames... they don't have any of the sea gla...uh...diamonds in them."

Shock, and then anger, flew over his face before fearful resignation appeared to hit. Lance growled, pulling her to a safe distance. Mitch and Grant hauled Skip upward, dragging him away from her.

"You...you said they were there," Skip accused, his voice now full of defeat. Looking at the surrounding officers, he said, "It's gone. All my work is gone."

As Colt's deputies read Skip his rights and pulled him away toward their vehicle, she looked at Bill. "How is he?"

Bill offered a wan smile, wincing as Zac had him moved to the stretcher. "Can't believe I got shot...over fish." Looking at Lance, he said, "What the hell was that about?"

Mitch stepped in, placing his hand on Bill's shoulder. "We'll fill you in, but for now, just concentrate on healing."

She stood, supported by Lance. Holding on to his arm, uncertain her legs would hold her up, she stepped over to Bill. "I'm so glad you were here."

Grimacing, Bill said, "I knew I kept hearing a noise by the gym door. I came down the hall to find you, but that's when I saw Skip in the room, holding a gun. And I realized he must have slipped in the gym door when I wasn't looking."

Lance, his arms around Jade, fearful of letting go, nodded at Bill as the stretcher was loaded into the back of the ambulance. "Thank you, man." With a smile, Bill lay his head back and the doors closed.

Turning Jade so he could fully see her face, he took in Bill's blood splattered across her. Cupping her cheek again, he peered into her green eyes, but saw no fear... only love. "Oh, baby, I thought I'd lost you—"

Shushing him with her fingers over his lips, she shook her head. "I'm here, Lance. I'm here. Just for you...I'm here."

---

The sunset painted the sky and Jade shivered in her jeans and sweatshirt, despite being wrapped in a blanket.

"Babe, come in," Lance ordered, walking to her side

with his hand extended. "You shouldn't be out here." He had gone to the station for a debriefing after making sure Jade was safely at his house, Belle keeping her company. When he arrived home, he found Belle standing at the sliding glass door, peering out at Jade, sitting alone on the deck.

"I tried to get her to come in," Belle explained, her eyes full of concern. "But she insisted that she needed to sit by herself for a little while."

Thanking Belle before seeing her out to her car, he walked back through the house and onto the deck, where he noticed Jade shiver in the evening breeze.

Jade peered up at him and offered a slight smile as she took his hand, allowing him to pull her to her feet. Tucked underneath his arm, she stepped inside the house, feeling the warmth surround her.

After they settled on the sofa, she asked, "How's Bill?"

"He's gonna be fine. It's a flesh wound and he's already discharged."

Nodding, she sighed. "What can you tell me?"

Lance stared at her for a moment before he spoke. "There's a lot of the investigation that is still ongoing, but when Skip was arrested, the gravity of his situation took hold and he began to confess. It seems that he and George did become close over the past decade and especially when their wives died within a year of each other. Both of their savings were almost drained by the cost of their wives' cancer treatments and the two men began to discuss how they could make more money. Skip knew of the many smuggling operations that went on in the bay so he was the brains of their operation. It took a while, but they began simply. They would go out at night on George's boat after disabling the GPS, and would approach a predesignated ship. They would take the diamonds from one and transport them to another ship, keeping a cut of the money before going back to deliver the payment to the first vessel."

Shaking his head ruefully, he added, "It was really brilliant in its simplicity. They essentially were transporters for hire."

"So, what happened? Why did Skip kill George?"

"According to Skip, he didn't. He says that as he learned more from the smugglers, he realized that, besides just moving the diamonds and money between the ships, he could use the diamonds as collateral for smuggling other, more lucrative items. And that's where George's moral code came into play, at least as far as Skip is concerned."

Twisting in his arms, Jade looked at Lance, her brow crinkled. "Moral code?"

Chuckling, he explained, "It seems George didn't have a problem transporting diamonds and money back and forth, but when Skip told him one night that the diamonds were going to get them money to use in buying and selling illegal fish, George balked. As someone who respected the sea he fished in his whole life, the concept of killing endangered fish or smuggling them to make money, did not suit him."

Eyes wide, she shook her head. "This is crazy. It doesn't seem real."

"I think that's how it seemed to George, also. Skip's plans got more elaborate and convoluted. George told Skip he wasn't on board with the plan and wasn't going to do it, but the deal had already been struck. When Skip wasn't looking, George must have tossed one of the bags of diamonds into the water and when they got to the next ship, they did not have all the diamonds needed for the transfer of goods. Skip said George told them he hid them somewhere. According to Skip, an argument ensued and the foreign smugglers, to make a point, killed George right in front of Skip then told him to clean up the mess and get the diamonds or the money."

"That bag I found was the diamonds and I just thought it was someone's lost sea glass."

"Skip had no idea how to make things right until the news article about you finding the body was aired and the Gazette had a picture of you holding up a bag of glass. He recognized what it was."

Leaning with a huff, she shook her head. "It makes no sense. Hearing the story, it still makes no sense. I sat on the deck, watching the sunset, hoping that I could rectify everything with the sweet men I knew, but now that I hear everything, I'm still stunned."

After a moment of silence, Lance's fingers gently smoothing her shoulder, she whispered, "What will happen to Skip?"

"He'll go to prison, baby. But, maybe with his testimony, it will break open the smuggling that has plagued the bay for a while. Callan says the Coast Guard will be actively involved in the case, so that they can identify the other participants. At least that way, some ships will be banned from U.S. waters."

"Do you feel sorry for them?" she asked.

"Sorry? Why should I?"

"Because they suffered so much when their wives died...I know you once talked about how difficult it is to move forward when you lose people close to you."

Lance shifted her body around, so that she was facing him, lifting his hands to cup her cheeks. "I did say that and, at one time, thought removing myself from others was a way to protect my heart. But after meeting you, I was willing to expose myself to pain, just to be with you. One day, one of us will have to face losing the other, but baby, there's no money in the world that would make that hurt less. The choices George and Skip made were wrong, and I can't help but think their wives would be hurt knowing how far the two of them had fallen."

"You're right," she nodded, leaning in for a kiss. Pulling back slightly, she added, "Thank you for taking a chance on me."

"Baby, with you in my life, I'm now whole again. Our love has put all my pieces back together."

## 35

### EPILOGUE

The bride beamed as she turned to face the gathering, her new husband on her arm. Lance looked up at Jade, gorgeous in her deep green bridesmaid dress, and winked as the organist began to play. Jillian and Grant's wedding was the town's union between the proverbial prom king and queen, the pier and surrounding area filled with guests.

He watched as Mitch, Brogan, Aiden, Zac, and Callan, standing up with Grant, paired off with Tori, Katelyn, Jade, Ginny, and Belle as they walked down the aisle, following the newlyweds. A sense of pride moved over him, knowing he allowed himself to call them friends...and be one in return.

Later, swaying back and forth on the dance floor, Jade in his arms, he looked at the crowd, now recognizing most of the people he saw. As their eyes caught his, they nodded and smiled, a few patting him on the back as they walked by. He waited to see if the old feelings of nervousness would settle in his stomach, but it appeared they had abated for good.

"Hey," Jade's soft voice sounded, capturing his attention. Her eyes, even more green with the dress she wore, twinkled. "Are you okay?"

Looking down, he said truthfully, "I'm great."

"The wedding was perfect and Jillian was so beautiful."

Nodding, he added, "It was and she was, but for me, I only had eyes for you." She laughed and the sound was sweet to his ears.

Quietly, letting the music flow through them, they held each other tight.

Six months later

Bright sunlight streamed through the window where the sea glass mosaic was hanging, creating a brilliant burst of color. The small gathering was awed by the beautiful pieces of art surrounding them, but the creator's eyes were on the back of the room. Lance's attention was held by the woman rounding the top of the stairs. Her long, ivory dress, stunning in its simplicity, flowed behind her. Her dark hair, pulled away from her face as the tresses waved down her back, held a light veil.

Jade, her hand on her father's arm, searched for

Lance, her eyes finding him standing in front of their mosaic, creating a halo of color behind his head. Her smile widened as she walked toward him, barely noticing when her father kissed her cheek formally before moving to sit next to her mother.

Her parents sat across the aisle from Lance's parents, both sets deciding to attend the wedding. She and Lance had simply ignored their parents' initial protestations over the engagement and then rolled their eyes when their parents approved upon discovering they were marrying into a family with money.

More important than their parents, were their friends gathered for the nuptials. Turning to Jade, Lance took her hands, smiling into her upturned face. After the formal vows and the minister pronounced them husband and wife, he leaned in to whisper, "Thank you for picking up my pieces, Jade."

As the gathering faded into the background, he kissed her, his arms winding around her body, pulling her in close.

Their friends began to clap, the sea glass mosaic casting its glow…and magic, over the kissing couple.

Don't miss any news about new releases! Sign up for my Newsletter

Don't miss the next Baytown Boys
Sunset Flames

Her father was a hoarder…

and now he's gone, and Madelyn Stover returned reluctantly to Baytown to bury her estranged father and clean out his house. Finding journals he had written left her wondering what secrets her parent's marriage had held.

A serial arsonist has the Eastern Shore gripped in fear. For Fire Chief, Zac Hamilton, he just wants to protect those he loves.

A fire on her property led Zac to the beautiful newcomer and as they grew closer, discovered they had more in common than either realized.

When the arsonist strikes too close to home again, can Zac keep his promise to keep her safe?

Please take the time to leave a review of this book. Feel free to contact me, especially if you enjoyed my book. I love to hear from readers!
Facebook
Email
Website

Jaxon

Jayden

Asher

Zeke

Cas

Lighthouse Security Investigations

Mace

Rank

Walker

Drew

Blake

Tate

Hope City (romantic suspense series co-developed

with Kris Michaels

Brock book 1

Sean book 2

Carter book 3

Brody book 4

Kyle book 5

Ryker book 6

Rory book 7

Killian book 8

Saints Protection & Investigations

(an elite group, assigned to the cases no one else wants…or
can solve)

Serial Love

Healing Love

Revealing Love

Seeing Love

Honor Love

Sacrifice Love

Protecting Love

Remember Love

Discover Love

Surviving Love

Celebrating Love

Follow the exciting spin-off series:

Alvarez Security (military romantic suspense)

Gabe

Tony

Vinny

Jobe

SEALs

Thin Ice (Sleeper SEAL)

SEAL Together (Silver SEAL)

Letters From Home (military romance)

Class of Love

Freedom of Love

Bond of Love

The Love's Series (detectives)

Love's Taming

Love's Tempting

Love's Trusting

The Fairfield Series (small town detectives)

Emma's Home

Laurie's Time

Carol's Image

Fireworks Over Fairfield

Please take the time to leave a review of this book. Feel free to contact me, especially if you enjoyed my book. I love to hear from readers!

Facebook

Email

Website

# AUTHOR INFORMATION

I am an avid reader of romance novels, often joking that I cut my teeth on the historical romances. I have been reading and reviewing for years. In 2013, I finally gave into the characters in my head, screaming for their story to be told. From these musings, my first novel, Emma's Home, The Fairfield Series was born.

I was a high school counselor having worked in education for thirty years. I live in Virginia, having also lived in four states and two foreign countries. I have been married to a wonderfully patient man for thirty-six years. When writing, my dog or one of my four cats can generally be found in the same room if not on my lap.

Please take the time to leave a review of this book.

Feel free to contact me, especially if you enjoyed my book. I love to hear from readers!

Facebook

Email

Website

12653947R00224